The Lady of
Misrule

By Suzannah Dunn

Quite Contrary

Blood Sugar

Commencing Our Descent

Venus Flaring

Tenterhooks

Past Caring

Darker Days Than Usual

The Queen of Subtleties

The Sixth Wife

The Queen's Sorrow

The Confession of Katherine Howard

The May Bride

The Lady of Misrule

The Lady of Misrule

SUZANNAH DUNN

Little, Brown

LITTLE, BROWN

First published in Great Britain in 2015 by Little, Brown

1 3 5 7 9 10 8 6 4 2

Copyright © Suzannah Dunn 2015

The moral right of the author has been asserted.

A CIP catalogue record for this book
is available from the British Library.

Hardback ISBN 978-1-4087-0466-0
C-format ISBN 978-1-4087-0467-7

Typeset in Fournier by M Rules
Printed and bound in Great Britain by
Clays Ltd, St Ives plc

Papers used by Little, Brown are from well-managed forests
and other responsible sources.

MIX
Paper from
responsible sources
FSC
www.fsc.org   FSC® C104740

Little, Brown
An imprint of
Little, Brown Book Group
100 Victoria Embankment
London EC4Y 0DY

An Hachette UK Company
www.hachette.co.uk

www.littlebrown.co.uk

For Katy Rensten, with whom I spent a lot of time cooped up when we were sixteen, but voluntarily, and listening to 'Low' and eating toast.

I

A good Catholic girl was what they'd said they needed, and, seeing as no one knew otherwise, I was trying my hand at being exactly that. And so far — on that first, mid-July, swift-sweet day — I was getting away with it, scurrying behind the Lady Lieutenant through the Tower of London. We were on our way to some lodgings, I thought: somewhere for me to kick off my shoes and lay down my head, fasten some shutters against the belting of London's bells. After two long days on the road, that was as far as I could think, it was all I wanted, and at seventeen I was naïve enough to think that whatever I wanted, I'd get.

Nothing about the unguarded door to which she led me was any different from all the others we'd passed in passageways and courtyards. Not that I'd had time to see much; she wasn't hanging around. Tight-lipped and bustling, she acted as if England's unequivocal proclaiming of the wrong queen, thirteen days before, had been an oversight for which she, with a hasty rejig of household arrangements, could make amends.

Follow me, she'd said at the gatehouse, and diligently I'd done so, almost tripping over myself to keep up, but as far as I was concerned I was under no one's orders. I'd chosen to come, surprising myself as much as anyone else, the evening before, by raising my hand. Me, who usually kept my head well down. Me, who, if truth be told, couldn't have cared less who had been or should be Queen.

The Lady Lieutenant knocked on that unguarded door cursorily before opening it and drawing back, leaving me to go ahead. The walls were silk-hung, the ceiling looked gem-worked and the floor was a welter of honey-coloured carpets, each and every one of the thousands of brush-touches and knots of silk there to honour the occupant of the centrepiece, which was a throne. It was empty, though, and its gold-cloth canopy was being dismantled by a man who was overdressed for the task, the close-stitched pearls of his doublet squeaking against one another as he strained this way and that. His foreshortened steps around the obstacle of the throne gave him a fractious air, and he snatched at the canopy as if it were a prop and the show was over. His every move was thwarted by that expanse of thread-thin gold, which slipped and slid, making him cower and cringe as it threatened to swipe off his jewelled cap.

It was quite a spectacle, but the others in that room weren't paying him the slightest attention. All four of them were standing around a table on which was a leather chest, lid open. Two richly dressed gentlemen, stiff with self-regard, faced a girl of twelve or thirteen and – to judge from the protective hand on her shoulder – her older brother or cousin. So stunningly dressed were the younger pair – she in her deep, glossy greens and he from top to toe in gold-embroidered white – that I didn't, at first, think of them as real. They were players, I supposed, on their way to or from something ceremonial.

I too was in borrowed clothes, although mine were notably less glamorous and also too big for me. My sudden, belated awareness of how bad I must look gave rise to my first misgiving: what was I doing here? This was no place for me. But the Lady Lieutenant was ushering me forward – *Get on with you* – as she pushed past me to claim attention from one of the men: a touch to his elbow, a whisper which I over-heard. 'The Tilney girl', she called me.

'Right,' was all the man said. I'd do, presumably, whoever I was: the catch-all Catholic girl that – in his eyes – I was. If he spared me a glance, I didn't spy it.

That green-dressed girl did, though: she regarded me briefly, and although there was nothing in particular to the look, there was light in it. And that was when I saw that she wasn't anything like twelve or thirteen, just small. The man who hadn't bothered to look at me continued his business: 'And the purse,' indicating the little drawstring bag that hung from the girl's girdle.

'Oh—' *of course*, and she obliged, unfastening it while the boy huffed and muttered on her behalf at the indignity, the pettiness of it. As soon as the man had hold of the purse, he stuck two fingers into its neck to stretch it, then upturned it over the table and shook it to release its cache. Two vigorous shakes yielded a splash of small coins, at which he jabbed with an interrogative fingertip.

That was when it occurred to me who that girl might be. But here, behind an unguarded door in the company of a couple of plume-crested, linen-spry dandies, along with that canopy-draped incompetent and a six-foot sulk? If she was who I thought she was, then the blond at her side – half as tall again – was no brother but a husband. Baby of the Dudley family, married off six weeks ago to the Grey heiress. Just in time, as his family would've seen it: just before she was bundled on to the throne. Mummy's boy, people were saying. What a pair they made. Not an ounce of flesh on either of them: any closer together and they'd cut each other. Six weeks, that pair had been married, and I couldn't help but wonder: were they actually, truly, man and wife? Hard to imagine, particularly of her.

There she was, the girl who had, until that morning, been England's queen but was now being divested even of her small change. Not that she seemed bothered. Her attention drifted again from the man's endeavours, to find its way to me, and she smiled. Only a passing smile, not pausing for me to reciprocate, but it was warm enough: it was a hello.

Which was all very well, but where was everyone else? Where were all her other ladies? Finishing his job, recording the sum and dropping the confiscated coins into the case on the table, the man relaxed, became jovial. To the little ex-queen he said, as if she were a guest, 'The Lady

Lieutenant here will show you to your rooms,' and to her husband, similarly, 'You come with us, we'll see you over to yours.'

The boy reeled as if to take issue with that, but the girl cut across him: 'Can't I go home?'

Home: despite the softness with which it was said, like a request for warm milk, it brought us all back down to earth, as if someone had blundered in among the gilt and tapestries in nothing but a nightshirt. With that one simple word the ceiling was suddenly just paint-encrusted and chipped, the carpets musty, and those statuesque silk-built figures on the walls turned whey-faced and silly in their wimples. This was no home, and didn't a sixteen-year-old girl – particularly one stripped even of her small change – need a home?

There was no denying it was well and truly over for her. The bells confirmed it: their ringing in a different queen. England was turning, and rip-roaringly. This girl's time had already been and gone, and none of it had been of her doing in the first place. And now she was left with a coin-collector and his lackey, a gentleman defeated by a piece of cloth, and a posturing boy-husband. Oh, and a lady lieutenant and me. I mean, we were no army, were we.

Freedom would come soon enough for her, was what everyone said. As soon as the clamour died down and the new Queen was crowned, the new reign established: then the girl-pretender could slip away as if none of it had ever happened. And where, I wondered, was it that she envisaged closing a door behind her, sinking on to a cushion and slipping off her little shoes? I had a home, back in Suffolk; she had one in Leicestershire, I knew, and she'd have one in London, but for a girl like her there'd be others. Perhaps there was even a marital home, too, for the newly-weds. Although, come to think of it, she'd said 'I', not 'we'.

No one in that room wanted to be the one to refuse her. The Lady Lieutenant lowered her eyes: she was just doing her job, no more, and even that – she had probably guessed – not for much longer. They were all caught on the hop, was my guess. No one – absolutely no one, of any persuasion – had expected, two weeks ago, to be facing this situation. Not even two days ago had there been the remotest possibility of having to decide what to do with a pretend queen. Because she hadn't been a pretend queen: she'd been the Queen proper and no pretence about it. The dying boy-King had chosen her over his Catholic half-sister and she'd been pro-claimed as such by every last councillor, all of them, reformist and traditionalist alike, and practically every nobleman in the land. Towns all around the country had declared for her, the royal guard and navy, too, and the Tower was hers and she was already in it, inside its very throne room. Home and dry, done and dusted: Queen Jane.

But now, just thirteen days later, she was being taken from this room to another to make a prisoner of her.

Here she stood, asking to go home instead and looking them in the eye, every one of them somehow all at once; she didn't waver, and it was quite something to see. Myself, I made sure never to look anyone in the eye if I could avoid it.

The officious man seemed ill at ease. He didn't reply, presumably hoping his colleague would step into the breach, but the other man busied himself shutting the leather case, its straps suddenly proving troublesome, so eventually the first man said, 'It's probably best you stay here for now.'

'*Best?*' This from the boy, who stalked away to glare moodily from a window; I'd have liked to deny him the satisfaction of being watched, but couldn't quite resist. He turned back to us. 'Says who?'

Again the girl spoke over him, to object but still in that reasonable tone of hers: 'My mother's gone home.'

I knew she had a mother – the dead King's cousin, no less – but for all that she was tiny, and the paucity of coinage in her purse, something told me that she didn't have much use for one. Perhaps we had that in common. Well, that and both our mothers being elsewhere, upriver, but the crucial difference was that my mother was thrilled for me to be in the Tower: it was cause at long last to be pleased with me, it was as good as it gets for a girl as useless as me. 'And –' the girl looked at the gentleman who was having such a job subduing that canopy '– my father's off home, just as soon as he's . . .'

The Duke of Suffolk, then, on the rough end of that gold cloth. Would he be shamed by our collective gaze into a declaration of paternal devotion? *Goodness, no, sweetheart, as if I'd leave you alone here!*

Nothing was forthcoming, so the officious man was probably right to say again, 'It's best you stay here for now.' With a father as spineless as that, she might well be better off with me, even if I'd never in my life looked after anyone. That was when the man gestured towards me: 'Miss Tilney here will attend you,' and there I was, conjured up in my new guise as her personal captor. She gave me another of her smiles but the speed of this one suggested that what he'd said was news to her. She hadn't realised why I was there. Her life, these past couple of weeks, must have been full of all kinds of people coming and going. Going, mostly, lately.

I saw her file it away: a good Catholic girl come to supervise her in her detention. Every girl in England now, under the circumstances, made sure to be a good Catholic girl. Except her, of course. And, if only she knew it, me.

The man had reckoned without remonstration from the regally attired boy-husband. 'My wife stays with me. No way am I turning her over to you bastards.'

Tough talk from Baby Dudley. I had to turn away or I'd have laughed. Who did he think he was? Baby of a traitor-family, married in what was still probably name only, to a girl who could barely bring herself to look at him. I did, though: turned and looked right at him. Creature, I thought: the cheekbones, the brackish eyes, the broad mouth. *Cold fish.* And clueless, to think that talk like that would get him anywhere, although it certainly livened up the proceedings.

The man didn't rise to it: 'She'll have her own rooms. You'll be able to meet—'

'On whose orders?'

He was probably right to ask, because whose orders, currently, counted? While one queen was being escorted from the throne room but the next had yet to arrive, who could give orders to whom?

'Lord Arundel,' the man replied, but barely, as if it were entirely by-the-by who'd given the order, as if it could be on anyone's orders: *Anyone's but yours.*

To which the boy said, 'Fucking turncoats. All of you. Fucking cowards.'

Judging from the lack of response from the two men, they'd heard all this before.

As if she'd not heard it at all, Jane said, 'Shall we go?' and then, to her husband, with a smile, 'I'll be fine, thank you, Guildford, don't you worry.'

Don't you worry your pretty little head. He didn't like it, but he was quick, recovering in an instant and changing tack: 'Jane—'

An entreaty, which struck us all: every one of us stopped sharp and stared at the pair of them. Now that he had our attention, he didn't seem to know what to do with it. His hand hovered and I could see he wanted to touch her cheek but didn't quite dare. That pleasant, patient demeanour of hers was somehow forbidding. She was facing him down, I saw, in her own peculiar way, and – perhaps not quite so stupid after all – he backed down, withdrew his hand. 'Till soon, then,' was all he could say.

She nodded and took us with her to the door.

Back down those stairs, then, the Lady Lieutenant and me, but now with a deposed queen in our keeping. We were on our way, I supposed, to join all the other ladies and girls, and

I could sink happily back to being no one in particular. Down that staircase trooped the three of us, into that exultation of bells, and I wondered what the girl made of the din. She'd know why they were ringing but, shut away in here, she couldn't possibly guess at the glee out there on the streets. England was proclaiming loud and clear and at length how very glad it was to be rid of her, but all she showed us was that faintly cheerful, freckle-sparkled look of hers.

Stepping ahead of me from the stairwell, the bottom of her gown spilled over the cobbles and it occurred to me that perhaps I was supposed to pick it up and carry it for her. I had no idea of any duties I might have; nobody had yet said anything to me about duties. Possibly her captors themselves didn't know how to treat a pretender-queen. Then and there, I made a snap decision, emboldened by the riotous bells: I wouldn't do it, I wouldn't take up her train. Why should I? She was no queen and never had been.

Our friends the Fitzalans had told us that when she'd come to the Tower, two weeks back, her mother had been the one to oblige. Up the riverside steps they'd come from their barge, the Duchess of Suffolk grappling with taffeta. 'Her own mother': a roomful of scandalised Fitzalans had wondered aloud how that could ever be right. Because even if the Greys had been the heirs to the throne, even if the cousin duchess was closer in blood to the King than his two supposedly bastard half-sisters – even if that could possibly have been true – then why hadn't it been the duchess herself swanning up those steps on her way to the throne? Why her daughter? The Fitzalans had asked it merely to express their disapproval. Like everyone else in England, they knew the answer: because it was the daughter who was married to the baby Dudley, and this was all his father's doing.

The father, the Duke of Northumberland, had ruled for the boy-King for years and wasn't about to give up and go home just because the boy-King was dying. He'd stayed beside the sickbed until that poor boy had accepted his helping hand in signing the throne over, not to the rightful heir, his half-sister, the middle-aged daughter of the long-ago Spanish Queen, but to his cousin's daughter, English rose and kindred spirit Lady Jane Grey, or Lady Jane Dudley as — conveniently for the duke — she'd only recently become. Watching her emerge ahead of me from the stairwell into the sunshine, it struck me that however bad this situation was for her, it was also freedom from the Duke of Northumberland: there was that, surely, to say for it.

We were retracing my steps, as if to make our way back to Lion's Gate and onwards into Petty Wales and the city, but once we were clear of the maze of courtyards and into the inner bailey, the Lady Lieutenant led us instead towards a house built hard against the wall, a house that would've belonged better on the other side of it: a three-storey, jettied townhouse, quince-hued around its timbers, incongruous among the old stone towers. It even had, beside the front door, its own little herb garden.

'Mr Partridge's house,' she said. 'Gentleman-gaoler. There's a Mrs Partridge, too.'

Indicating the neighbouring tower, she told Jane, 'That's where your husband's going to be,' adding hastily, 'Good rooms, too, those,' *don't worry*. 'Just better, we thought, for you girls to be here.'

Making it up as they went along, probably: I imagined a meeting last night, someone's anxious question, *Where shall we hold the Queen?* and someone else's rapid reminder, *She's not the Queen.*

Girls, the Lady Lieutenant had called us: Lady Jane was just a girl now, like me.

Girls, both of us, together, in need of a home for a while and this, it seemed, was to be it.

My heart contracted as we walked into the shadow of the house where we'd be living until the new Queen was crowned and the pretend one could be released.

It was an unlikely prison, but that was what it was.

'Nice house,' the Lady Lieutenant mused.

But small. Where was everyone else? The Lady Lieutenant honoured its tenants with a knock, which failed to elicit a response. Not someone to be fazed by a locked door, she selected a key from the jangle at her waist. 'I'd have liked this house for myself, rather than our big old place,' she confided. 'Ours is too close to the river: damp and draughty,' at which she gave a comical shudder, but this chumminess was rather late in the day and we stood there in silence, we two girls, on that threshold. 'Still . . .' she finished as she disappeared ahead of us into the house, by which she probably meant it no longer mattered.

Directly inside the doorway was a staircase, up which we followed her to the top where she opened an unlocked door, releasing into the stairwell a scent of floorboards, of prolonged unoccupancy. As we shuffled in, the long-undisturbed air shifted and rearranged itself around us. The room seemed wary, doing its painful best for us: a chair angled artfully at the fireplace, a jug of roses dead-centre on the table. On one wall was a hanging too big for the space, bunched at one end on its rail although its subjects were unimpeded in their little drama: Susanna and the elders, Susanna conveniently already having done her naked bathing and well wrapped up as she always was by the time the tapestry makers got to her and, unbeknown to her, the repugnant elders lurking behind her on a hiding to nothing.

'Well, make yourself at home,' said the Lady Lieutenant in the sceptical, resigned tone with which, at the door, she'd muttered that one word, *Still* . . . 'I'm off to get your boxes brought up.'

Or, just as likely, to pack her own.

No switch of a key in the lock, just retreating steps doled out stair by stair until there was silence. If this was it – if there really was nowhere else but the room we were standing in, and a bedroom behind the internal door – then there could only be the two of us who would be living here. Alone together for the first time, we were too close for comfort. I went to the window, and Lady Jane opened the bedroom door, ostensibly in exploration but probably as desperate as I was for a snatch of solitude. What had I got myself into?

How could I have been so stupid as to get myself shut up like this? What had I been thinking, last night, when I'd volunteered? It had seemed a good idea at the time. And it wasn't as if I was doing much else. There I'd been, newly arrived to stay at the Fitzalans', when word had come home from the earl that a girl was needed. No doubt he'd have expected one of his own daughters to volunteer but it had been me who'd raised my hand, *I'll do it*.

Hearing the door drop home against its jamb, I turned around to the room, which came back at me with a blank stare of its own, but down in a corner was something – alive, dark, fast – and my heart cannoned into my breastbone before I understood I was seeing a cat. It froze, mirroring me: the pair of us in a stand-off. I must've exclaimed because suddenly Jane was back in the doorway, alarmed: 'What?' I slid her gaze with mine to the animal, which glanced between us, affronted, and took a single, exaggerated backwards step. 'I can't breathe,' I gabbled as if my breath were already gone, 'if there's a cat in the room.'

She snapped into practicality: 'Well, you're in the right place, because I can't stand them,' and in a couple of strides she was at the main door, throwing it wide and ordering the cat on its way. It was an impressive performance for someone so small and, had it been directed at me, I'd have been falling over myself to oblige. But the cat, being a cat, feigned confusion and terror, shrinking and cringing, and only when I'd resigned myself to a merry dance did it surprise me by knowing what was good for it and streaking for the stairs.

There we stood, Jane and I, looking into that gaping, unguarded doorway: both of us, I think, embarrassed to be complicit in her captivity. If she ran, though, she'd only get as far as a gatehouse, which was where the guards were. And, even if she could possibly get past those guards, then where? There was no one, now, who would have her. She closed the door, saying decisively, 'We don't have to have that in here.'

We did have to be in here – or *she* did – but we needn't submit to further indignities. There were limits.

'Thank you,' I said.

'Oh –' she shrugged it off '– my little sister's the same,' and went to open the window. 'With my other sister,' she said, easing up the catch, 'it's horses,' and turning back around to me, she raised her sketchy eyebrows: *Imagine!*

'Why don't you like them?' I asked her. 'Cats,' I clarified, *not your sisters.*

'Devious,' pronouncing it as if it were the final word on the subject.

With the window open came the banging of those bells.

'What's your name?' she asked me, and for an instant the devil in me almost had me claim my cousin's identity, Cat, but of course I stuck to the truth: 'Elizabeth.'

'Well, Elizabeth,' and she presented her back to me, 'would you help me out of this?' She raised her arms a little, offering herself up for unpinning. 'I hate the thing, and it's hot in here.'

'The thing' was made of such heavy damask that the pins were in it up to their necks. I wondered whose dress this once might have been: a dress fit for a queen, but it couldn't have been made for this one because there wouldn't have been time. Just because the Duke of Northumberland had wanted his daughter-in-law on the throne hadn't necessarily meant that it would happen. He'd had his work cut out for him, and right up until the last moment. Only a month or so back, according to the Fitzalans, he'd been playing safe with big smiles and fine wines for the King's Catholic half-sister whenever she had come visiting. No, this dress had once been someone else's, some dead queen's, then rustled up for this pretend one in haste from the Queen's Wardrobe. Perhaps it had belonged to the tiny queen of the old King, Katherine Howard, Queen for a year when I was a girl, because I remembered it being said that she'd had a new dress for every day she was on the throne. Afterwards, they must have been packed away somewhere.

I asked whether we shouldn't go through to the bedroom for her unpinning but she was nonplussed, happy for us to stay where we were, and similarly when I reminded her that her other clothes hadn't yet been delivered, she was cheerfully unconcerned: she could sit in her kirtle, she said; who was to see her? Well, no one, if we didn't count me. How I'd have loved to ask the same of her, for her to unpin me from my gown – the room was so stuffy and I'd had such a long day – but one of us needed to stay respectable to open the door when her chests were delivered and supper served. She asked me where my own boxes were, and when I said they were still in Suffolk, she exclaimed but I said no more, avoided telling her how my mother and I had travelled light and fast, incognito, to flee the fighting that everyone had feared was about to start there. As it had happened, we needn't have worried, because when it came to it, there'd been no fighting anywhere: no one had fought in Jane's name.

'This dress isn't mine,' I said, 'it's borrowed.'

'From?' She was merely making conversation, I knew, but still she'd have to have an answer.

'Mary Fitzalan.'

'Mary!' – but the pleasure of recognition dropped into an uncomfortable silence, because if her own cousin was lending clothes to her captor, then surely there was no one left for her.

When she was free of the gown, she took off her hood and then there she was, kirtle-simple and bare-headed, so that – disconcertingly – it could've been me in that room who was the ex-queen.

An hour or so later, the first chest of hers was delivered but she was less than pleased to find it held no books. 'I don't need clothes,' she complained, raking through the contents, as if the very notion were absurd, as if no one ever needed clothes, 'I need my books. Where are my books?'

What books? And how would I know? What was I, her personal librarian?

'Elizabeth, I need my books,' as if it were me who was denying her.

'I'll ask.' What more could I say?

'Ask whom?' She paced as if caged; caged, bizarrely, in a kirtle, in swathes of silk.

She had a point, though: no one had told me what to do — where to go, to whom, how and when — if we needed anything. And, ridiculously, I hadn't asked. 'Someone'll bring supper,' I improvised, 'and then we can ask.'

Which earned me a sharp sigh.

But, honestly, I wondered, what could she possibly need, before then, with any books? And anyway, who was she to be demanding? She was a prisoner.

There was an impressive jut to that little chin of hers. 'They *said* I could have my books.'

'And I'm sure you shall,' *if you just wait.*

She turned her back on me. Well, so be it. Two can play at that game. I withdrew to the window seat.

Then, from her, '*You* don't read, I suppose.'

'I *can* read,' I countered. *And* write. Not with any ease, true, but I could manage shopping lists and household accounts, or I could have a stab at them, I could make myself understood, and wasn't that enough?

She came to the window. How I wished those bells would stop; the air itself whooshed and boomed so that I felt a bit sick, as if I too were swinging. Together, we looked out over the courtyard. 'What do you do, then,' she asked, 'to pass your time?'

Your time, I noted, not *the* time: I was someone who had time to pass. But time passes anyway, is what I'd always found. If I made myself scarce, it passed. I shrugged:

'Whatever needs doing.' The truth was that I made a point of spending my time trying to get out of whatever needed doing because I only ever seemed to do it wrong. I'd be safe here, then, it occurred to me: there was nothing here that needed doing. In that sense, I supposed, I'd made a good move.

There was another sigh from her – heavy, this one – but beyond which, I hoped, I heard something else. 'Supper,' I announced, in anticipation.

'You can have mine.'

'You have to eat' – although why should I care if she starved herself? Why should I feel sorry for her? The worst that would happen to her was that she'd spend a couple of weeks in this room before gliding off to a life in a big house with a pretty-boy.

Whatever I'd heard, though, it wasn't supper; we ended up waiting a while longer for that, but at least by then she'd asked me to help her dress again. When eventually we did dine, she was in Protestant black. And there was me in all that finery, which I could hardly help because it wasn't actually mine and anyway, if she'd looked beneath the table she'd have seen my boots. Did she really think God looked approvingly on her for her sartorial self-denial? Not that it was anything of the kind, if you looked closely, because for all that it was black, that dress of hers was sumptuous.

And it was all a pose anyway because, however much she might want to pretend otherwise, we were both Edwardians: his reign was all we'd properly known, which, for all our apparent differences, made us first and foremost Edwardians.

Having that oh-so-Protestant ex-Queen across the table pushed me into a Catholic corner, which was unfair because although we Tilneys certainly weren't reformists, we weren't anything much else either: we just *were*; we were what we'd always been, doing pretty much as we'd always done, if – admittedly – a little more cautiously. It was the same for everyone else we knew. There'd been changes – of course there had, lots of them – but we'd dealt with them one by one as they'd come along: some we'd taken on; others we'd adapted or circumvented. We'd mixed and matched and muddled our way through the reforms, just as everyone else had. Protestant or Catholic, reformist or traditional: just about everybody I knew was a bit of both. We supposedly traditionally minded Tilneys kept close company with some who called themselves reformists. Harry, for one, although he'd changed his tune a few days ago when push came to shove. And Harry was a case in point because it was only ever happenstance in the first place that had made him back the reforms when my father, his neighbour, his best friend, resisted them. A different priest for Harry when he was growing up and then a different wife, back when he'd had a wife. The point was that nothing was simple, and during the past few difficult days there had been plenty of so-called Protestants rallying behind the Catholic Lady Mary, for various reasons, and many so-called Catholics better disposed towards the primly black-clad girl who was sitting across the table from me.

When the chambergirl returned to clear away our supper,

the Partridges came up the stairs with her but waited politely in our doorway for Jane to act the hostess and invite them inside, whereupon they settled together on the window seat like good children. Mrs Partridge looked about the same age as my sisters – in her twenties – but there the similarity ended, because even in repose her moon-face bore the trace of a smile: it seemed to have been cast that way. Bemused and shy, she might've been the one of us in the room who was reliant on good will. Her husband was older and smaller, with a lopsided smile and something off-kilter, too, about the eyes (different colours? a scarred iris?). He looked as if he'd dashed in the general direction of his clothes and kept running. If his wife brought to mind a bowlful of freshly picked apples, he was a windfall.

They'd come to welcome us but also to talk over various practical arrangements (meals, linen, exercise), and their emphasis was firmly on flexibility. Listening to them, it was possible to forget that Lady Jane was a prisoner. They were good company, and in return Jane was perfectly pleasant, more so than she'd been to me all afternoon, but then, understandably I supposed, I'd be the one to bear the brunt. When they left, unease balled in my stomach and I had to remind myself that it was in their house that I was living, not hers. I was living with those nice Partridges at least as much as I was living with Lady Jane Grey: that, I told myself, was how I was going to have to think of it.

They left us with a whole evening to spend in each other's company, but luckily they'd located the missing books, so

Jane was busy. And me? Bone-tired, I curled up on the window seat to breathe the evening air and watch daylight pale away, lamplight claiming the corners and doorways. I spotted Mr Partridge venturing from the house with a hound and returning a quarter of an hour or so later. The bell-tolling beyond the walls petered out until it was its absence, instead, that made itself felt.

I suspected we were both putting off going to bed. We might've managed a tentative accord for the evening – her at the table with her books and me at the window with the view – but our other room was uncharted territory. It felt odd, too, somehow, to be deciding our own bedtime, extinguishing our own candles: I felt as if we should ask permission of someone. Eventually, though, I could put it off no longer, and declared I was turning in.

'Me too.' She closed her book and stood, ready, which had me despairing that I hadn't gone earlier to use the chamberpot – I'd missed my chance, now, of some privacy. My light, as I followed her through the bedroom doorway, struck the bed's coverlet, the silk-depicted, ruby-fruited vines. 'Isn't that beautiful!' I wondered if it was Mrs Partridge's own work.

'There's no truckle,' was all Jane said: no second, little bed to pull from beneath the main one for me. She must've ascertained it when she'd first looked in, back in the afternoon. We'd have to sleep together in the big bed. Well, at least we were both small.

First, though, we were going to have to undress each other. And how, I wondered, should we go about that? Because if I started with her, as presumably an attendant should do, then she'd be undressed while I was still clothed and that didn't seem right. Come to think of it, though, she'd been stripped down to her kirtle earlier, at her own request. So when she'd removed her headdress and the string of pearls that was her girdle, I offered – 'Shall I?' – and, yes, immediately she turned her back to me, her row of pins, and there I was, undressing a queen for bed, or an ex-queen, and thinking of Harry – *Look at me, Harry, undressing a queen* – because that was something he hadn't ever done. One up on Harry, then. Then again, one up on just about everybody.

When I was finished and had lifted away her gown and her kirtle, she pulled her shift up over her head with a dismaying lack of self-consciousness, reaching for her nightdress but unhurriedly, not attempting to hide anything. But, then, really, what was there to hide? We were both the same, underneath.

Then it was my turn. At home, I'd have roped in my mother to unpin me, or her chamberlady, or any of the other girl-servants: I'd call down from my room for help or waylay someone somewhere and stand still in a stairwell or passageway while the pins were extracted. But here I had an ex-queen at my disposal and in the event she proved satisfyingly deft, sheen slipping around on her hair as she bent this way and that, the better to tackle the task.

Having finished with me, she went blithely to the chamberpot, which was when I made sure to disappear briefly into a flurry of linen: shift off and nightdress on. I decided I'd have to forgo the chamberpot: I'd hold on, if I could, until morning. And if I couldn't, if I woke during the night, I'd be very quiet about it. She combed her hair, then prayed beside the bed. I only ever prayed in chapel, and only because it was expected of me. As she knelt there, I busied myself folding and stowing away our various garments. What confidence, it seemed to me, to think God would listen to her here, in her own room. But then maybe He would, because what did I know.

She got into bed in the same manner I'd seen her do everything else that day — brisk, resolute, no equivocation or trepidation — and thus she had the choice of sides. She left me to close the shutters, too, and light the night-light, draw the hangings, do the proper work of the attendant that I now was. It was when I was dealing with the shutters that I noticed a lit window in the neighbouring tower and almost said so — *Look! Your husband* — but then didn't because perhaps it would've been improper for me to remark on it when she hadn't.

I climbed into bed. She smelled of almonds.

'Do you snore?' she asked.

I said I didn't know.

'Well, if no one's ever said, then you probably don't, do you.'

I had to explain that no one would've told me because there was no one to know: I didn't share a bedroom with anyone. 'I'm the youngest': my sisters grown up and gone before I was ever in any bed with them.

'Well, you're lucky,' she said. 'My littlest sister coughs, and the other one talks in her sleep.'

Which had me curious: 'What does she say?'

She had to think about that. 'Oh, nothing really.' She cast around: '"Put it in the bucket." That kind of thing.'

And I laughed, because how was that a 'kind of thing'?

'Mind you,' she said drily, 'she doesn't say anything much more meaningful when she's awake.'

When she said nothing more, I asked, 'And what do *you* do?'

She turned to me, uncomprehending.

'In your sleep.' What, if anything, should I be prepared for?

'Me?' She sounded surprised. 'Nothing. I sleep like the dead.'

And she was true to her word, turning over then and there to do exactly that. Me, I was ready to lie awake for a long time, pondering my predicament, but actually all I wondered before I fell asleep was whether Harry had noticed I was gone. Had he turned up at home yet, and asked casually, as if it were nothing much, as if I were nothing much to him, 'So, where's your Lizzie?'

He would have expected to find me, earlier in the day, in the clock alcove in our chapel. At the start he hadn't liked the idea, which was mine, but in no time he'd come to appreciate it, as I'd known he would, because, even if I said so myself, it was a good one. Perfect, no less: we Tilneys

27

weren't the most observant of families; none of us was ever in chapel unless we had to be. That alcove, behind its own door, was the quietest corner of Shelley Place's quietest room. No one was permitted anywhere near, however laudable the intention, except for my father, who wound the mechanism every morning, and the clockmaker, Mr Farebrother, on his infrequent and well heralded visits. Otherwise, my father decreed, there was to be no cleaning or polishing, no sweeping or tidying, no coaxing, tinkering, easing or tightening; none of the meddling and ministrations to which everything else in the household, living or inanimate, was subject. That clock was my father's pride and joy and we were all to leave it well alone, to let it get on with its work.

I didn't find it hard to shut myself away inside that bell chute because no one was ever looking for me. I'd grown up trailing in everyone else's footsteps; it was second nature for me to drop back and slip from view. And so it had been paying off, lately, at last, the benign neglect with which I'd been brought up, as perhaps I'd always had an inkling it would do.

Harry, though, was impossible to miss. Ordinary enough in his looks – forties, portly and mousey, although the smile was certainly something, the glee in it – he was none the less a presence, always at the centre of everything, even of our household, to which he didn't even belong. 'Like family', my father always said of his boyhood best friend. And more like family, perhaps, than our actual rather sorry excuse for a family, although in his company we did rather better because somehow he brought out the best in everyone. How did he do that? Even he himself probably didn't know, because there was nothing calculated about him. He was a natural, a man's man who was just as comfortable in the company of women. A big character, literally so in girth if not in height, although of course, back when I was younger, he'd towered over me. And now, if he was past his prime – still wearing it, but outgrown it – at least he'd had one.

He was unmissable, but more than that, he was a guest, so how did he contrive to disappear into his host's chapel's clock cupboard? He couldn't even pretend to want to go to our chapel, reformist as he was. No genuflecting, for him, in front of our secret St Sunday.

I never saw how he managed to slip away because I was always already there, ahead of him, waiting, shoulder to shoulder with that skeletal clock-mechanism, its bared teeth. He probably did it in plain sight: to my parents, a breezy *I'll see myself out*, and then, in the courtyard, no word at all to his own men, just that good-natured shrug, and then off, who knew where or why. Because who was going to ask? Servants don't ask. Or perhaps he'd even have mounted his horse, he'd be taking leave of my parents but *Oh!*, a sudden recollection of some task that needed doing and then, mindful of their comfort, *You go back inside, keep warm, don't mind me, I can look after myself*, and they'd assume he had business to do with our cellarer, or perhaps our stablemaster or warrener, because there was always business to be done between our neighbouring households. And anyway, he was family, as good as. *Your home is my home.*

Sometimes, I imagined, he'd have said nothing at all but just walked away, a hand raised in his wake, a half-wave, as brazen as that, just because he could. Harry could get away with anything. No one ever doubted him. No one ever thought anything but the best of him, because he always did his best for everyone.

When he opened the alcove door, it didn't matter how he'd got there; all that mattered was fitting him inside there with me. It was difficult enough to get the door shut on the pair of us and then there was the clock's foliot of which to keep clear, the arcing of that arm one way then back again, as slow and steady in the semi-darkness as a sleeper's breath.

Old kneeling-cushions were heaped in there but even so I'd have Harry underneath me – better padded, he should be the one to suffer the flagstones – and no sooner was he down there than I'd be on top of him, ducking beneath the two hunks of stones that dangled on their chains, edging blindly downwards, and I'd be kissing him: kissing and kiss-ing, my tongue circling his as if that were a way to wind myself open, because we didn't have time to feel our way and I never found it much easier at the start than the first time. I wanted him sliding into me with ease; I wanted instantly the ease that I knew was coming, but at first it was a blundering, an ill-fit because this was new, for me: I was seventeen and this was all still new. I'd have to work my way down on to him and for a notch of one of those clock-wheels we'd be getting nowhere but then, before I knew it, my resistance was instead a grip, I'd have him in my grip and then we were laughing as much as we could with our mouths pressed together because there we were, and we were on our way.

However much I'd needed my sleep and however swiftly it had come, I woke exhausted in the morning, having lain braced all night for the courtyard clock-strikes which were all too ready to extract another hour from the night's dwindling store. But at least the bells did what they had to do and then, for a whole hour at a time, left me in peace – unlike sweet-breathing Jane, sleeping soundly beside me and only ever shifting, or so it seemed, precisely as I'd succeeded in nodding off. I'd rather she had snored: some proper disturbance to justify my grievance.

When she rose, some time after the clock struck five, I played dead. If this was habitual for her, this early rising, then we'd have a problem, because I'd never been one for mornings. Rigid in my refusal to face the dawning day, nevertheless I must've drifted off because some time later there she was, beside the bed, regarding me with animal-like curiosity, as if about to extend a paw to worry at me.

She asked, 'Are you all right?'

Doubtful that plain old tiredness would be sufficient excuse, I made a bit more of it: a headache, I told her, and it did the trick: 'Sleep it off,' she advised, turning away, and clearly glad to be going.

Well, good riddance. And anyway, what would I be doing if I did get up and follow her into the main room? She was more than capable of looking after herself and this was very much her world, even if she was now held prisoner in it. Me, I was all at sea, hunching beneath the coverlet to make the most of my precious time alone in that bed with only the odd sound from next door – an occasional off-carpet footfall, some object placed on the table – to ripple my half-sleep.

Later, when I surfaced, my head was full of nothing-noises from home, of summertime early mornings at Shelley Place: a shutter let go too soon; a pail dropped on to cobbles; my mother sneezing extravagantly; and my father whistling for the dogs. An odd music that I hadn't realised I'd ever heard, let alone could sing to myself in my sleep, but there it was, as familiar to me as the rhythmic nudge of blood in my temples. Then suddenly it was gone again and irretrievable.

When eventually I went through to the main room, Jane was dressed, at the table with a book open in front of her and the fortification of several more to one side. The glance she gave me was ready and friendly enough but her focus lagged, reluctant to leave the page. She flapped a hand towards a tray. 'Breakfast, if you'd like.'

God, no, no breakfast, thank you: not at the best of times and this certainly wasn't that. But if I didn't sit down to breakfast, then what? I ambled over to the window, where I noticed – down below, outside – something that had escaped me in the afternoon light of the previous day: the green was failing in patches to live up to its name, because on it were the ghosts of tents that had been put up, some days back, for the men charged with the defence of the then-Queen. Those tents had made their mark but within a few more grass-growing days it would be as if they'd never been. The men would in all likelihood be back home now, drinking with everyone else to the proper Queen, the real one, the rightful one.

And what would I be doing, if I weren't here? Nothing much more productive. Practising the art of slipping by, sliding from view, making myself minimally useful in the hope of keeping everyone off my back. 'Help your mother,' my father always said. But my mother's line was 'If you want something doing, do it yourself.'

And anyway, she was beyond help. Everything was too much for her – it never stopped raining or instead it was stifling; the servants were shifty, her physician sceptical, the dogs a disgrace, her daughters didn't know they were born and her husband hadn't the time of day for her. She couldn't possibly feed any more people and the house was falling down around our ears while the tenants asked more and more of us and her headaches were worse than ever. Me, she'd given up on years ago. 'Head in the clouds', was what she said of me to anyone who'd listen, and anyone else too.

Jane – across the room from me – had her head in a book. Did she do that at home? Did she get into trouble for it? We had no books at home; I couldn't even imagine what books we would have, if we did, and they wouldn't be covered, as hers were, in midnight-blue corded silk or filigree-lavish vermilion satin. What could we possibly learn from books that we didn't already know?

Dreamer, my mother always said of me, and always with irritation – although, to be fair, that was how she said pretty much everything. She couldn't have been more wrong. Secretive, she'd said of me, even back when I wasn't. I didn't dream. I daydreamed sometimes, yes, but never had anything as serious, as hopeful for myself as an actual dream. Other girls had dreams of anything and everything, it seemed to me. My cousins and the girls who came to visit us and in the houses we visited, girls whom I could've called friends if I'd wanted to kid myself: those girls were always wide-eyed and hopeful, hugging themselves, barely able to contain themselves when they speculated on a coming Christmas, or some new piece of clothing, or a potential suitor. But what was the point? No one was ever any prettier for a length of ribbon or gold stitching – not really, not if you really looked – and Christmases come and go.

It wasn't that I didn't think of my future. On the contrary, there was no escaping it; it was everywhere ahead of me like the horizon. Though like the horizon, ever-receding. But even if I did ever manage to catch it up, it would be – bar the details – more of the same. I could never quite imagine myself married but I supposed one day I probably would be and then I'd have my own floors to sweep and linen to patch, my own grumpy servants and tetchy priests to placate. More of the same, bar the details, and the problem was that I'd already had enough.

Jane was staring into nowhere, gnawing her lower lip: she was thinking, as far as I could tell, and strenuously. She was already in her future as a wife – albeit little more than a child-wife – and I wondered what she made of it. I didn't envy her being married to a boy. The boys I came across were boring: their high opinion of themselves, of what they considered themselves due, and their contempt for me as a girl. At least Harry was past all that.

I gestured at her book. 'What's in it?'

My question threw her. 'It's – I'm translating—' but she halted; it was probably obvious I'd already lost interest, or, more accurately, had had no real interest in the first place.

And, anyway, it had been none of my business to ask.

Translating for whom, I puzzled: who was here to translate for?

Returning to her page, she added, 'There's Mass, apparently, at ten.' *If you want it.*

I said nothing. *You think you know me, but you don't.* I had no intention of going to Mass while I was here. There was no one watching me, so why should I go? Whatever else this incarceration was, it could be freedom from chapel; it might as well be that. Lolling on the window seat, listening to housemartin-chunter beneath the eaves, I drew up and clasped my knees. I'd stay here: this space at the window would be mine. She could have that table and those books, and the breakfast if she wanted it, and I could have this view of the outside world or, for as long as we were here, what would have to count as the outside world. It might not be much, but it was something.

The soon-to-be-crowned Queen would be stopping *en route* at least once a day for Mass; every respectable household between here and Ipswich would be frantically preparing to welcome her. Ipswich was practically home for me; she'd been in my home town while I was here in what was about to become hers. She was heading for the Tower to prepare for her coronation. How different her journey from Ipswich to London would be from mine: no dressing down, no keeping her head down (although in her time she'd had to do more than enough of that). And no rush, because she had her subjects to receive in their thousands, all along the way. They were flocking to her, the Fitzalans had said: the earl had sent news home of people in their thousands tripping over themselves to kneel at the side of the road. Thousands upon thousands of them, relieved and overjoyed, as if it had taken Mary Tudor to come riding along as Queen to liberate them. We, her subjects, hadn't come to her support but instead she'd come to ours: we'd needed her, and there she was. Just as well that no one, anywhere, during the troubled days, had fired a shot, because now absolutely everyone could claim to have been for her all along, but just cowed, hoodwinked, led astray.

I had asked Harry about it, a couple of days before my mother and I made our dash to London. I'd asked him what was going to happen. If anyone knew, he would. 'We'll ask

Harry,' my father so often said. Harry knew whatever there was to know, not because he was all that frequently at court – he was happier at home – but because, being down-to-earth and commonsensical, he was trusted.

On this, he'd been reluctant to speculate, but I'd pressed and eventually got an answer, which was nothing: nothing, he said, would happen. It's done, he'd said, done and dusted: the Grey girl is Queen. He'd sounded pleased enough about it; he was reformist, but, anyway, he liked things decided. I'd persisted, though, because I just couldn't quite believe it: would no one try anything? *Try anything*: I hadn't wanted to say *fight*; I didn't want to think of any fighting, even on behalf of poor, benighted Lady Mary.

Harry didn't think so; but if they did, he said, they'd be stupid, because they hadn't a hope in Hell. And anyway, he said, why would anyone want the Lady Mary on the throne? She'd take the country back to Rome, he'd said, and we're done with Rome. All of us, of any and every persuasion: we're free of Rome, he said; Catholics are English Catholics now, not Roman Catholics. No one in England had any need of a pope.

But it just wasn't right, I said: the King's sister should be the one to succeed him.

Half-sister, Harry corrected.

But a half-sister is closer than a second cousin.

'Lizzie,' he said, 'listen: the Lady Mary is a spinster. A queen needs an heir and there's scant chance she'd marry and produce, nearly forty as she is and always ailing and anyway only ever wanted to be a nun. There'll be no heir from there,' he said. 'Whereas the Grey girl is young, healthy and married. Married to a Dudley, true,' he allowed, 'but' – and he said it cheerfully, unconcerned – 'it's not as if we aren't used to Dudleys.'

Dudleys: down below our window, someone came into view, chucking a ball for the Partridges' dog, and only a double-take confirmed for me that he wasn't Baby Dudley. This particular blond, whoever he was, lacked the finery and the attitude. Taller, this one, too, although perhaps I'd have thought him an older brother of the baby's if I hadn't known for a fact that the four older brothers were elsewhere with their father. The Dudleys were a close family, everyone said. Well, now they shared being the only people in England who couldn't possibly hope to get away with the pretence of having rooted secretly for the Lady Mary. Not that the duke hadn't had a good try, according to the Fitzalans: hurling his cap into the air when he'd realised the game was well and truly up, hailing the new queen as if he'd never marched his own daughter-in-law on to her throne.

No, the duke and the four sons who'd flanked him were the only people in England who couldn't, by any stretch of the imagination, get away with it. But the baby of the family, the one who'd actually sat himself down on the throne, would be the one of them to go free. Because the new Queen, in magnanimously sparing her girl-cousin, would have to pardon the boy-husband, too.

*

There was absolutely nothing for me to do in that room at the Partridges' house. No noble girl could be held alone, hence me – or someone, anyway, and in this case the someone was me because I'd been the one to raise my hand. A body, then, was all I really was. Funny to think it: me, of all the girls in England, there for the sake of propriety. I took full advantage, did nothing in those first few days and did it to excess, losing myself in the view from the window, the comings and goings of workmen at their various tasks in the inner bailey, the strutting of ravens almost too corporeal to be creatures of the air, and the slow winding of the sky behind the White Tower. Inside the room, I developed an interest in Susanna – not the bovine lady herself, too long soaked amid a clutch of bone-bright water-lilies, nor the gimlet-eyed elders leching around the corner, but in how exactly the tapestry had been done, how those folds of the laundered linen had been depicted, and the shuddering of the sunstruck water. Tilting my head, I could glimpse that pond for the differently coloured, differently shaped sections of stitching that it really was – *I see your little trick* – but, tilting again, could summon back the cool blue depths.

One happy effect of retiring early and rising late was the shrinkage of the days. I got no complaint from Jane; on the contrary, she encouraged me. At the table amid an abundance of lighted wicks, she'd look up and suggest – nice as pie – that I take myself off to bed. She had work to do, as she saw it, but obviously I didn't and I must've been a hindrance, sitting there staring into space, yawning, waiting for her to finish. I was in the way: truly just a body in the room, rather than a companion. Then again, our eagerness to accommodate each other made us perfect companions.

I was only ever ashamed of my indolence when the chambergirl came waging her war on dust and dirt, infestations and untidiness, or bringing us food and ale, pitchers and clean chamberpots, linen and lights. Mrs Partridge had introduced her to us on our first evening as 'Goose', with no qualification or explanation nor any apology. Goose was bafflingly ungoosey: a vivacious, snub-nosed redhead, her hair so vivid as to be closer in colour, I felt, to purple. A gap between her front teeth made a smile within a smile, both of which came for me whenever I offered to help, along with a reassurance which sounded anything but: 'You stay where you are.' Or sometimes even a triumphant 'Uh-uh-UH!' as if my attempt to be less of a burden had somehow been underhand. Did she think – as my mother did – that I'd end up creating more work? All I was ever offering to do was lift my feet for her broom, or run a cloth over the panelling, or plump up the pillows – what scope was there in any of that for disaster? Perhaps she feared she'd get into trouble with the Partridges if she allowed it. Perhaps, though, she just liked to refuse me. She had an accent I couldn't place – which, come to think of it, did have a rather honking quality – despite our having to hear a great deal of it. Amazingly, her ceaseless, wide-ranging commentary – food prices, weather conditions, bowel habits, gardening tips, corruption, witchcraft and deformities – never had Jane so much as look up from her books.

It didn't take long for me to get sick of flopping around; it was strangely exhausting to spend so much time in bed or at a window. Mrs Partridge came visiting several times each day – often a little too dusted with cat fur for my comfort – with solicitous enquiries as to our well-being, and on the fourth afternoon I cracked and begged her for something – anything – to do. Shelling peas, perhaps, I said, or tying lavender bunches. She looked doubtful – no peas that particular day, apparently, and already more lavender that summer than boxes and chests in which to make it useful. Polishing plate, then, I suggested, or folding linen; but by then she seemed almost scared.

'Goose—' She didn't have to finish. I understood. Repairs, then, I offered, in desperation; never in my life had I thought I'd hear myself actually offering to patch and darn, but any household, even one as small as the Partridges', would have more patching and darning to be done than any single person could manage. All those sagging hems and missing hooks-and-eyes, the detached belt loops and ripped linings: Goose would be cutting off her beak to spite her face if she objected to some help with those. But if it did have to be repairs, I warned Mrs Partridge, they'd need to be hidden. Sweetly, she tried to laugh that off as false modesty on my part until I allowed her a glimpse of a seam on my sleeve, after which she was good at coming up with jobs on which it was safe to let me loose.

So there I was, for hours on end, fidgeting a needle and thread around in floppy old linen against the backdrop of

Susanna, whose stitches were hidden in the clear light of day, packed so tightly as to forge a single, continuous surface.

On my fifth afternoon, I found a means of regular, brief escape: I'd fetch our meals from the Partridges' kitchen and return the tray when we'd finished. This too, though, was the job of no-nonsense Goose, and nonsense was exactly what she thought it was for me to be making what she called unnecessary trips up and down the stairs. I stood my ground until Mrs Partridge was called to adjudicate and pronounced it fine for me to do so if I wished.

And I did wish, I definitely did. It wasn't much of a free-dom but it was something, and much more than just a break from Jane. I liked being elsewhere in the house, even if it was just on the stairs. Usually I'd come across someone – if on occasions only the Partridges' cheerful hound, Twig – and we'd greet one another in passing as if I were just another member of the household, not captor or captive or whatever I was, and the house not part of the Tower. Country girl that I was, I'd never lived in a townhouse. I'd been a guest in the London residences of family friends, such as the Fitzalans, but those places were grand and intimidating, whereas I rather liked the Partridges'; and there were times when I was on the stairs or standing in the kitchen doorway when I felt it wouldn't be so bad to be living Mrs Partridge's life.

Back home, the kitchen had been no place for me. Shelley Place did all its own growing and milling, baking and brew-ing, butchery and preserving, and I'd grown up wary of the tumultuous kitchen which had to feed at least thirty people twice every day. Not that it was somewhere I could have stumbled upon: reaching it, behind the buttery and the various larders, took some doing. Catering at the Partridges', though, was an altogether more homely affair, just for the immediate household, a consequence of which was that, as I made my way through the house, the kitchen was quite suddenly there. Along the passageway I'd go and then there it was. So much smaller than the kitchen at home, it was much hotter, too, and I'd have to take some deep breaths and let my stomach settle as I stood there watching the cook and his boy. At Shelley Place, our cooks and kitchen boys struggled to keep on top of the work, but the Partridges' cook and boy had the luxury of being able to take pride in what they were producing. The cook was a small, energetic man, endearingly vole-like, bright-eyed and long-nosed; the kitchen boy, by contrast, broad-featured and serene, a steady pourer and stirrer of sauces. I got no acknowledgement there in the doorway until they were ready for me, but I never felt conspicuous and it was as if I were taking a place that was mine, as if my witnessing their work was a small but vital part of the process, or so I liked to think. Only when the fruits of their considerable labours had been decanted into various dishes would they come over and patiently talk me through the courses: ' ... and this sauce, here, is for this little dish, here – just a spoonful on the side ... '

I must have looked a sight, the first week, in that doorway of theirs. My belongings hadn't yet arrived from Suffolk and Mrs Partridge was kindly lending me clean linen of her own but her shifts did me no favours, swamping me and rucking up fatly beneath the seams of the fancy Fitzalan-loaned kirtle.

Size, though, was the least of the physical differences between Mrs Partridge and me. Like it or not, I was very much a Tilney girl in looks, and more than several times I'd overheard one or other of my sisters described with a kind of bafflement as 'striking'. To me, back when I'd been growing up in their wake, they'd had an inside-out look to them: their skulls staring from beneath their faces, their limbs all shanks and sockets. They chewed their nails, bit their lips, shrugged their shoulders, and their glances were swift and accusatory. Always about to scarper, was how they'd looked: ready to hitch up their skirts in their claws, turn tail and run.

As for me, I bristled with lashes and brows and even the whorls of my fingertips were, I imagined, declamatory, whereas Mrs Partridge's might well make their mark by weight alone: a perfect oval, a dark dimple. But for all that she was substantial, she was light on her feet and often at our door before I'd heard her, and I couldn't help feel somehow improper in her benign, steady presence. I was tough, though, I knew, whereas she, with all that soft flesh, was vulnerable. At night, when I drew the expanse of her linen up and over my head, I'd slip entirely free of it, but she, undressing in her bedroom below me, would, I imagined, bear a criss-cross of seams and she'd have to rub those chafings away, ease the blood back into her skin to reclaim her lovely lunar glow.

Personal items, she had added, smiling nervously, to the

discussion of linen and laundry on that first morning: bundle them up, she said, yours and Lady Jane's, and hand them to Goose; don't try to wash them out yourself. *Personal items*: I'd loved that. My mother would've said – *did* say – 'your rags', and at Shelley Place I did wash them myself.

At the end of our first week, Mrs Partridge – coming across me on the stairs – invited me to accompany her to the Queen's Garden. All those flowers in there, she rued, going to waste. A queen's garden without a queen, it seemed, was a garden up for grabs. Jane wasn't mentioned and I understood that under no circumstances could she be allowed back over there, even for innocuous flower-gathering. Not that she'd miss it, I thought; she probably hadn't ever left her books to go down there even when she could. She didn't strike me as a girl with an interest in flower arrangement. Mrs Partridge said we could look on it as a bit of deadheading, which, given where we were, struck me as an unfortunate choice of word.

I told Jane I was off to pick flowers, but avoided saying where. Mrs Partridge's short-cut started at an unremarkable door in a wall on the far side of the bailey and took us into the first of a series of courtyards which could've been rooms but for their lack of ceilings. On the walls, which were rendered an apple-skin red, were stone carvings the hue of honey, of beatific faces or bucolic scenes, and in the third courtyard, high up, was a sundial incongruously painted with an arc of inky sky, a lick of moon, a gaudy splat of stars. Beneath our feet were no cobbles or flags but tiles, creamy-coloured in the first two courtyards and river-green in the third, where each square depicted a kiln-blurry beast of some kind – tails, horns, paws – or a perky fleur-de-lys. The soles of our shoes, though, scored tracks in grime, and here and there in corners lay last autumn's leaves. 'Hardly anyone ever comes this way,' Mrs Partridge explained, 'because it was built for You-know-who.'

Actually, I didn't.

'Queen Anne.'

Queen Anne?

'Boleyn.'

'Oh!' – I'd forgotten that Anne Boleyn, or 'the King's whore' as I'd more usually heard her called, had ever properly been Queen. But yes, I remembered, she had indeed been crowned, unlike the bevy of queens who'd followed her. All those queens, young and old, pious or irreverent, clever or silly, but none of them, in the end, in the old King's eyes, quite up to the job. So there I was, in the courtyard of a thousand-day queen now almost twenty years dead. Second wife of the old King, second of the six and the start of all the trouble.

Until now – until Jane, until Mary – all a queen could ever have been was a wife, a mother: chief wife, chief mother, her job to sit beside the king and grow bigger for nine months of every year, praying for the baby to be a boy. River-lit rooms had been built for Anne Boleyn but in return she was supposed to produce a prince, which, to judge from her gusto in pursuing the throne, she hadn't doubted she'd do. But how

46

had she reckoned on that? Faith in God? Or trusting to luck? Or perhaps she'd tried not to think about it: perhaps she'd told herself that it's possible to think too much.

Standing there in the courtyard and looking up and around at that building, I wondered how many men had sketched the designs for its staircases and fireplaces, then resketched to make them bigger and better, then how many masons and carpenters, plasterers and glaziers had pored over those plans. All the candles, too, to light their labours, and the chandlers who'd worked late to make those candles, and the boxes upon boxes of tapers they'd burned as they'd done so. A mountain of bills, but all adding up in the end to nothing. Jumped-up, French-spouting Anne Boleyn: you could build queens' rooms for her, you could plant a queen's garden for her, dress her in queens' clothes and take her to Westminster for a crown to be put on her head, but she was never any queen. You could banish the real Queen and her little princess and kill any number of nay-sayers – a bishop or two, a chancellor – but even that wouldn't turn a commoner into a queen and everyone had known it.

Everyone except the King, or not for a while, not until that woman had sat beside him for a couple of years, growing thinner and sharper, carping and meddling and feuding and disparaging until eventually even he couldn't fail to see her commoner's bones showing through. But a king never makes a mistake, so the fault must've been hers. She must have been a liar, a beguiler – perhaps even, you could say, if you didn't say it too loudly, a witch. A king never makes a mistake but he'll always right a wrong. He can raise someone up but much quicker cut a person down, and soon that so-called Queen was even less than the commoner she'd once been, she was a traitor and her bones not even a body but a heap, and only buried anywhere at all because bones have to be hidden or they'd be dug up by dogs.

But the shut-away daughter had lived on – if only just, in those various faraway houses in Essex and Suffolk and Norfolk, keeping to her four walls, to her chapels, confessing to her priests and consulting her physicians. For years she'd lived the quiet life, reconciled to her lot: elder half-sister to little half-brother. But then the half-brother had died and after a quarter-century that half-sister was on her way back into the very heart of the kingdom. In a few days' time, she could well be standing where I was, I thought, and perhaps she'd ask for the doors that Mrs Partridge had just locked behind us to be reopened, and then she'd walk where we'd just walked. Perhaps she'd go where we hadn't, up into the building itself, into the rooms that, twenty years ago, had housed a woman who'd been so completely sure she'd got it made.

Mary Tudor was the first ever queen coming to the Tower not at the invitation or on the order of any king. She *was* the King, if a female one. The invitation she had accepted was that of her subjects. The day Jane was declared Queen, the Lady Mary had written to everyone in England and the letter had been copied then and there, and the copy copied and so on, down row upon row of trestle tables in the hall at her Framlingham house, those copies passed hand over hand to the ready riders for dispatching anywhere and everywhere. Within two days England was blanketed with what she'd had to say. Which was, basically, *Remember me?* That was all, more or less; that was all it took: *Remember me, the old King's eldest daughter? Well, here I am, if you'll have me.*

I'd been leaving the Fitzalans' house for the Tower, for my Jane-minding duties, when news had come of Queen Mary's imminent declaration at the Eleanor Cross. The Fitzalans' excitable fourteen-year-old son, Henry, little Lord Maltravers, had taken to the streets to see what was what, and he returned just as my mother and I were heading down the garden to their barge. 'You should see it, out there,' he called after us, and then suggested we do exactly that: forgo the Fitzalan landing-stage in favour of somewhere slightly downstream, just a few streets away, where we could take a wherry and he'd see us personally to the Tower. It was safe, he assured us, perfectly safe: there was nothing in the air, that morning, he said, but good will.

'London's in love,' was, I remembered, how he'd put it. Smitten, he'd meant, by the dowdy lady who had, against the odds, just become its queen.

My mother claimed a headache but I was curious and keen to stretch my legs after two long days in the saddle. Even keener, if truth be told, to delay venturing on to the water, which was to be a new experience for me. Surprisingly, I didn't have to argue too hard: my mother agreed I could go with Henry as long as we promised to stick close to our Fitzalan minders.

Our own goodbyes didn't detain us, so there I was, minutes later, leaving the gatehouse in the company of the funny little Fitzalan heir, although, as I teetered on the threshold, there seemed to be no place in that packed lane for a single extra footfall. Somehow I managed it, took the first step and pitched myself in. Once inside the crowd, I discovered it to be built of shoulderblades. United, too, those shoulders: everyone hugging everyone else as if they were long-lost friends, but me in the midst of them knowing no one, not a soul. My heart drummed a warning but I kept calm: it had been a mistake to think I'd be up to this, but no harm done, easily remedied, all I had to do was reverse that single step of mine back up into the gatehouse. I turned but, behind me, my minder misunderstood and pressed what he intended as a helping hand into the small of my back, and dodging it took me a couple of steps further adrift. *Get me back*, I should've said to him, *please*, but my mouth had shut itself against the viscous stench: the lane reeked like a ditch, like skin and bone dumped, although actually the source was broad grins and armpits opening up for all that hugging.

Dancing, too, even in that dense crowd; a rhythm being beaten on something and a handful of people barging into bystanders, of which I was about to become one. On tiptoe, I glimpsed the feather of Henry's cap: no chance of me catching him up, saddle-sore as I was and sweltering and swollen inside my boots. Boots which then blundered into a body down on the ground, battering at a clutch of child-ribs, bringing my heart to a screeching halt; but no, I saw, looking down,

50

thank God, no body: a child, yes, but busy, unbothered, filching coins from the cobbles. Coins: that was what they were, then, those splashes of glare: handfuls of coins chucked into the air. But something else was in the sky, too, and rushing our way: black smoke, a great roiling of it. 'Bonfire,' the minder blared into my ear. He could prod all he liked but I was going back. Glancing round, though, I found the gatehouse had gone from view: my tiny steps, with which I'd been keeping my ground, had in fact been taking me deeper into the city. We were too close to the fire, its shocking incandescence, and I saw that whatever was at the heart of it was keeling over, rigid, as if agonised. But that was when Henry Fitzalan's hand took mine, and how he'd made his way back through the crowd to me I simply couldn't imagine: but there it was, his hand in mine and his smile over a stranger's shoulder, and from then on we were on the move, we were unstoppable and I was tripping over my own boots, my breath no longer hampering me but blowing me along the streets. Little Lord Maltravers threaded us expertly between elbows and then, when we turned a corner, there it was, above our heads and higher than the rooftops: a gilded tower topped with a cross. And then came the roar – Mary Tudor proclaimed Queen – and my bones were singing with it and me too, yes, even me: I was yelling, because you couldn't not, you just couldn't not.

We'd been at the Partridges' for a week when the invitation came, via Mrs Partridge: the boy husband wished his wife to join him for a stroll. They were free to meet, we'd been told on our first evening, as long as they remained in public – the herb garden in front of the house was Mrs Partridge's suggestion – and under proper supervision, which, to judge from Mr Partridge's glance in my direction, was down to me. Jane's only response to this message from Mrs Partridge was a nod. No clue as to how she felt at the prospect, although a week in her company had taught me not to expect any. She'd made no mention of that husband of hers all week, but why would she? I wondered if he might be easier, on this occasion: calmer, perhaps, than he'd been at their parting; it was possible, I supposed, that under less fraught circumstances he'd manage to show himself in a better light.

So, I'd be playing gooseberry: I'd have to stand alongside the pair of them in that herb patch – although of course I could stand at a distance, or at as much distance as a herb patch could offer. Actually, I didn't care where I'd be standing as long as I was out of that room. A week in the Tower, and playing gooseberry was something to do, a herb garden somewhere to go.

That afternoon, on the strike of three, as arranged, we closed the Partridges' front door behind us and there they were, Guildford Dudley and his attendant on the far side of various herbaceous tufts. Guildford was testing something – animal, vegetable, mineral? – with the toe of his boot, but left off as soon as he saw us. The white and gold of a week ago had been replaced by a tawny silk which inevitably did a little less for him, but still, he was a vision next to the pallid, sunken-eyed attendant. Jane should take a look at that attendant, I thought, and perhaps she'd realise she didn't have such a raw deal after all. I was quite possibly a world of fun, compared.

I loitered by the door, absenting myself as best I could, resolving not to eavesdrop nor meet anyone's eye and definitely not that of my counterpart; I couldn't envisage any cause for solidarity with him, and if his turning his back was anything to go by, he felt similarly. Jane was barely past the bee-fizzy lavender before Guildford – making no effort to lower his voice – demanded to know how she was being treated. I didn't have to be watching to know she'd shrugged the question off. The detail of her reply escaped me, but the tone was unmistakable: non-committal, if not rather positive. Undeterred, her husband launched into noisy complaint: 'Because *I'm* getting all manner of shit.'

A notable lack of response from his wife – just a frown, I glimpsed, a dutiful expression of concern but her heart not in it nor anywhere near.

Leaning back on to the wall of the Partridges' house, I gave myself up to a warming by sun-struck brick. Being at ground level offered no obvious advantage over my usual view of the green so I closed my eyes and was entertained instead by the play of sunshine on the inside of my eyelids. Perhaps, I thought, I should've called Twig along for company; then again, he might have expected a walk; it would've been mean to lure him on false pretences.

'It's pathetic,' I heard Guildford protesting, 'it's just a

chance to throw rotten eggs at a king and queen, and it's too much for them to resist; they just can't stop themselves.'

That did grab Jane's attention. 'Rotten eggs?' I imagined her frown of concern deepening into one of incomprehension.

Which he gave short shrift. 'You know what I mean.'

I wouldn't bet on it.

'Our being stuck in here,' he seethed, 'is the biggest fucking excitement they've had in years.'

'Who?' Jane asked, and her interest was audibly genuine. 'Who's doing this—' *throwing of rotten eggs,* as it were.

He was predictably hazy on the details: 'Oh—' and I imagined the dismissive flap of a fine-boned hand, *just everyone.* 'Every last one of the bastards. Even the bloke who brings in my breakfast.'

Not having the benefit of the Partridges' kitchen close at hand, he was buying meals in from the Tiger Inn, the Partridges had told us, for himself and his attendant.

'Lording it over me, all of them. You can see it,' he insisted, 'you can see it in their eyes.'

My own eyes half opened, to see him strutting up and down a row of sage. 'I mean, is it too much to expect them to think for themselves?' Then, vehemently: '*Little people.*'

At which point, as if summoned, Goose banged through the Partridges' door, flinging me an acknowledgement as she did so ('Lady Lily-Loola,' on this occasion) then stalking off across the bailey. Was Goose a 'little person'? The day before, I'd asked her where she came from and with a glorious laugh she'd said, 'A long way away, but not far enough.'

'And you know what? You know what?' Guildford's petulance knew no bounds. 'Why not just have done with it? They want to string me up, do they? Well –' he flung his arms wide '– here I am.'

Don't tempt me.

Jane's response was merely 'We've been treated well.' *We*: she and I, it seemed, were a we.

'Oh, well, yeah,' was his gloomy rejoinder, arms slapped back to his sides, 'but they'll be easier on you because you're a girl.'

Or tougher on you because you're a prick.

She changed the subject: 'Any news of your father?'

'On his way.' Guildford didn't elaborate, snapped off a sprig of rosemary to lob it over his shoulder.

Being brought in, more accurately: his father wouldn't be dropping by of his own accord for the pleasure of some flower-gathering.

'My brothers, too. Tomorrow, probably.'

Then came fulsome nose-blowing from the attendant, for which Guildford made a point of pausing, head cocked as if ascertaining some fine detail and resuming only when any more discharge would have been life-threatening: 'But she can't hold him to blame.'

The attendant coughed, perhaps from physical necessity but possibly in surprise.

Jane closed her eyes, emphatically: this, by the look of it, was old ground. *She*, the soon-to-be-crowned Queen, and *blame*, for having advanced the claim of a pretender.

'She can't.' Guildford circled her, stepping over a patch of chives but not quite clearing it, which drew a disconcerted glance from the attendant, as if we were responsible, too, for the welfare of the herbs. 'I mean, how can she blame him? What else could he have done?'

Jane must've signalled impatience or scepticism because then he was remonstrating, 'No, no, this needs to be said,' and even taking her by the shoulders, from which she recoiled into a fold of arms.

I'd given up the pretence of not watching. I was just keeping an eye, I told myself. Someone had to, and Guildford's attendant was more interested in the contents of his handkerchief.

'Because how convenient for everyone to forget what the King wanted.'

Jane started a small pacing of her own, to shake him off.

'You,' he said. 'He wanted you. Not her.'

Keep your voice down. This helps no one.

He aimed a kick at whatever it was that had been suffering his attention when we arrived.

'The King's dying wish was that you succeed him. Has everyone forgotten that?'

I wondered what was going through Jane's mind. People said the boy-King had been her soulmate, but people said all sorts of things – whatever best served their purpose – and lately more than ever. It was hard to imagine her being anyone's soulmate. She gave nothing of herself. Well, not to me, but then again, why would she? Nor to her husband, although if what I'd seen of him so far was typical, that was hardly surprising.

'And you know very well he'd never have chosen his half-sister as his heir. You do know that.'

She admitted she did, although she allowed no more than a defeated-sounding 'Yes.'

'But because he wasn't old enough to write a will—'

A gesture of exasperation from Jane: *Guildford, I know all this.*

'—my father had to see it through for him.'

His father, Lord President, protector of the boy-King, his facilitator, the man in charge.

'Because whatever the King wanted to happen, my father had to make happen. And he always did. Nothing ever mattered to him except whatever the King wanted.'

She didn't deny it, but nor did she give ground: continuing her pacing, wrapped in her own arms.

Quieter, he said, 'My father's loyal. That's what he is. Loyal to a fault.' Then, 'It's easy for everyone else: sloping off, switching sides.'

Which was what Harry had done, although of course it had been more complicated than that. Or, no, simpler perhaps. His son had been captured *en route* to London by the other side and that had been enough for Harry: he'd do whatever they wanted, say whatever they wanted – and what a prize for them, the turnaround of an earl's brother – just as long as they let his son go. Which they did.

'Everyone's pretending it was someone else's idea to

declare you but they should ask themselves what they'd have done in my father's place. He's loyal,' Guildford repeated. 'Nothing matters more to him than loyalty to the Crown. He'll be loyal to our new queen, too, if she lets him.'

That, I hadn't expected. Nor, from the look of her, had Jane.

There was a defiant glitter to Guildford's eyes. 'My mother's gone to the Queen. They've let her go to the Queen, at Newhall.'

To pledge her husband's loyalty, he meant. To beg for his life.

Jane's response was no response, just a straightforward, unrelated question which took them back to where they'd begun: 'Why did you want to see me?'

He didn't seem to have an answer. 'Well, to — *I* don't know,' and an edge of complaint to it, as if she should be the one to know.

'I must go,' she announced, to no one in particular but I was quick to peel myself from the wall. He didn't argue, but he did ask her if she'd come again. 'We'll see,' was all she said, and wisely he didn't pursue it.

I couldn't have been less prepared for what happened when I followed her back inside the house: her whirling around to me in the gloom to seethe, *'Did you hear that?'*

Hear what? I couldn't even properly see: my eyes hadn't adjusted and for that moment she was just a deeper darkness ahead of me in the stairwell.

'Did you *hear* it?'

I couldn't think: with her there, breathing fire at me, I just couldn't think. Hear what? About the loyalty – was it that? The mother-in-law begging for mercy?

'*King*,' she quoted, the word dredged with disgust. 'Guildford was never King.'

Then I remembered: *king and queen*, he'd said; *throw rotten eggs at a king and queen*, meaning, as I'd understood it, the boy and girl who'd briefly been taken to be King and Queen. That was all he'd meant, I was fairly sure; no more than that.

She said, 'He would never have been King and he *knows* it, he *knows* it,' as if I'd dare stand there and deny it. Then she was off, stamping up the stairs. 'I couldn't have been clearer about that.'

And I, for one, wouldn't have wanted to be on the receiving end of that clarity.

Halfway up, she halted and turned to drive it home: 'If he hadn't gone around *acting* as if he were King, we wouldn't be here now.'

Really? Did she really think that? People said he'd assumed airs, and I'd seen for myself the white and gold suit, but was that so bad? I was as happy as the next person to ridicule him – he did rather lend himself to it – but the fact was that he'd had a part to act, as queen's consort, and wasn't that all he'd been doing? Did she think the Queen would be so petty as to seek vengeance for that? Did she really, seriously blame her being held at the Tower on Guildford's white and gold suit?

'He's my husband – I can't help that – and maybe the King

did want me to be Queen, but since when did he want the next *king* to be *Guildford Dudley*?' and it was as if she couldn't even bear his name in her mouth. 'I'm telling you,' and it came barrelling down the stairs like a threat, 'he was never going to be King, whatever his father said.' With that, she stomped off, calling behind her, 'My husband could've been Duke Whatever-he-liked, but King?', the words ringing out in the stairwell: 'Over my dead body.'

The following afternoon, I watched from our window as perhaps a dozen horsemen arrived together at the far side of the inner bailey and rode unhurriedly across to our house. They were impressively dressed, and their horses beautiful. I'd seen horsemen before down there, of course, but only in pairs at most, distantly, and mid-assignment. Never a show of them, like this, and never at our door. What could a dozen mounted gentlemen want with anyone here? Not that I was worried, because whatever or whomever they'd come for, they were in no hurry, staying in their saddles but slackening their reins and indulging in some back-stretching. Through our open window, I caught snatches of conversation: sons, dogs, a troublesome reeve. Chit-chat. Definitely an off-duty air to the gathering. I didn't hear anyone leaving the house to greet them, nor did they seem to expect it; they sounded happy enough to be there beneath our window in the sunshine.

Then came a second, similar group, joining the first with comparable languor, and a third, by which time I'd realised their riding up to the house was simply to leave room for those behind: this was some kind of procession coming to a close here.

Before long there were dozens of noblemen down there on their wonderful horses. Was Harry somewhere among them? Harry, taking his place as the fine, upstanding man he was supposed to be. And if he was there, would he know I was here? Should he spot me, he might come up. It wouldn't be easy, though, to have him here; he'd be out of place. I didn't want him coming up here.

So, I drew back, unable then to see much more of the oncoming archers than a protracted jostling of bows, and behind them the flashes of sunlight on silk suggesting the presence of standard-bearers. Well over a hundred men in all, was my guess. The green's already-patchy grass would be getting a good kicking. Absorbed as I was, I jumped when Jane spoke up: 'Is that the duke?'

She spoke up but didn't look up: I could tell the difference, by then, from her voice alone; I didn't need to tear myself away from the spectacle to know she had her head in a book. I wondered if, in turn, had the hubbub of the crowd and the haze of horses not been drifting through our window, she'd have known from my demeanour that I was witnessing something quite different from the everyday, humdrum business of the bailey.

The duke? Could all this be for the duke? He'd be arriving under escort, I knew – but this? Horsemen and archers and standard-bearers. A hundred or more men, in all.

How would I know if he was there? Even if it were easy

to distinguish anyone in particular down there, which it wasn't, I didn't have a clue what he looked like. But then actually I did – I did see him and I did know it was him in the very instant that Jane offered the clue: 'Scarlet cloak,' adding, 'He always wears it,' as if he did so specifically to bore her.

Mid-crowd, a man was indeed dismounting inside an eye-catching bloom of that finest cloth. *Got him.* 'Yep, he's there,' I crowed; and then, when she didn't respond, 'There he is!'

'*Is* he.' Sarcastic, as if she'd never been interested.

Suit yourself. Me, I was avid to see whatever I could of the man who'd run England for the past couple of years then had the gall to ignore a king's daughter and, in her place, declare his own daughter-in-law.

The scarlet-sporting duke was joined by four others, fine figures of men but with a residual delicacy of boyhood and an air of dejection. These, I guessed, were the sons, the beloved sons. A huddle of sons, around whom other men busied themselves, conferring and casting around for direction. The duke showed no sign of discomfort, didn't cower as his sons did; at ease and busy, he appeared, as if he were at least equal to those other men in the matter of bringing about his detention. Which, conceivably, he was: the outstandingly capable duke. Only when he turned in pursuit of one of those men did I see that there was something amiss with that heavy-swinging but light-as-air cloak of his; but not until he turned again did I properly see the splatter, all down the back. An extravagant, glistening mess. Real, actual egg-throwing, then, and it took my breath away to see it because that must've been some ride through London. No wonder the sons were unnerved.

But egg was all it was, and perhaps a little of whatever else people had found to throw that would do damage – which was anything, really, because it wouldn't take much to put paid to fabric as fine as that. It wasn't what they might have thrown that shook me, though, it was that they'd thrown it at all. Anyone who wears such a beautiful cloak does so in complete surety that nothing adverse will come its way, and it was that confidence which the Londoners had wanted rubbished. Could I have joined in? However horrible the duke was, however much he'd cheated the people of England, could I have gone to some street corner with my egg or eggs and whatever else, my hands full or with a bagful, and perhaps even scooping up some dung: could I have stood there at the ready and, as he'd ridden by, taken aim and actually lobbed it? No half-measures when it comes to throwing – a throw's a throw or it's a mere letting go. Could I have lobbed an egg with the force to have it smash on his back? And then what would I have felt to see its impact, its momentary cling, its nasty slide? There's no fighting a thrown egg, no negotiating with it; you just have to take it. *He always wears it,* Jane had said, and there he was, wearing it still, ludicrously sullied though it was. He could've taken it off, but there he was, toughing it out. As I watched, he joined the man whom he'd addressed and together they strode from view, leaving the sons at a loss, which was when one of them began to cry:

right there, in the middle of that crowd, openly crying, wiping his eyes, his bearing gone. My intake of breath had Jane ask, 'What?' and I was just about to tell her – the ruined cloak, the young man overwhelmed – but I found I couldn't. Not because she'd be upset but because, I feared, she wouldn't.

Guildford's father and brothers were taken to the Beauchamp Tower where, the following morning, Jane's own father became a fellow-prisoner, although he'd arrived with no procession of any kind and we'd have been none the wiser if not informed by a carefully sympathetic Mr Partridge. Jane didn't ask Mr Partridge if she could send any message and none came for her, and then within days her father was free again, perhaps because he was the Queen's cousin's husband, or perhaps – as Jane seemed to suggest – because he was a harmless idiot.

'Oh, he's no danger,' she'd said airily, when I'd raised it.

We were getting ready for bed at the time: she sitting on the bed and me kneeling up behind her, combing her hair. Her ivory comb was carved with four figures and once, spotting me looking at them, she'd said, 'Paris,' which had me ask who she knew in France and she'd had to explain that Paris was a man judging which of three goddesses was the fairest; and when I'd asked whom he'd chosen, all she'd said was 'The wrong one.'

Now she was saying, 'My father's no threat to anyone. Full of talk, that's all. And all of it about himself.'

She raised a hand to signal I'd done enough combing, and we scrambled to swap places.

'To his mind,' she said, 'he's a thinker, but he's easily impressed and the Lady Mary knows it.'

The Lady Mary, not 'the Queen', but that was an oversight, surely, a slip of the tongue. I said that she too would soon go free, because if her father – an instigator – was already pardoned, then it couldn't be much longer before that privilege was extended to her. Not that I particularly relished the prospect, although of course I didn't mention that. Whenever she went free, so would I, but I didn't feel quite ready to go. Sometimes – times like these – I quite liked being here in the Tower. Or perhaps it was that I quite liked not being at home.

Jane said knowingly, and not without satisfaction, 'Oh, I don't think she'll be quite so forgiving of me.'

I turned to object, but was stilled by her touch to my head. She said, 'We didn't part, last, on good terms,' then told me how, when she and her family had last stayed with the Queen, back when she was still the Lady Mary, she'd gone into the chapel with one of the household's ladies in search of her little sister, and the lady had genuflected to the reserved sacrament. Jane said, 'I asked her why she did that and she said, "Because our Lord is there." So I said, "Where?" Inside the reserved sacrament, she meant, on the altar. "Because *I* don't see him."' The combing ceased, and fabrics rustled as she slid down from the bed. '"*I* see something the baker made." And of course she went and told the Lady Mary, who was –' she paused to indicate the next words weren't her own '–"very disappointed" in me.'

Exasperated, I said, 'And that surprised you?'

After all, the Queen had lived for years in fear for her life for exactly that belief.

Inspecting her stockings for holes, Jane was sharp in return: 'No, it didn't surprise me. But it needed saying.'

'Did it?' I almost laughed. 'Did it, though?' What difference had she hoped it would make? Had she thought the Lady Mary might suddenly see the error of her ways? *Oh, how silly of me! Because now that you mention it . . .*

She said, 'It's the truth.'

Which only exasperated me further. 'Well, maybe it is and maybe it isn't' – because who could ever know the truth about bread and bodies? – 'but you can't go around saying it to the Queen.'

She didn't shift, not an iota, just sent it straight back at me, 'It's the truth,' and I saw it was pointless for me to persist.

Later, lying in that bed, trying to sleep, I pondered how I didn't believe half of what I was told. At least half. And did most people, really? Just stories, surely, so much of it. But did I rub anyone's nose in it? No, I kept it to myself. As did most people. Because that was the price of peace. Smile and nod. Each to his or her own. I would never dream of trying to ruin anything for anyone else. But then again, perhaps the smiling and nodding was truer of me than of most people. I was well practised at keeping out of trouble. I'd grown up a little girl in a big house, the last daughter by a long way, accustomed to slipping by unseen, and I wouldn't have had it any other way. Jane, though, heiress of a family with the strongest of royal connections; perhaps she felt that she couldn't keep out of trouble if she tried, and so had nothing to lose.

Not many days after I'd seen the one of the Dudley brothers sobbing, I watched the tall, fair Dudley brothers' lookalike loping across the green with a lute. 'Who *is* that?' I wondered aloud, not so much asking as venting an inexplicable impatience with him. Something about him irritated me. Or everything: the capering with canines, the lording it about with that lute.

It wasn't a question, but it would get an answer because Goose was in our room and she had an answer to everything. Sure enough, she was past me to the window in a trice. 'Ohhh,' as if she had a treat in store for me: '*that*, Lady Loopy-Lou, is Edward Courtenay.'

To my amazement, Jane was up from the table and across the room: the first time I'd seen her show an interest in anything but books, and even more extraordinarily, she and Goose were suddenly a team, subjecting that young man to dual scrutiny.

'So *that's* him,' Jane breathed.

But, '*Who?*'

She didn't relinquish him, spoke to the window. 'Edward Courtenay.'

No, but, '*Who is* Edward Courtenay?'

Which then made me the object of curiosity: both girls turning wide-eyed – incredulous – to me.

But how on earth would I know? Whoever he was, down there with his fancy lute, he hadn't figured in Suffolk.

Goose started to gabble, 'Oh, but he's been here years and years, he's been a prisoner here since long before I came, back in the days of the old King.' She'd got that wrong, though, because back then he'd have been a boy. 'Since he was a boy,' she said.

'But why?' That was horrific. 'What did he *do?*'

Jane shook her head: it wasn't what he'd done, 'It's who he is,' at which I almost laughed, despite it being anything but laughable, because we were going in circles. 'Yes, but who is he?'

'*Some*one,' said Goose, turning away, leaving him be, happy to have the details beyond her.

Jane knew, though. 'Plantagenet heir; heir to the house of York.'

A possible rival claimant to the throne.

Was Jane here because of what she did – of what was done in her name – or because of who she was?

Goose was back to her sweeping. 'Too young, though, he was. His father –' she shrugged, *fair enough* '– but you can't do that to a kid, can you,' which was when I realised she was talking about an execution: Edward Courtenay's father, executed, but his son held here in the Tower.

Settling herself back down at the table, Jane said, 'But now he's going to be free.'

'Is he?' I wanted to hear more of that. He might well have irritated me, but I couldn't begrudge him his long-overdue freedom.

Goose flexed her eyebrows. 'Oh, very much a man of the Mass, that one.'

So, he'd be one of the new Queen's men.

Jane said, 'She'll wait, though, until she gets here, then make something of it.' His release, his pardoning: the new Queen would do it with some ceremony. It surprised me to hear such a worldly, even cynical observation from Jane.

'How long,' I heard myself asking even as I couldn't quite bear to ask, 'how long has he been here?'

Jane didn't look up. 'He was ten.'

He looked to me as if he were well into his twenties. I tried to remember myself at ten but it was an impossibly long time ago, a lifetime ago.

Goose said cheerily, 'Been spoiled rotten by the bishop, though.'

Jane turned a page, didn't look up. 'He's not a bishop.'

Goose countered, '*Bishop* Gardiner.'

At which Jane did look up, to reiterate, 'He's *not* a bishop. He *was* a bishop but he wouldn't accept the new teachings so the King put him in here, and if he's in here, he's not a bishop, is he.' Then she was emphatically back to her book, which left Goose's roll of the eyes for my benefit alone. It didn't go unappreciated: I should learn from Goose, I thought; I could do worse around Jane than a bit of eye-rolling of my own.

'Well, yes, *was* Bishop Gardiner,' Goose revised, put-upon, '*was* Bishop of Winchester, and I imagine *will* be again, soon.'

A barely veiled reference to regime change, which I couldn't help feeling was a bit insensitive in the circumstances, but Jane allowed it with a muttered, acerbic 'Perhaps.'

Not someone to suffer fools, was probably how Jane saw herself, if she gave any thought at all to how she conducted herself around people. Not that Goose was a fool; Jane underestimated Goose, I felt, at her peril. But then, who knew how Jane saw herself? Not me, for all that I spent every hour of every day and night in her company. We didn't talk much. Inevitably, we conversed a bit over meals, if only about the food, and also, a little, when we dressed and undressed each other. And she'd chat to me from the chamberpot, whereas I didn't use it at all unless she was on the other side of the closed door.

Several times she spoke of her sisters, which was several times more than I'd spoken of mine. She didn't hear from her family because, for her, letters were forbidden. I didn't hear from mine because my mother couldn't much write and my father wouldn't have known what to say. Instead, our steward, Mr Locke, would be checking on me whenever he was in London.

Once, Jane had described her sister Katherine to me as a rescuer of kittens and I told her about my father, about how everyone for miles around knew he'd take in any old hound. Somebody would only have to remark how they had a good ol' fella past his best and what a shame to see how he couldn't keep up, and there'd be my father leaping in with the offer of a home. Harry rescued people and my father rescued dogs. Dogs nosed into Shelley Place to throw themselves on our mercy, of which they got plenty along with a place on the hearth and the odd tasty scrap, and plenty of fussing of their ears – or what remained of them. 'Old boy', my father would address them, 'Old girl': no names, freeing them from being called upon (to which they'd have been deaf in any case) and even, in their dotage, from having to have a character. My mother had grown up in a household where dogs stayed outside and, for her, my father's adopted companions were at best a source of irritation, at worse of disgust. 'Under my feet' was one objection, although had those dogs been physically capable of having it any other way, I was sure they would've. 'Stinking' was the other, which there was no denying.

All this I told Jane, only to have her say that she couldn't remember her sister ever having actually rescued any kittens; all she'd meant was that she was the type to do so. This was the sister she'd once described to me as 'nice', in a tone to suggest that niceness was suspect.

I was amused. 'And you're not?'

Which she'd dismissed with 'You know what I mean.'

Actually, I'd said, I didn't.

'What I mean is, she knows exactly what to say to people.'

And you don't, I thought. Well, there was no arguing with

that. The surprise, for me, was that she knew it of herself, and, feeling slightly awkward in the face of that revelation, I'd turned jovial: 'Family favourite, then, is she, your Katherine?'

Po-faced, Jane said, 'All three of us are disappointments to our parents in our own different ways. None of us is what they wanted.'

'Which was . . . ?'

'Sons,' and she gave me a look, *Ask a silly question . . .* 'Although they do now have a son-in-law . . .' But he too was a disappointment, it seemed, if, for now, of an unspecified nature. 'My mother would've been happier if we girls had taken to hunting, but . . .' She sighed: 'Katherine,' *rescuer of kittens*, 'and Mary . . . Well, she can't help how she is.'

Mary, I knew from what Jane had once earlier told me, hadn't grown: Mary, the little little sister. 'And me . . . Well, my mother's always asking, what use are books?'

Best left uncommented upon, I decided. Instead I asked, 'Do your parents get on?'

She shrugged, then, to my surprise, asked me, 'Do yours argue much?'

'Might be better if they did,' and I told her how they had little to do with each other, their exchanges limited to information or instructions given in passing as they went about their separate lives. Even in each other's company they talked as if the other weren't there:

'Your father is going . . .'

'Your mother says . . .'

Then she asked me, 'Who are you going to marry?' Just like that, she asked it. Not a personal question, in her view, I didn't suppose, because in her world marriage was a matter of arrangements. But I came from a different world and there'd been no arrangement made for me, nor was there ever likely to be: me being the third girl, any dowry having dwindled and Tilney money in general having run low after the difficult years we'd had. Unlike her, I wasn't valuable. Any arrangements, I'd have to make for myself. Which, of course, was no bad thing. I couldn't have married Harry even if I'd wanted to, because although his wife had gone off with someone else before I was old enough to remember her, they were still married. And they'd stay that way if England went back to Rome, because divorce would only come with the reformists.

It was my turn to shrug, which seemed the best answer.

She said, 'I was going to be married to Edward Seymour,' and, seeing my confusion, clarified, 'His son.' Edward Seymour's son Edward: eldest son of the Lord-Protector-as-had-been. The Lord Protector, seen off to the block for his various incompetencies by the fearless duke, who'd replaced him as *de facto* ruler of England and styled himself Lord President. Jane had been going to be married to the first one's son but had ended up being married to the son of the second: shunted along to keep up with the times, to maintain her advantage.

I asked, 'Did you like him? Edward Seymour?'

Like was regrettably lame, but she answered unhesitantly:

'Yes.' Unreadable, though. 'Yes, I did.' Then she was back to her book, and I didn't like to press her.

There had been no mention of Guildford.

The day when the soon-to-be-crowned Queen reached the Tower would be the day, as I understood it, when everything would change. If Jane didn't actually walk free that day, she could certainly get packing. Queen Mary's arrival would herald a new era: calm, kind and dignified; no place for scheming and self-promotion. Lady Jane Grey would quickly become a relic, a curiosity, barely more than a story. Consigned to the past, she would, however, discreetly be handed back a future, albeit a small Jane-sized one, but nevertheless a future all of her own — well, apart from Guildford being in it, because it was too late now to do anything about him.

When the all-important day did eventually come, though, two weeks after my own arrival at the Tower, it would have passed us by had we not been up on the wall. The section of wall behind the Partridges' house had become Guildford's preferred, Partridge-approved venue for time spent with his wife, but from where, elevated though we were, we still had no view of the river.

His invitations came daily and his persistence was, I felt, genuine enough; I didn't think the intention was to browbeat Jane. Probably, he saw himself as doing her a favour: new husband behaving honourably towards his young wife. Certainly he took every opportunity to bore on about honour, which, unsurprisingly, he judged as lacking in others but to be the very lifeblood of the Dudleys.

Any good intentions aside, though, he must've been lonely, denied contact with his nearby father and brothers, and shut in a room with that baleful attendant. His eagerness for walks outside on the wall was understandable. What was unaccountable was Jane's giving in, every day, and agreeing to see him. Because giving in was clearly what it was, for her. Why did she do it? From what I knew of her, she was hardly someone to favour the path of least resistance. Perhaps she saw it as a choosing of battles, and regarded this one as beneath her. Much of their time together was taken up with his recriminations, his misguided efforts to get her attention, but never once did I hear her make even the faintest of sympathetic noises, and I had to admire her resistance to being drawn in.

All those unbidden invitations for her, day after day, but no word for me from Harry. Not that I was expecting any. Nor had I tried writing to him. And even if either of us had been any kind of writer, what would there be to say? We'd never spoken much except to make our arrangements, pressing and complicated as they were. And then, even when we'd been together, we hadn't really dared speak for fear of giving ourselves away. Nor, of course, had we had the time for it.

On the day of the new Queen's arrival, Jane could well have cried off her walk because she'd started her monthly and was notably below par. Not that she'd have had to give Guildford the real reason, although it would've been amusing to see him squirm. She'd woken pale and puffy-eyed, and had asked me what to do with her used cloth, which was how I knew.

She was uncharacteristically hesitant about handing her cloths to Goose, which was fair enough in a sense but I suspected there was more to it. After all, this was a girl who stripped off at the drop of a hat and didn't think twice about using the chamberpot in company. Nor had Goose's sensibilities ever seemed to be much of a priority for her. And anyway, we all bleed.

No, there was something beyond the mere fact of her bleeding, I felt, that she didn't like Goose and me knowing. That there was no heir on the way? But that was good news, surely, because look at Edward Courtenay: a pretender is trouble enough, but an heir to a pretender is a complication too far. Before the new Queen was in London and everything was settled for good, Jane would do best to stay unencumbered and have the fact well known. My guess was that she balked at anything at all being known about her and Guildford's marriage, even if only that they weren't so far producing an heir, and even if no one was sure that they'd ever actually tried. My suspicion was that she hated even to figure in the same thought as her husband.

She was with him up on the wall, though, that early-August afternoon when the new Queen rolled up. It was incredible that we hadn't been informed that the procession was about to arrive, that someone or everyone had forgotten to let us know: Jane's becoming irrelevant not about to begin but, it seemed, already happened and in one fell swoop.

Unforewarned, though, we inadvertently had the best possible view. As it unfolded, none of us spoke a word, but all four of us leaned over the parapet, drawn to the edge and held transfixed as if we were in the middle of it, although that was exactly where we weren't.

The inner bailey was filling up as it had when the duke had been escorted into custody, but on this occasion everyone was on horseback and there were at least as many ladies as gentlemen. The expanse and depth of velvet down there had me half tempted to clamber over the parapet and try walking on it. I would never have guessed there were so many nobles in England. Harry would almost certainly be down there among them, ostentatious Mary-supporter that he'd needed to become for the sake of his son. It occurred to me that he was always completely taken up by whatever or whomever was directly in front of him – no bad thing if that was where you happened to be, which on plenty of occasions since Christmas I had – and there was more than enough going on down in the inner bailey to keep him there. I was safe from him bowling up to see me, full of that characteristic bonhomie which, I somehow just knew, would leave Jane cold.

As we stood watching, one gentleman in particular managed to ride right through the gathering crowd. His horse was amazingly dressed – the gentleman himself, too, but it was the horse, draped in gold, that stole the show. Riding behind were two ladies, one hooded and her gem-beaded purple gown redolent of a winter fireside, the other shining blossom-white with a caul of silver threads over loosely knotted, honey-golden hair. I knew who they were; no one could fail to know them for the royal half-sisters who hadn't seen each other for so many years. The old maid was the one who was to be crowned our queen; the other, half her age, was her heir.

The Queen dismounted stiffly, which had me tense, as if to catch her should the need arise. Small, she didn't stand tall, landing on the grass like a clot of something. Her radiant half-sister dropped like a skein down the flank of her horse. So much taller and standing taller still, that half-sister had the bearing of the old King, people said, if the sharp face of her mother. She looked at a bit of a loose end, with a self-conscious sway to her hips and her hands clasped in a stab at modesty.

Her older sister crossed the grass, stepping cautiously but hopefully, as if to approach a cat, and that was when I saw the figures on their knees: a lady and three gentlemen, one of them the lute player who'd been the boy-prisoner. It was him to whom the Queen went first, crouching down as if to the child he'd been when he'd been taken from home, offering him her hands, raising him up, that lanky lad, and gathering him to her.

Look at her, that spinster of nearly forty, exiled for three-quarters of her life in a succession of backwaters, that old-fashioned dresser with her high colour and stooped shoulders: how on earth had she done it? How had she managed to walk into the Tower and take it from the King's designated successor? Not with any charm or charisma, nor any army, but simply by believing in her people. She'd appealed to her subjects' sense of fairness and if the sea of velvet down there had failed me, the sense of righteousness alone would have borne me up.

Guildford snapped back from the parapet as if severed from it. Nothing unusual in Jane keeping her thoughts to herself, but Guildford's silence during the past quarter of an hour or so was as much a marvel as anything else I'd seen. He couldn't hide what he was feeling, though: it had hit him, I saw, that nothing was as he'd thought. He'd believed what he'd been told, he'd swallowed it whole – the King's half-sister's unsuitability for the throne, the inevitability of his own wife's succession – but now saw how wrong he'd been. I might've expected to feel vindicated – *See?* – and in a way I did, but at the same time I understood something of how he felt and, quite unexpectedly, my heart flipped and I had to quash an instinct to get hold of him, turn him away from the scene.

Back in our room, Jane still said nothing, and didn't even look at me. More unusually, she didn't go to her books. Didn't go anywhere. Stood as if undecided quite what to do, as if there were actual options. For once, she was the distraction. I took up my stitching but she began pacing and then she said, 'It wasn't my doing.' She didn't specify what, but she didn't need to. Her being here, the reason she'd been escorted across the Tower precinct and why she was still residing in the Partridges' house. I didn't offer any response because I hadn't been addressed: she was merely thinking aloud. And anyway, it was hardly news, it hardly needed remarking on.

It was impossible to imagine her having hatched that particular plan, going to her father-in-law and saying, *Here's an idea, how about me for Queen?* And if anyone ever doubted it, they should spend a couple of days shut up in a room with her, because all she cared about was whatever was in her books.

Nothing else mattered to her, not the smallest of pleasures – or none that I'd ever detected. No touch of sunshine to her back, nor dish of strawberries on our tray, nor blackbird-brilliant dusk at our window. Never had I seen her pause to breathe something in, unlike me. Compared, I was a mess of hankerings. Even in the few minutes we'd been back in our room, I'd longed for a noseful of honeysuckle scent, a mouthful of pastry crust, the circling of my wrist by a glass bead bracelet that I'd left behind at Shelley Place.

What would Jane have wanted with being Queen? The throne would have taken her from her books, her councillors would have interrupted her reading. Becoming Queen wasn't something she'd done but something that had been done to her. It was the usual situation writ large, although very large, granted, because for most girls of any standing it was marriage that was done to them. Not that she hadn't also had to endure that.

She stood looking out of the window, her back to me, and said, 'I didn't want to be Queen.'

I wasn't stupid enough to believe that she cared what I thought; she was rehearsing her account, if only for herself. 'I did say no. I said it and said it.' *For all the good it did me.*

Yes, but for girls such as her, from families such as hers, there was no saying no: not to the husbands chosen for them, nor, as it happened, to thrones. Books, though, by contrast, didn't make her do anything, didn't ask anything of her. They didn't even speak until she opened their covers.

She glanced at me and now it was definitely me, rather than the window, to whom she said, 'Guildford's mother was the one who said it first.' Then, 'Which was why I didn't take it seriously.'

I didn't know Guildford's mother – but I got the gist.

'I was visiting for the day,' she backtracked to explain. 'I'd married Guildford but no way would I ever stay with the Dudleys.'

Which was no explanation at all, because what did *that* mean? Married but not married. A very Jane sort of marriage. A so-far-celibate marriage, probably. Was that, then, how she'd resisted her parents' plans for her? Useless though that resistance was, of course, because what did she think would happen in the end? For how long did she think she could refuse to stay with the Dudleys? I put down my sewing, to show I was listening. I might not be able to make sense of everything that she was saying, but I did want her to keep talking.

She was back to speaking to the window, away from me, into the distance. 'His mother was always trying to get me to stay, and I just thought this was some new ploy of hers. She said the time was near, the King was really ill, and I was his successor so I needed to be close by.'

She shrugged to show how she'd regarded it at the time – unworthy of any credence – and added in her defence, 'My own mother didn't say anything.' But in the silence that followed, she might've been hearing again her mother's withholding and listening anew to the betrayal in it, because what was the betting that her mother had known very well what was going on. 'She didn't say anything, but she did make me stay. There was the usual huge row, but this time she didn't back me up and I ended up having to stay.'

She related it to me as if it were something I'd understand – *the usual huge row*, the being backed up or not, the staying or not staying – but I had no idea how her kind of people lived their lives, no idea what understandings existed between them.

And where was Guildford in all this? Presumably he'd been there, at the Dudley home: he must've been the purpose of those visits; surely she wouldn't have gone there to visit his mother. But I didn't dare ask, for fear of putting her off her stride. I'd sit tight and take whatever I was given.

'So, we all had dinner' – a deliberately false chirpiness to make clear it hadn't been the most convivial of evenings – 'and then off we went to bed.'

Her and Guildford? If there'd only ever been day-long visits to the Dudleys before, then that could've been the first time. No longer a celibate marriage, then, perhaps. Although only perhaps. 'But next morning, I went into my mother's room and lay down on her bed and said, "I'm ill and I need to go home."'

Well, that told me something, if only that she hadn't spent the night alongside her mother. No grounds for concluding she'd been in the same bed as her husband, still less for thinking that anything had happened between them. But wherever she'd slept and whatever had or hadn't gone on, clearly she hadn't been reassured because come morning, she was at least as desperate to leave that place. If she had slept with Guildford, then she was no convert to what my mother called 'marital relations'. I felt the sting of pity for her. Mind you, I doubted it could have been all that much better for Guildford.

'And my mother said,' here she turned sing-song, to disparage her, '"No, you're not, and stop playing up, and don't show me up" ...'

Then she dropped the act to give me a direct look – *Mothers* – and before I knew it, I'd raised my eyebrows in reply: *Mothers indeed*.

Funny, though, to think of Jane as showing anyone up. Her mother should try me for size.

'But I just lay there and said, "I'm ill," and I just kept saying it, and in the end she took me back to Chelsea.

'But then a couple of days later, Guildford's sister Mary was at the steps.' She added, 'Mary's all right.' Then, 'Which was why they sent her.'

Because she'd find it hard to refuse Mary.

'Poor Mary in her barge, refusing to come indoors, crying and saying, "You've got to come back, you've just got to come back." Saying something had happened, but she wouldn't – or couldn't – say what.'

83

In my mind's eye, I saw a fragile, overdressed Mary Dudley, distraught in her lavishly cushioned barge. I might've been tempted to untie that mooring rope.

Jane said, 'Even if I did suspect it was all some nonsense of her mother's, we couldn't just turn her away, could we.'

No?

'We couldn't send her all the way back on her own.' She threw up her hands: *What could we do?* 'So, we went all the way back with her, our barge behind hers.'

She left the window for the table and settled, chin in hands. 'When we got to the Dudleys', we went into Hall but no one came. All that time on our barge and then there we were, just standing in their Hall for ages.'

I almost smirked at this, it held something of the pique of a small child in need of a snack.

'And there was Mary, looking nervous but insisting we stay. It was ridiculous.'

And then I did feel for Mary; regardless of whatever she'd been put up to, I felt for her, stuck there with a fuming Jane. 'And my mother pretending she was clueless, and then at last in came Mary's mother' – she was babbling now, in a bid for my sympathy – 'and it's all Hello-dear to me and to my mother it's May-I-have-a little-word-please-Frances, and off went the pair of them' – a sweep of her arm, doorwards – 'and I said to Mary, "Right, that really is it, that's enough, I'm off—"'

I interrupted, curious: 'Didn't you worry that this was something to do with Guildford – that something had happened to Guildford?'

'No,' and not a missed beat, unless you counted my own because it was breathtaking, that nonchalance of hers regarding her husband's welfare. Ridiculous he might well be, but harmless enough, surely; I didn't think I could have been so dismissive of him. 'But then the door opened and there was Guildford's father and some of his cronies' – her pitch and pace on the rise – 'and they came up to me and they *knelt.*' Here, at last, she did pause, to glare at me. A response was required, it seemed, but what was I was supposed to feel, picturing those men on their knees at her feet? In truth, I couldn't quite see them because I was still lost somewhere in the various comings and goings, the barges here and there, the lack of snack.

'*Knelt,*' this time the disgust loud and clear, so I could oblige with a disapproving frown. 'And you know what I thought?'

No, but go on, tell me.

'I thought they were making fun of me.'

And there I did have to catch myself because for one disloyal moment it was irresistible, the vision she'd conjured. Because she did act superior: even if she couldn't help it, she did, and, from what she was saying, everyone else knew it too. It wasn't just me who suffered the rough end of it.

'They think,' she said, 'that I see myself as too good for Guildford.'

Which brought me to my senses. *But you are,* I wanted to say, *aren't you? I mean, anyone would be. Even I would be.*

She sat back in her chair. 'Well, I wasn't going to stand there and take that; I asked Mary to tell my boatmen I was leaving. But then in came my mother, to tell me the King had died.'

It seemed to strike her anew, and suddenly all the belligerence was gone; instead, she was wide-eyed and bereft. 'I just couldn't believe it. I mean, I'd known he was ill, really ill, of course I had. Everyone knew it –' she looked to me, and I didn't deny it '– but, well, I don't know, but . . . '

And I saw it, then: how she lived her life in the certainty that thinking everything through was enough to protect against the untoward.

'And then' – and now she sounded truly amazed – 'I couldn't stop crying.'

Not merely tearful in front of people but later owning up to it, and to me of all people.

'And I said no. I said the crown was his sister's. I said no, and I said it and said it.'

And really, I wondered, what more could she have done? Punched and kicked the duke and bolted from the room? And then what? Because if everyone said she was Queen, then she was, and for one suffocating instant I felt the horror of it closing down on me, as if that fate had been my own.

'But the duke was saying, "It's not for you to decide," and my mother said that if I didn't do it then England would be taken over by papists and Spaniards; and in came my father and it was the same, Stop snivelling, do your duty, think what happens to this country if you don't. And then Guildford—' The recollection brought her up sharp. 'All lovey-dovey.'

Amazing that he'd thought that would cut some ice.

'And then...' A huge sigh, she'd had enough. 'Then there was a banquet, that evening, for those who could stomach it,' of which she clearly hadn't been one, 'and the next day we came here,' she concluded, 'and there you have it.'

Did I, though? I wasn't so sure that I did. This was the most — by far — that she'd ever said to me, but somehow I was none the wiser. All that barging about, and Chelsea and banqueting, the duplicitous mother-in-law and the husband who wasn't quite a husband. Then again, what would I have said to anyone if I had to explain what had been happening, at the same time, to me? Would I have managed to make any more sense? A clock cupboard, a house like a lantern, a lady of misrule.

It had begun the previous December. The days were no more than daubs of light, not that we at Shelley Place glimpsed much sky from behind the hefts of door, the fastened shutters and lined hangings, sore-eyed as we were in the spew from the long-smouldering fires and fatty, spitting wicks. We too were burning up: sick of preserved food, salt-addled and dry-mouthed, our headaches worsened by the interminable candlelight. How can such short days feel so very long?

But then, as the month crawled towards its miserable end, bang came Christmas and Shelley Place shook off its torpor to put on its glad rags. We Tilneys threw a party for everyone from miles around — those mud-mired miles, scoured by wind — not because my parents were sociable but because it was a Tilney tradition, and most of Suffolk, it seemed to me, came trekking through the biting gusts to knock red-nosed at our door, all but insensible until revived with our spiced ale and pastries and a fire lavish with logs.

It had been a good year, with a harvest at last and, for once, no war or plague, and more people than usual turned up that Christmas, many of whom I only ever saw at our annual party. Crowded into Hall were the kersey-bundled with the silk-draped, those who were lively with lice and others decked with gems, all of them side by side and then, later, hand in hand as the dancing demanded, and the volume of chatter was a physical presence of its own, strong enough to lift the roof. By early evening, we'd been fed twice and fulsomely, dinner and supper: Hall was girded with tables, the dishes breathing steam and the air zinging with cloves. And for those of us at the top table, there'd been special delights — jewel-bright sugary jellies and gilded stars of spice-bread, and a wine heavy with honey that kept coming my way.

I'd lost track of how long I'd been there with the food and drink coming and going, the musicians sawing at their strings: it could've been days, judging from how tired I was. But, I knew, I'd need to be back on my feet before too long, because there was more dancing to come, and sure enough the tables were soon being cleared, dismantled and stacked against the panelling, and the musicians were manfully preparing to strike up, summoning the verve from God knows where so that it would've been churlish not to honour their efforts.

And I knew I'd manage it: somehow I'd be there with everyone else and be glad of it, and not too bad at it. Light-headed, I was game, which was everything, and within minutes I was there, doing my bit, shoulder to shoulder with my fellow-dancers.

Harry turned up opposite me in the line, as eventually everyone would: taking his place as the dance required, part-nering me for that particular move. Harry, in a hallful of people I hardly knew; there he was, being so very much him-self, so very ready to give of himself, and there was something close to comical about him — the ale-ruddied cheeks and cowslick hair, the popped buttons — but he was definitely in on the joke, which only made it funnier.

'Hello, Lizzie,' he said, and that too was funny, to have a greeting voiced as if we were anywhere other than passing each other, flushed and breathless, in a dance. No one ever greeted anyone during a dance; everyone just danced. And what a funny pair we made, too: the big man and the scrap that was me. But a proper pair in that hallful of fair-weather friends, because we'd known each other for my whole life and for a moment, just one moment, as he took my hand, I felt that no one else would ever know me so well. But it was only a moment, gone in a flash and if nothing more had hap-pened later then I'd never have remembered it, I'd have danced on down that line, partner after partner, with Harry long gone as he should've been.

A little later, the music stopped and that year's lord of mis-rule came running on to the dais to direct the festivities. I knew the face – he was one of our stablelads – but the face wasn't what drew the eye. Skipping on to that little stage to cat-calls from the audience who'd voted him there, he was preceded by an absurdly swollen codpiece which spoke of high jinks behind the scenes: a host of stablelads having had a hand, as it were, in its creation.

Their handiwork had been slapdash, though, and now it was skew-whiff, the stuffing slipped, not that our puny sta-blelad seemed bothered. He was keen to display his appendage with swirls of an over-sized cloak which would've been loaned by someone twice his size.

With a particularly vicious swirl, he regaled us: 'Oh, you lover-ly lot.' A snarl, but scamp-eyed in the delivery and I recalled him as meek and mild-mannered at the stables, much more so than the other lads, which was probably why they'd voted him up there. The gleam in his eye said he wouldn't disappoint them: if he really did have to don an outsize cod-piece and whip up a crowd, then he'd not be doing it by halves. 'You lover-ly lot down there.' The dais elevated him all of a hand's breadth above us, the advantage of which was lost by his diminutive stature. 'Call that dancing, do you?' He was deriding us as he was supposed to do: we dancers who'd halted dutifully to become his audience. 'All that lover-ly little neat-stepping of yours,' and he took a couple of niggardly, prancing steps which had the codpiece bouncing horribly and of course we all laughed. 'Well, you know what?' He stood tall, as much as he could. 'Life's been too kind to you.' At this, the laughter turned slightly guarded, although the deal was that we should give ourselves over for goading, that we should lay ourselves open to it, and anyway there was safety for us in numbers. I hoped those who'd volunteered him had his interests at heart, because I saw now that he was a little unsteady on his feet; I hoped he knew his limits. 'You don't need to enjoy yourselves, do you.' He lunged accusingly and the crowd, as one, drew back, but then he was swirling again, working himself up to being a spectacle for us, and letting us off the hook. 'Because every day's a party, for you, isn't it. Not just for you. . .' he seemed unsure how to name us, '*finer* people,' said, though, with no detectable rancour, 'but *all* of you,' he crooned it to the roof before snatching it down into a playful sneer, 'with your oh-so-lover-ly indoor lives.' A flamboyant swirl of the cloak almost unbalanced him. 'But you know what? You wanna be outside with the *real* men.' His relish of the word 'real' garnered him a roar of approval: he was playing to those friends of his, now, and specifically addressed them: 'Work hard, play hard, eh, lads?' and to the rest of us, 'Out in the stables there's a lot of . . .' he paused for effect, '*horsing around.*'

Everyone obliged with the predictable collective groan, at which he giggled, losing his composure before changing tack and calling ringingly through the room, 'But who's going to be my lady of misrule, eh?' Arms flung wide, codpiece on its way to his knees. 'Where's my lady? What's the point of being a lord if I don't have a lady?' and suddenly his eyes were on mine simply because I was nearest, at the front, just because that was where I'd been when the music had stopped, and how hadn't I seen it coming? Why hadn't I realised how exposed I was, there? Why hadn't I stepped back to lose myself in the crowd?

'You,' he implored me.

Instinct had me take a backwards step, by chance into Harry – I knew it was him from his laughter in my hair, wine-scented – and he put a hand on my shoulder, possibly just to stop me from treading on his toes but it was enough, it was all that was needed to claim me from the Lord of Misrule.

Later that evening, on a dash outside to the jakes, I was sufficiently stoked on indoor warmth to be able to take a moment on the way back to appreciate the sky, which held most of a moon amid a pack of stars. The midwinter sourness was gratifyingly bracing and I left the courtyard for the rose garden. Just a minute more, I decided, but then I glimpsed a figure ahead, sitting on a wall, and the figure turned and it was Harry. Harry, here in the dark. Harry, who was never to be found anywhere but in the thick of things.

'Fresh air,' he offered in explanation when I approached, although I hadn't actually asked and if fresh air was all he'd wanted, he could've kept to the steps by the door. So, I checked, asked if he was all right, and he said he was.

Not cold?

No, 'But *you* are,' and there was no denying that, my breath seething with shivers.

Nodding towards the house, he gave me his blessing: 'Off you go.'

But Shelley Place, across the garden from us like a giant

lantern, was suddenly not where I wanted to be. And anyway I balked at being ordered; I'd go in my own time. Which perhaps he detected, because then he got to his feet, saying, 'You're right, it *is* cold,' and although he had my interests at heart, it rankled; I was quite able to look after myself. I didn't need saving from myself. But then he made me smile by adding, 'Back to the fun,' making clear that he regarded it as anything but. He was right: it was unconvincing, that fun in there. Good-natured and well intentioned, definitely, but I'd had enough of it. I'd had what I wanted of it and there were so many people who were better at that kind of thing than I was. But we were already in step on our way back, even though we didn't believe in it. We were going back indoors because we had to, and perhaps in recognition of that, we were holding hands: a conciliatory gesture. Who had taken whose hand first, I hadn't noticed, but it didn't matter because they were a good fit, our hands, and the warmth was welcome. There we were, walking along with our linked hands swinging between us as if this were something we regularly did, although in truth no one had held my hand since before I could remember.

And just as we were reaching the door, just as we were about to step into the light of the bracketed torch to be reclaimed by Christmas, just as we needed to release each other, I stopped but didn't let go. Perhaps I wanted a little more of what we'd had – the easy companionship, the sly solidarity – and possibly I'd have been satisfied with a smile, an acknowledgement of what we'd shared; but halted, Harry

93

turned, surprised and quizzical and unbalanced, and then it was not just our hands that were together but our mouths.

I'd never been kissed before, and how extraordinary it was, how much mouth he had; it was all I could do to stand there and take it. His tongue, tentative though its touches were to mine, seemed to reach right into me, and so the whole of me was held there, hanging from our joined mouths. There was nothing precarious about it, though: I'd never felt so certain about anything in my life. And all the time my heart hollered, and how exhilarating to ignore its clamorous warning, to let it ring on and on regardless, and to go ahead anyway and do just as I wanted.

But suddenly his mouth was off mine, leaving it wet and cold, and he breathed something like a bashful laugh, saying, 'We should go back inside.'

We, was what I heard of it. And *should*: how sceptically it was said. My life was all about what I should and shouldn't do and here at last was someone who understood them for the risible words they were.

And better still, and whoever would've guessed it: that someone was Harry, ever-obliging Harry, everyone's favourite. Well, I knew a thing or two about Harry, now, that no one else did. And no one but he knew the first thing about me.

II

The Queen was in the Tower but nothing had changed. If we hadn't seen her arrive, we wouldn't have known she was there. We'd had the very best view of her that afternoon, but in the following days and then weeks, despite her living just a stone's throw from us, there was nothing more, not a glimpse. She was there, though. They were both there, she and Jane, either side of the Tower, in a peculiar kind of balance: victor and vanquished. Jane wouldn't be in the Partridges' house if it weren't for the Queen, but neither, it seemed to me, would the Queen be quite the victor she was if there had never been a pretender. The jubilation jamming the streets on the day I'd run hand in hand with Henry Fitzalan, and, two weeks later, the elation hovering over the green like its own little Heaven: for all that, I suspected, the Queen had Jane to thank.

What, I wondered, would Jane – or, more accurately, her father-in-law and his cronies – have done with the Lady Mary, as she'd been, had England gone *their* way? Would they – *could* they – have left her be? She'd given Council so much grief for so long – more a bargepole in its side than a thorn – but those battles had always been about her freedom to worship as she wished. But if her second cousin had been successfully elevated over her to the throne? Would she have kept to skirmishes over altars and priests? Eldest daughter of the old King and his first, true queen, she was at least as importantly a niece of the Holy Roman Empire: not only rightful, but dangerously closely related to all the right people. True, Spain had made no move before, but back then no one – not even England's vastly powerful adversary – had quibbled over her half-brother's right to rule. With the boy-King dead, though, would the Holy Roman Emperor really have sat back to watch his niece passed over in favour of some English Protestant pipsqueak second cousin? The Lady Mary would've been trouble for Jane's regime and might well have ended up in Jane's place at the Partridges', but, I suspected, facing a far worse fate.

As it was, though, she was safely installed in the Tower's royal apartment, from where all kings and queens go to their coronations. Or, in the case of two of the old King's unfortunate queens, to the scaffold. Well, where queens go from, then, be it for good or bad. Good, though, in this case, and so much so that there was no rush, no date for the coronation. This queen could afford to bide her time; the crown was hers for the taking at her leisure and anyway, August had turned too hot to risk crowds in London.

The heat had taken us all by surprise, steaming into the sky one afternoon and setting up camp to make London its dominion. We suffered particularly badly at the Partridges', the house, hard against the Tower's west-facing wall, absorbing every last touch of the slow-setting sun. Opening the windows only seemed to let more heat in. Keeping them shut, though, didn't spare us the flies.

By mid-August, Jane and I were shrinking from each new day, not even dressing but just changing nightshirts in the morning for fresh ones. Jane looked harried and flushed, so utterly unlike herself that sometimes, despite the misery of it, I'd want to laugh. Any foray of mine beyond our room had me wearing a kirtle, but only a kirtle and as loosely as possible. I still did the runs to and from the kitchen, although they'd become anything but runs. It would have been unfair, I felt, to have expected Goose to step in just because the going had got tough: no fair-weather tray fetcher, me. But I didn't hang around the kitchen doorway, and the sweat-slathered cook and his boy didn't have the energy to talk much to me about their dishes nor even properly to acknowledge me. Which was a blessing, really, seeing as I was in their company in nothing but a slack kirtle. In turn, shamefully, Jane and I couldn't face eating much of what they strove to provide for us.

Until it turned cooler, Jane was refusing to go outside to meet Guildford. I wondered if the Queen was braving her garden, and if her blossom-white sister with her golden hair, wherever she was, was retaining her radiance. In my fevered memory, Shelley Place had become a palace of shade – the draughty old hall, the scrubbed-bare dairy-house, the slimy cobbles of a kitchen courtyard that never got the sun. I longed for it so hard that the very marrow of my bones was leaching homeward. Not that the Tilneys, huffing and puffing as I knew they would be, appreciated what they had. They should try this, I'd think – being in the basin of the Thames, cupped inside walls opened to a tight, white sky.

The moat stank. Or something did, sliding into our room and sticking close, yet keeping just the far side of identifiable so that we could never be sure it wasn't we ourselves who were at fault, that there wasn't something we should've washed or discarded, something of ours for which a pit should've been dug. In truth, all that was hanging around us was the tang of fresh linen and the faint animal scent of our hair which we'd left loose.

The nights were harder even than the days to bear, because of the confounding of the anticipation of relief, the persecutory edge to the heat, the redoubling of its efforts, *You thought you could escape me, did you?* We tried lying on top of the bedclothes but I couldn't sleep exposed so went back under while Jane didn't, which only made matters worse, the linen around me like a winding-sheet. All day every day, we were witnessing the naked greed of flies, their galling sense of entitlement, but at night came the turn of the fleas left to us by that bastard cat. The heat had them jumping for joy and winkling into our folds so that we woke every morning rubied with bites. Despite taking the heat much worse than we did, Goose was on our side against those fleas and it was just a shame they couldn't be scared to death. While we sat around dabbing our bites disconsolately with lavender water and honey, she bashed her broom everywhere and swabbed the floorboards with verjuice.

Her appetite for gossip blissfully undiminished, though, she told us that Edward Courtenay, who'd done so much of his growing up inside these walls, was already gone: skedaddled, she said, as soon as he could, and who could blame him, and good luck to him. The Queen hadn't only raised him from his knees but had restored him to the earldom of Devon, which meant that he had riches coming his way and could get credit extended to him, not least by the Queen herself. She couldn't do enough, according to Goose, for the boy who'd been shut in for as long as she'd been shut out. Rumour had it, she added, that he was spending hundreds of pounds on clothes. No longer kicking around with an incarcerated bishop, he was off into town and keen to look the part.

Dressed to the nines, Goose told us, he'd headed across the river to Southwark, where he'd made himself amply at home. Arching an eyebrow, she specified with relish, 'In houses of ill-repute.' Voiced in that accent of hers, there was something of the goose-honk in 'repute'. 'And fair enough,' she said, 'because he's a lad with a lot of catching up to do. But first things first: it's horses he should be learning to ride.'

Jane said, 'But if he's sticking to Southwark, he doesn't need a horse, does he.'

Goose continued, 'Everyone knows what he's up to' –

Well, everyone but Jane.

– 'but there they were, only a week ago, saying he'd be the ideal husband for the Queen. Now they know better, even if the poor lady herself doesn't. Everyone knows what he's up to, except the Queen herself.' Then came that gappy smile of hers at the very idea of the pair of them: the pious lady and the popinjay.

In the face of Goose's glee, Jane made something of turning back to her book. Whatever she felt about the Queen, she didn't feel it appropriate, it seemed, to make fun of her. Or for Goose to do so, anyway.

Guildford had much the same story when, on the first of the cooler days, Jane gave in and went up on to the wall to walk with him. It was still hot up there; the herb garden would have been a better choice. None of us actually walked, or even stood; all four of us sat heavily on the hot flagstones, below the jeering gulls, in as much shade as the parapet could offer. How I would've loved sight of the river inside its skin of glare. Guildford seemed to have his own source of stories, a Goose-equivalent. 'No one's impressed,' he said several times of Edward Courtenay's alleged vanity, but for someone so keen to stress just how unimpressed he was, he couldn't stop going on about it. Don't push it, I thought, because that was more or less how he was regarded by his own wife.

'. . . and,' he said at one point, 'he's gadding off south of the river—'

'In houses of ill repute,' I interjected in Goose's accent, or as close as I could get, just for the sheer pleasure of it.

Guildford looked startled, as well he might because I'd never before breathed a word in his presence. I was about to explain myself – *So says Goose* – and detected that Jane was ready to do the same but then neither of us did because it was too hot to bother, and in a moment Guildford looked away, let it go.

The bishop – Goose had been right, Stephen Gardiner was back to being a bishop – had departed too, although not, of course, for the delights of Southwark. He had work to do, serious work, not only as bishop but as Lord Chancellor, now, and Keeper of the Great Seal. This we gleaned not from Goose – not known for her interest in official appointments – but from the Partridges, over dinner one evening. That morning, Jane had looked up from her book as I'd returned from a kitchen trip, and announced, 'We're dining with the Partridges later.' The offer had been there since the very first evening, but she hadn't so far taken them up on it. When I asked if I should wait up for her, she frowned, puzzled and a little displeased at the misunderstanding: '*We*, I said: you're coming.'

I'd assumed she and Guildford were to be the guests.

'So, be ready,' she said, 'for six o'clock.'

That evening, at the Partridges' table, Jane was keen for news of the outside world and unabashed in pressing her hosts for it. This was a side of her I hadn't seen before, and hadn't imagined. Who, she wanted to know as we tucked into beef pie, had the Queen appointed to her Council? I anticipated a long list of names I didn't know but actually Mr Partridge just said, 'Everyone,' and checked with his wife, 'Wouldn't you say so?'

Mouth full, she nodded.

'All persuasions,' he elaborated. 'She wants to listen to absolutely everyone. It's a huge council,' which was when Mrs Partridge chipped in with the news of Bishop Gardiner's promotion, adding, 'And I didn't think she liked him, because he didn't help her mother back in those days.'

Mr Partridge said cheerfully, 'Oh, I don't think *any*one much likes him,' and Jane almost smiled when she added, 'And I think that's mutual.'

'Makes him a good choice, though, I suppose.' Impartial, I took Mr Partridge to mean.

Jane said, 'He does like Edward Courtenay.'

'No, *did*,' Mrs Partridge whispered, 'because have you heard about him?'

Jane said, 'We hear of little else.'

'The only person who hasn't heard,' said Mr Partridge, 'is the Queen herself, who's still thinking she'll marry him.'

But Mrs Partridge wasn't having that: 'So people *say*. That's what they like to think, Nathaniel, but I'm not sure she's that—' *stupid*? Whatever the word, she thought better of using it.

Nevertheless, there was a pause, in recognition that she might've gone too far.

Then Jane piped up, 'Is Mass being said?'

The Partridges appeared embarrassed by this cutting to the

chase. Mrs Partridge looked to her husband, who nodded in reply but busied himself with his piece of pie.

Jane asked, 'And does the Lady Elizabeth go along?'

Mr Partridge considered. 'Well, we've heard she's been ill, lately.'

'Headaches,' Mrs Partridge explained. 'Chills.'

Jane said, 'Well, she's going to have to become an invalid if she wants to escape it for much longer. The Queen won't allow her to keep getting away with it.'

An uncomfortable lack of response from the Partridges.

'She's either going to have to start going to Mass,' Jane said, 'or come out and say she won't, and – I can tell you – she'll never do that.'

Would you, though? But yes, I realised, she almost certainly would. And already had, with her comment in the chapel about the baker. But now she was shut in the Tower, with no one to hear what she had to say, whereas Elizabeth Tudor was still at liberty, in the public eye: a vision to sustain those who needed it, which might just be what she was keeping in mind as she trod her careful line, and wasn't there something to be said for that?

'Yesterday,' Mrs Partridge said in a hushed tone, 'someone threw a knife at the Queen's chaplain at Paul's Cross,' adding hastily, 'It missed, but—' *imagine the commotion.*

Jane shrugged, as if to say it was nothing, it was only to be expected. 'It's all already happened,' she said; 'we already know better. People won't be turned back to the old days. No one will take it.'

No one. She was talking as if I weren't there – nominally Catholic me – which didn't much matter because I was accustomed to her bluntness. But as far as I was aware, we knew nothing of the religious persuasion of the Partridges, even if there was the suggestion of nothing-hard-and-fast about it.

'Well,' Mrs Partridge said, with her serene smile, 'the Queen has said that everyone should practise according to their conscience, unless Parliament ever chooses to rule otherwise.'

Jane made a face, derisive. 'Yes, but you know why that is? It's because she can't imagine that anyone, given the choice, would be anything other than a Roman Catholic. Still, I'd like to take her up on it – can we have someone preach here at the chapel?'

'Actually, no.' Mr Partridge, apologetic. 'Because that, I'm afraid, she *has* forbidden.'

Jane was puzzled: 'Preaching here?'

'Anywhere,' admitted Mrs Partridge.

I watched her take it in. *Forbidden.* The clergy back merely to conducting Mass, and nothing more to say for themselves.

'Not that it's stopped some of the bishops,' Mrs Partridge confided: 'because there've been arrests.'

Jane put down her spoon. 'Who?'

'Bishop Hooper,' said Mr Partridge, 'and Ridley.'

'Rogers,' his wife spoke over him, 'Latimer.'

'And the archbishop?'

Cranmer, the author of all the changes, and the champion all those years ago of Anne Boleyn.

The Partridges demurred.

Jane was confounded. 'Really?' she pressed them. 'Not Thomas Cranmer? Are you sure?' Because him, surely, above all others.

The Partridges looked equally perplexed.

Matter-of-fact, Jane concluded, 'Oh but she's biding her time, isn't she. She's making him sweat. Because he's the biggest prize. She'll save him for last,' and I marvelled again at her worldliness. Then, 'There's the King's funeral still to do, of course, and I imagine she'll claim him, now, for Rome.'

A Catholic funeral for the Protestant king.

'There's been no decision, is what we've been told,' said Mr Partridge cautiously.

Jane dismissed this. 'But it's what she'll do.'

Mr Partridge still wouldn't quite have it: 'I really don't know, you know: the vigil, for instance, is still in darkness.'

'Darkness?' I hadn't been able to stop myself, because what kind of vigil was that?

Jane said, 'Candles are papist.'

I knew what she meant but, really, '*Are* they?' because weren't they also just candles? Pointedly, I looked around at the various candles that lit our soirée. Candles also just light up darkness. And darkness around a coffin was just wrong, surely, because what comfort was that to a soul?

Jane ignored me. 'It'd be monstrous of her,' she said, 'to do that to him, to go against his final wishes, against everything that ever mattered to him.'

The Partridges looked sympathetic.

'I mean,' she insisted, 'to do that to her brother! The brother she always said she loved so much.'

'Yes, but it's *why* she'll do it, isn't it,' I said. 'I mean, if she does. She'll want him to have a proper burial—'

Now Jane did turn to me, fierce-eyed.

'—as she sees it,' I finished.

'After everything he did,' she said, tight-lipped. 'After what he lived for. His whole life was dedicated to moving his people away from this . . . ' words failed her, 'pointless . . . magic.'

I managed, 'I suppose that's not how she sees it.'

Icily, she made sure to have the last word: 'I don't care how she "sees" it; she's *wrong*.'

And so it was, too, the following day, when Goose flourished one of the new coins, like a child with a find: 'Look!'

Jane didn't look, or not properly, bar the merest glance to ascertain what it was that Goose had in the palm of her hand.

I did though, craning, making an appreciative noise for the sake of politeness.

Goose carried on, artlessly: 'What's it say?' She followed the inscription with the tip of her index finger.

I doubted I'd be able to make sense of it so I drew back, but she didn't let it rest. 'What's it say, here?' She advanced on Jane, who tutted, glanced and said, '*Veritas temporis filia*,' as if Goose were somehow at fault for something.

But Goose laughed because for her – as for me – that answer was no answer at all. 'No, but what does that *mean*?'

Again Jane's response was brusque. 'It *means*, truth is the daughter of time.'

Goose's protest was predictable: 'What's that?' *If you've got something to say, say it.*

'It *means*' – impatiently – 'you can't hide the truth for ever.' Then she looked at Goose full-square to pronounce, 'But it's superstition.'

Which didn't help matters, because, 'What is?'

'Everything that she' – the Queen – 'regards as the truth.' Said as flatly as if she were passing on news, of, say, a blocked thoroughfare: some inconvenience of which a person might like to take account. 'It's just superstition.' And as if that decided it, she went back to her book.

'But ... she thinks it's the truth,' Goose tried: a genuine effort to comprehend what she was being told.

'Yes,' Jane didn't look up. 'She does. She thinks it's the truth.'

Goose slid her gaze to mine but I looked away. I was saying nothing.

I was thinking, though. I was thinking that if Jane believed the Queen to be deluded and ignorant, then presumably she judged her unfit to rule. But if not Mary Tudor, then who did Jane deem worthy of the throne? Not the sly sister, as she saw her: I didn't imagine Jane was any supporter of the Lady Elizabeth. And the Lady Elizabeth could never rule in place of the current queen because, if not one half-sister, then how the other? So, no half-sisters. But if no half-sisters, then who? Who, to Jane's mind, should be ruling England? She'd claimed she didn't want to be Queen, but for someone who made such a lot of noise about telling the truth, my suspicion was that she wasn't being entirely truthful with herself.

Jane's scathing comments were nothing compared to how far some people would go to make their opposition known. A knife aimed at a chaplain later that week was wielded rather than thrown, which made it brutally effective. And perhaps the new Queen did end up listening to her conscience, but perhaps it was the increasingly knife-happy populace that worried her into playing safe. Whatever the reason, her brother was given a Protestant funeral at Westminster Abbey, conducted by his beloved Archbishop Cranmer, while the Queen kept to a requiem Mass said at the same time in her own chapel by the newly favoured Bishop Gardiner.

The radiant half-sister stayed away from both, Mrs Partridge told us that evening, when she was up in our room. Not even the laying to rest of a little brother, it seemed, would have that princess show her true colours. Jane made no comment while Mrs Partridge was with us but as soon as we were left on our own, she said, with a longing the like of which I'd never heard from her, '*I* should have been there.' She was standing at the window as she spoke, looking away over the green, and I felt I should back away, leave her be, but I'd have only gone into the bedroom and what good would that have been to her – me on the other side of the door as if waiting for her to finish her mourning? So I stayed, standing there – almost, but not quite, at her side – until, with a sigh, she returned to her books.

At least her friend was at peace. I hoped she hadn't heard the rumour – as I had, at the Fitzalans' – that he'd have died sooner and more mercifully had her father-in-law not engaged the services of a woman to administer potions which prolonged his agonies. The King had been kept alive, people said, day after day, bloating and peeling and leaking until he'd signed that document in favour of Jane: splintering his ribs with his coughs and vomiting up the lining of his stomach, and all the time the duke at his bedside with that piece of paper and *Sign this, why don't you sign this* . . . Was it possible to keep a dying boy alive? I didn't know, but certainly the Fitzalans had been convinced.

The duke's own death would be over in an instant and there'd be no fighting about his funeral because traitors don't have funerals: a dead traitor disappears as if he never existed in the first place. Guildford had been saying that his father wouldn't even come to trial but then, when the date of the trial was made known to us, he'd switched instead to predicting a favourable outcome. 'She's pardoned everyone else,' he'd hector Jane, as if it were her personal failing that the pardon hadn't yet come. And in a way, I understood his refusal to believe it, because what did we know, shut up in the Tower while the new world took shape outside? It was possible, I supposed, that at any time we'd hear that the duke had indeed walked free. After all, Jane's father had, so it was no wonder that Guildford continued to hope for the best for his own father. And proper, too, surely. And hadn't he and Jane themselves just been indicted but reliably informed that they had nothing to fear? Their own forthcoming trial, Mr Partridge assured Jane, was merely for show. But then, they were children, or almost, not far off, and I remembered Goose's words, *You can't do that to a kid.*

But the duke's trial went ahead on the 18th of August and he was found guilty. The following day, up on the wall, Guildford was testing Jane's patience. The wind was testing mine, although it seemed churlish to resent it, given the stifling conditions that we'd recently endured. *Be careful what you wish for.* Guildford's attendant was the only one of us in relatively good spirits: hopping up, startlingly, to perch on the parapet. I'd been at the Tower for exactly a calendar month. Sometimes it seemed to me that we'd been living at the Partridges' a long time, and sometimes it didn't. That particular day, it did.

I was no more keen on Guildford than Jane was but his reaction to the verdict was understandable, because hadn't he been Daddy's little prince? Literally so, in the end, if only for a matter of days. Surely it was natural, to say nothing of honourable, for him to be believing the best for his father until the very last moment, and I wished Jane could find it in herself to humour him, if not for his sake then for ours, so that we didn't have to listen to his whining. But I might as well have been wishing for the moon.

He was saying yet again, 'She's pardoned everyone else.'

'Not everyone,' Jane corrected him. Mr Partridge had told

us of two other men who'd had trials and guilty verdicts. Their names had meant nothing to me, but he and Jane had agreed they were odd choices for the block.

'*Practically* everyone,' Guildford dismissed those two unfortunates, 'including your own father.'

Her traitorous father.

'My father's a fool,' she said mildly.

'Yes,' he seized on it, 'whereas my father's useful. He ran this country for two years, he got England on an even keel after all the mess. He did an amazing job, you know he did. Everyone knows it. No one else could've done what he did. And I'm sure the Queen's a good woman and everything, but so what? She has to govern this country now: that's what she has to do, and she'll need all the help she can get. And not' – this was said with disgust – 'from a load of clerics.'

His father reinvented as good-natured helpmeet: I had to admire his gall.

'And everyone listens to my father.'

Not any more, they don't.

'And he'd give it all he's got.' He kicked distractedly at the parapet. 'He's incapable of doing otherwise: you know that. He lives to work. And he's loyal.' We were back to that. 'He'll do anything to stay loyal to the monarch.'

'Yes; on which note,' Jane remarked, 'have you seen him lately?'

Guildford was thrown: it was a nonsensical question because 'You know they won't let me see him.' He gave her a searching look: what did she mean? What was she up to?

'Oh, but you can see him anyway.' Her upturned little face, in the sunshine, was unreadable. 'You can see him if you look out of your window towards chapel when the bell's ringing for Mass.'

He was still staring at her, clearly as baffled as I was, so she spelled it out: 'He's recanted, Guildford. Turned his back on everything he fought for, all these years, just like that. Down on his knees again for the Virgin Mary. That's how far he'll go to be loyal.' And with that she was off, leaving him gawping in her wake, the wind contemptuous of his hair. At a complete loss, he turned from the sight of her, which meant that inadvertently he turned to me and then he was staring at me as he'd been staring after her, confounded. To spare him, I rose – it had me reel, the rush to my feet – and was on my way, hurrying after my charge.

When the door to our room was shut behind us, I demanded of her, 'Is that true?'

She looked affronted: why else would she have said it? So it was true, then: she had seen the duke. She was rarely at our window but she'd seen him on his way to Mass, which meant she'd been watching for him, she'd known to wait for his capitulation. Something else that look of hers said was: *Who are you to question me?* Well, I was the one with her husband's stare burned on to the back of my eyes. She'd delivered that most hurtful of blows then hadn't so much as glanced back at him. 'Did you really have to tell him like that?' He hadn't deserved that.

'*Listen,*' she was at least as loud back at me, 'his father is despicable. Imagine betraying your most fundamental beliefs for a few more years of life.'

Yes, and imagine telling his son like that.

And, yes, actually, anyway, *since you ask*, I could imagine it, I could imagine perfectly well trading a prayer book for my life.

'Elizabeth, all this –' she threw an arm wide, encompassing who knew what, but her anger was unmistakable '– is the duke's fault.'

All that had befallen her. And of course she was right: what did I know? A mere month of her life, I'd known her, and it had felt like a long one, but lived pleasantly enough in here. I knew just about nothing of her life before our time together here in the Tower. Except this: the duke had taken her up, which she hadn't wanted in the first place, and now he'd dumped her, which was even worse.

The duke's recanting got him nowhere: he was to be executed in four days' time. The Queen had left London even before his trial. She'd spent a couple of weeks at the Tower but she could leave whenever she wanted and one mid-August day she'd upped and gone to another of her palaces. Richmond, we heard from Mrs Partridge, which for me had a lovely ring to it: upriver, to Richmond. We hadn't seen her leave. She'd entered with pomp and ceremony but perhaps her greatest luxury now was privacy; she could choose what, if anything, to give of herself to her public and on this occasion she'd chosen to leave via her private gates. All those years of her every move being subject to scrutiny and objection, but now she could come and go at will and all England had to fall in with her wishes.

Her leaving before the duke's trial was pointed, Jane told me over supper that evening: the duke's fate was to be seen as a matter of justice rather than personal vengeance. But for all its supposed impartiality, in the end the trial hadn't, we'd heard from Goose, been dignified. He'd made a scene, broken down and begged for mercy. I wondered how Jane had felt to hear this bit of Goose-gossip, because she herself had pleaded in his Hall on that day of her barge journey from Chelsea — not for her life, true, but near enough — but he hadn't listened to her, had he.

In the final two days of his father's life, Guildford made no mention of nor even the merest allusion to the pardon that might possibly be on its way from the Queen. All that talk of his abruptly stopped and was so thoroughly gone that the prospect might never even have crossed his mind. No word, either, of the many various injustices or indignities that usually he perceived himself to be suffering. Up on the wall, he kept instead to observations, which were either overly enthusiastic, like those of a little boy ('That man down there really doesn't know how to handle that horse') or cautious and perplexed, like those of an old man ('I don't like the look of those clouds'). Where was the Guildford we knew and didn't love? I'd spent a month willing him to shut up, but now I was missing his rants. Rather his rants than her silence.

I was sure he hadn't stopped hoping for the best for his

father. He didn't look as if he'd given up: on the contrary, he had the look of excitedly nursing a hope but sensibly keeping it clear of his wife's scorn. Her impatience with him was all too obvious, probably not least to him. But God only knew what she expected from him, under the circumstances. To him, his father had been a hero, a leader, a man of vision, but in a matter of days he'd be obliterated and Guildford himself would be no one, or less than no one: son of a traitor, his life ahead of him merely to be got through. His wife standing unsympathetic beside him, clearly bored to stupefaction, could only have served to stress how alone he was. Which made two of us.

On the morning of the duke's execution, Jane and I rose sluggishly, in unspoken accord, so that the deed would be done before we were up. As on all other days, breakfast came; Goose persisted in serving it daily even though neither of us ever touched it. We'd both made clear more than once that we didn't want it but all we'd ever got for our pains was a big, loose Goose-shrug to suggest that our wishes on the matter were irrelevant. *You can wish all you like*, said that shrug, *but for as long as the sun rises over the Tower, jam will be decanted into little dishes at dawn.*

So, the breakfast tray came in that morning as usual, with the usual niceties observed: linen-wrapped rolls; glaucous jam; eggs with shells so clean as to seem supremely pleased with themselves. The bread would keep for later or find its way to Twig if he was lucky, and the untouched jam could be spooned back into its pot, but what happened every day to our rapidly cooling eggs? Goose ate them, was my guess, just as she probably made neat work of the bread and jam.

And who could blame her? She needed all the help she could get: she was never at her best, first thing. That particular morning, we were treated to a truncated acknowledgement in place of anything that could accurately be termed a greeting: 'Ladies . . .' Blur showed on Goose more than on most people because of her colouring: those red-rimmed eyes got her off to a poor start. Jane was unusually dishevelled for the hour, but that was the extent of her indisposition; her Goose-greeting was as crisp as ever.

So the formalities were observed in our room while, on the other side of the wall and a short walk away, someone lugged a pail of water towards the site of an atrocity, preparing to tackle the sullen cling of blood to wooden boards; blood that had, just an hour beforehand, richly filled a man. While we'd dozed, the duke had presented himself for his own butchering. Ending a lifetime of being respected, consulted and deferred to, he'd knelt for an anonymous beefy bloke whose only recommendation was a sure hand and a hefty swing.

Had that day dawned for the duke in any recognisable way, or had it been a mere weakening of the dark? I'd bet that whatever he'd decided to believe about bread and wine hadn't changed the God to whom he'd prayed during those hours of darkness, nor what he'd said to Him.

Long before Jane and I had emerged from beneath our pretty coverlet, most Londoners had gathered on Tower Hill to witness the killing of the duke and simultaneous confirmation that England's throne belonged to the eldest child of the old King and his first wife. The mess of the past twenty years – the string of dead and disgraced queens, the wrecking of churches and murdering of men of the cloth – had been a mishap, and all it would take was the love of a good woman for England to be England again.

Something told me, though, that no one really believed it. What had Jane said, that night at dinner with the Partridges? *It's all already happened.* Change was everywhere, and everybody knew it, and the problem for the Queen, it seemed to me, was that a lot of people had known nothing else. How could those such as Jane and Guildford be returned to the old way of thinking if they'd never actually known it? This queen was a generation too late, it seemed to me; if she wanted to return England to how it had been in the days when her mother was Queen, then she would have to get rid of us all, she'd have to put us all up there on that platform and no number of bucketfuls of the Thames could ever wash all that blood away.

The crowd at the execution that morning would have been its own worst enemy, keeping thousands too distant from what they'd come to see, but still they'd have felt it: the rippling recoil from the thump of the blade. We two girls, half asleep in our bed, felt nothing. One advantage of captivity, then: our heads resting oblivious on pillows while a man on the hill outside was losing his to an axe blade. But however much we acted otherwise, we weren't untouched by what happened on that morning. Jane was a step nearer freedom.

She was no longer allied to the Duke of Northumberland because there was no longer a Duke of Northumberland. It was a big step forward, for her; a big step nearer being a normal girl, or a normal noblegirl, give or take the small matter of Guildford. And I'd soon be on my way home.

After our Christmas kiss, Harry didn't reappear at Shelley Place for weeks, it being the hardest time of year to travel, but in all that time I jumped at every single answering of the door. Whenever he did manage to come, how, I wondered, should I be? I'd never been anyone in particular before: little Lizzie, carelessly unberibboned and always late to the table. Youngest daughter of his oldest friend. But now I was the girl who, in December darkness, had worked her mouth against his.

Incredibly, he arrived on St Valentine's Day. When I came into Hall for supper, there he was, taking his place at the table, and, 'Lizzie!' he laughed, as if it were a joke, which I supposed in a way it was.

It was Lent, which our household – unlike his – observed, so the evening was subdued, with dutiful servings of God-awful stockfish rissoles, not that Harry let it dampen his mood. He was his usual self, his talk as ever of his house and farm, his sons and staff and tenants, his dogs and horses. All I could think, though, all evening, was how he'd taken hold of my hand when everyone else was indoors having the type of fun they were expected to have, and under the vigilant stars he'd licked my tongue from my mouth.

If he could be his usual self, then so could I – laughing at his jokes – but surely he knew as well as I did that he couldn't just kiss me like that and walk away. A physical impossibility, was how it felt. There he was, at that table, in the firelight, as a guest of my parents, with our chaplain and our steward, one of my brothers-in-law and one of my uncles, and he was playing to them all but I knew my time would come.

It being Lent, no spiced wine was served after supper, nor anything else that might make a February evening bearable, so, despite the company, bedtime came early. At Shelley Place, Harry slept as we did, alone, with no need of his principal servant in his room. Unguarded, trusting to us.

Well, more fool him.

Up in my own room, undressed and ready for bed, I waited for the house to settle, the brief increase in activity downstairs putting me in mind of how the dogs turned around and around before bedding down. Below me, tables were cleared, folded up, stacked away, and various doors locked, bolted, barred. Then at last was the silence for which I'd been listening: there it was; it, too, holding its breath.

It was into that silence that I would venture. I'd have to be the one to go to him: he couldn't come to me, not least because he didn't know the way to my room.

Closing my door behind me felt like a launching, a giving up of myself to Fate. Never before had I walked through Shelley Place after everyone else had gone to bed, so it was all new: the listening hard and treading light, the sniping floorboards and fugitive shadows. My nightdress was voluminous around me so that I felt I was flying. Down my staircase I flew, and past the oriel window. I carried no light and had no need of one; I saw myself luminous in that window: I was my own light. Up the stairs, to the gallery; everyone else, all around me, earthbound. All those Lenten-cold bones, everywhere around Shelley Place, huddled into bedclothes. Was that, I wondered, what God wanted of them? I might've believed it, once. And if I knew at the back of my mind that I wasn't flying but falling, I didn't care, because who better to break my fall than Harry.

Hurrying along the gallery, it was as if I were coming free of an old skin, although actually I'd only ever been a good girl in so far as I'd never been actively bad.

I didn't know what was going to happen in Harry's bed. I didn't even know what I wanted to happen. I'd grown up fearing the indignities of a wedding night, but this was no wedding night. What, though, was it? I didn't know and didn't care, and that was the wonder of it: to be trusting to luck, to have faith in Harry. Nothing bad ever happened when he was around.

Which was all very well, but at the top of his staircase I found a closed door. Ridiculously, I hadn't anticipated that. Intent on leaving my room and finding my way, I hadn't thought as far as his actual bedroom door. Which would, of course, be closed. There's no winning over a closed door, no talking it round; its sole purpose is to stand there asserting its brute resistance. And so there I stood, brought to a halt, feeling silly, wondering how to get past it.

Knocking, I felt, would be oddly impersonal (*Anyone there?*). Should I call him? Call him what, though? I'd never called him anything, he was a friend of my parents and it hadn't been my place to call him anything. My place had been to laugh at his jokes, answer his dutiful enquiries as to my well-being, and welcome his flattery. Nor could I announce myself, because he always called me Lizzie but no one else did and that included me. So, both of us nameless there in the dark.

That door was so much bigger than I was but I'd come this far and couldn't let it refuse me. I settled on the simplest course of action: I'd to give it a try, even if I was likely to come humiliatingly up against a lock, a bolt.

To my surprise, though, when I turned the handle, there was give, and actually it was too much too soon because then there I was, in an open doorway but no nearer knowing how, in all that darkness and silence, to make my presence known.

But for a moment I forgot about that, forgot about me, because the darkness and silence inside that room was so different from everywhere else in Shelley Place and the difference of course was his being in it: he was there, I knew, even though there was nothing of him to see or hear. He was there, *he was there*, and for a moment that was enough.

But then it wasn't. I paused in the crack of the door, hoping he'd become similarly aware of me. But no word, so I was going to have to do a little more. I pushed the door wider although I myself didn't move.

Still nothing.

I made myself speak: 'You awake?'

Within the bed-hangings was an abrupt and drastic shift: him, caught unawares. '*Lizzie?*' Startled, but a squeak of protest in it too.

I closed the door behind me.

'*Lizzie?*' pitching upwards, towards panic, with a buffeting of the hangings: he was up and at the edge of that bed to ward me off.

And I felt for him, I really did, even as I wanted to laugh, because I knew he had to do the protesting and objecting, and I understood he even had to *feel* it, too. But it was pointless, it was wasted effort, because whatever would happen would happen. I wouldn't be discouraged. This was for me to do; he couldn't do it – family friend, older man, household guest – but I could. He had to let me do this, he had to leave it to me. I was the one who had to cross that room. Me: walking tall, luminous.

He kept up his complaint as I moved towards his voice. 'Lizzie, you can't do this, you can't come in here.'

But it was nonsense, and undeserving of a reply. What I said instead was, 'I'm freezing,' which was true, although coming from the staircase into an ember-lit room, I should've been warming up. 'Let me in.'

He had no choice, I was climbing in anyway and the onus was on him to shift.

The warmth of him alone was an embrace, snatching me up so that there was no turning away, and instantly I was lost to it.

'You *are* cold,' and he had to take hold of me because not to do so would've been unkind. With a little laugh at my audacity, he asked, 'What are you *doing*, coming here?'

'This,' I said, and kissed him.

And so there we were, kissing again, just as we'd kissed before: all the time in between collapsed to nothing. The muscularity of his mouth, yet nothing softer. He took a breath to say, 'You should go back,' and I said, 'I will,' which was true: I would, sometime. But in the meantime, there was no one to know I was there. This night was not the mere dark half of a day; it was made of different stuff. It was vast – stretching from the bed, the room, the house – and it was all for us.

I laid myself down along the length of him. I'd landed: fallen, and landed. I was heavy on him, substantial, real. We lay bound in linen, a tangle of limbs, every bit of me dwelling on the sensation of every bit of him. This was my world, now: I was home in the grain of his stubble, on the plane of his breastbone, up against the uncompromising collarbones. But we stayed wrapped chaste in our nightshirts: kissing was all we did, that long first night, and at the time I assumed that his reticence came from consideration for me, but later I wondered if he'd been scared.

I should go back: we both said it often enough but there came a point when it was indisputable; I really did have to go back to my room or I'd fall asleep and be found by his servant in the morning. So, back I went to my room, but lost no sleep over it; it was, I knew, no more than an interruption.

From then onwards, all I did was wait for the next time. Whatever was going to happen would have to keep to the moments between moments and to places that didn't really exist. Spring was coming, the better weather making for easier rides home, for fewer occasions when Harry would stay overnight. I had to find places other than the guest room. I needed to furnish our shared time, and who better to do that than me? Me, who'd spent my life in the numerous nooks and crannies of Shelley Place. Now, suddenly, I was running the show and I was good at it, delving into corners which previously I'd avoided, where before perhaps I'd been scared or lonely or cold or bored. I had good use for them now.

On the day of the duke's execution, Guildford's presence in the neighbouring tower lay heavy on me, but I watched in vain for any sign that it was the same for Jane. What was it that I wanted her to do? I had no idea. *Something*, though. Shouldn't we be doing something for him? Weren't we in this together?

No word came from him for many days afterwards and eventually I felt compelled to raise it. Over dinner, uncomfortably aware that I was straying into territory that wasn't mine, I asked her, 'Do you think you should see Lord Guildford?'

I wasn't sure I'd ever even spoken his name before.

She looked up from her slice of apple tart. 'Why?'

It was the most open of looks, but then again, was it? Or, in holding my own gaze as it did, was it a tad defensive?

If it was, she won, because I found I didn't know how to answer. And if she truly didn't know, then I couldn't tell her.

Returning her attention to her tart, she said, 'You go, if you want to,' and again, there might've been some indignation in it but it could as well have been genuine, because when did she ever say something that she didn't mean.

You go, if you want to.

But that was ridiculous. And I didn't want to. Did I? Of course I didn't. And it wasn't for me to do, anyway. What could I do for Guildford?

But I did end up going to see him, and at her behest. It was September before he broke his silence, via Mrs Partridge; and to Mrs Partridge Jane was all acquiescence, properly wifely, agreeing to be there for her husband as long as the rain held off; but then, that afternoon when the chapel clock struck three, we were still in our room and she gave no indication of being about to leave. I stood abruptly, attempting to look purposeful, hoping to prompt her. But she glanced across at me to say, 'Tell him I'm ill.'

Him.

She'd intended this all along, I realised, and now it was too late for me to do anything much about it.

And *ill*? A lie, from her?

I stood there, gormless, dropped right in it, charged with doing her dirty work. She looked back down at her book in order to dismiss me – but guiltily, I was sure of it, as well she might because what had happened to only ever telling the truth? And I could've said so, I could've thrown a hissy fit, refused to go – '*Your* husband, *your* duty' – because she couldn't have made me do it. But he was already waiting, that bereaved boy, up there on the wall, composing himself for the encounter, perhaps even rehearsing silently for it as he watched the rooftop door for her arrival. I didn't have to like him to feel sorry for him. I simply hadn't the heart to leave him there like that. It was common courtesy and cost me nothing to go and put him out of his misery.

As I stepped up through the doorway, he watched me intently. No, actually, he didn't, he watched intently for Jane and let me go across his vision. I could almost see myself gliding across the surface of his eyes. What I saw of him was how awful he looked, and I had an urge to explore precisely how, but was wary of staring. His attendant, surveying London, kept his back to me. When Guildford realised I was alone, he focused on me just enough to hear me out.

Apologetically, I said, 'She's ill,' delivering what I knew was a lie, which he didn't deserve, and squirming in case he saw through it.

But he looked a bit dazed. 'Ill?' It seemed to worry him and

I realised too late that she hadn't provided me with details as to what else I could say, what explanation I might give. He shouldn't have to worry, I thought: he'd had enough to worry about. I should let him off that hook, so, 'Oh—' and I shrugged, *just general, nothing serious,* which could've been an oblique reference to ladies' problems.

He looked at me – kept looking at me – in that same expectant manner, then almost shook himself, remembered himself. 'Oh. Well, tell her I'm sorry to hear it.' Which was of course the right response.

And it was a dismissal, too, but as I turned away, I realised I didn't have something similar for him and he was the one who'd suffered. So I turned back, just enough to say, 'And she's sorry—' but stopped because it was another lie and the hunger in his eyes was a blade to my heart.

Sorry that she hadn't turned up? Sorry that his father had been killed? It could've been either but anyway it was a lie and he knew it. What I'd done was worse than if I'd merely left it be.

But then came just the faintest concession – I couldn't have called it a smile, it was nowhere near as much as that although there was something of a smile in it. It was an acknowledgement, or an acceptance: he knew very well she hadn't said she was sorry, he knew that had come from me, but he took it for what it was.

The very next day, Jane dropped me in it again – but at least this time she was honest about it: 'I can't,' she said, and it was a plea: *I can't, but you can.* She'd waited until we were at the door before saying it and those amber eyes of hers held mine in a way that was new; she was hanging on my response, offering herself up in her helplessness, which turned me upside-down.

'Jane,' I said, a plea of my own, *don't make me do this.*

'I just can't do it,' and this time it was said with a note of panic, although there was something stronger, too, in it: a certain reckoning; she'd asked nothing of me so far, in all the time we'd been together, but now she needed my help.

Without another word between us, I undertook to do it, which meant I was on my own as regards the excuse. But then, what would it matter what I told him? Because whatever it was, it would be a lie.

I stomped up to the wall-walk, frazzled and flushed. I had a job to do, as I saw it, and I'd do it, I'd do whatever needed doing, but however quickly I was able to get back down to our room, it wouldn't be soon enough. Even sewing, I told myself, was preferable to Guildford. As for what I was going to say to him, I decided I'd think about that when I got there. I'd think of something.

There was a nick of rain in the air. Guildford looked worse than before – was there really nothing that gloomy attendant could do? He was obviously disappointed to see me in place of his wife. He said, for me to confirm it, 'She's no better,' but there was no recognition, this time, of it being a lie: he'd said it gravely and so we were to take it as the truth. Well, if he could do it – if he were generous enough or deluded enough to be able to do it – then fine. I shrugged, leaving it up to him. He could think what he liked.

But then came a flicker of reflection, and he kind of laughed it off: 'Well, you know, I'm not so great myself.'

No response from me would've been less than trite, but nor could I just turn and go; a respectful pause was required, and mine was genuine enough. So there I stood, resisting the urge to reach over and somehow tidy him up, perhaps reset his cap, do the job of that loafing, London-fixated attendant; just something – anything – to help restore him to himself. A buzzard drifted overhead, a moth-like underside to its wings.

And then he was asking me, 'Are *you* married?' Although he didn't sound much interested.

I shook my head, which got me a lofty, world-weary 'Oh well, then: just you wait.'

As if he were an old hand, but I bet I knew a great deal more about any number of things from the times that I'd spent in the Shelley Place clock cupboard than he did from a few months of his so-called marriage. And anyway, how pitiful, this attempt to make his wife's refusal to see him into some run-of-the-mill marital spat. And why bother? I mean, it wasn't as if I cared.

And, *just you wait?* I resented that assumption. He knew nothing about me. I was nothing like his many sisters, all of them – I knew, because everyone knew – so very well married off: there'd been a roaring trade, in recent years, in Dudley-daughter marriages.

'I might never marry,' I countered.

He was unruffled: 'Oh, a life of contemplation, is it, then, for you?'

A religious life, he meant, and I didn't know why he just didn't say it.

'No.'

He smiled, sort of, to himself. 'Not your style.'

Which was one way to put it.

'What *is* your style?'

He was merely prolonging the encounter, but mine wasn't the company he wanted or needed. Making to move off, I said, 'I'll tell her you asked after her,' although actually he hadn't.

He asked, 'What's your name?'

I couldn't help but know his – everyone knew it, for good or bad – but had I not come up here to make Jane's excuses for her, I might've got away with him never knowing mine. When I told him, he said, 'Well, Elizabeth, it's worse for you, in a way, isn't it, to be stuck here, seeing as you haven't done anything wrong.'

He'd said my name as if he were examining it at arm's length, or tasting it.

We've all done something wrong, I thought, if you look hard enough.

And, anyway, what was it that *he'd* done, really? Swanned around in white and gold silk, from what I could gather.

I simply said, 'Here's as good as anywhere,' and there was some truth in that.

When I got back to our room, Jane barely even looked up from whatever it was she was writing; I might've been no more than a draught coming through that doorway. No acknowledgement, either, of where I'd been, of what I'd just done for her. And I wasn't having that; perhaps it was petty of me, but I just wasn't going to allow it. Something should be said, I determined, even if I was the one to speak up. So, I said, 'He was all right.'

She gave me the look that was in fact no look, and I could've sworn she didn't know who I was talking about. Then, turning back to her writing, she muttered something that I missed but which might have been 'That's good.'

Retreating to the window, it occurred to me that actually it hadn't been so bad after all to go and see him: it hadn't been the ordeal I'd feared it would be. In his wife's company, he blustered – furious or defensive or wheedling – but he didn't have to do any of that with me.

From then onwards, his requests stopped, he backed off, didn't push it, appeared to have got the message and instead sent enquiries after her health, which, I felt, couldn't help but be pointed. Mrs Partridge, stuck in the middle, was rigorous in keeping the knowingness from her voice – 'Your husband's asking how you are, whether you're feeling any better' – but she herself never asked about Jane's alleged indisposition, which suggested she knew it for what it was. Not that she was, I sensed, necessarily unsympathetic.

Jane's responses were carefully vague, 'So-so,' 'Not so

bad,' 'A little brighter,' and I marvelled at how she kept it up, she who usually made so much of telling the truth; I would never have guessed she could lie so well. It couldn't last for ever, though, this keeping of him at arm's length. And hadn't she been cutting about Princess Elizabeth's playing the invalid? Yet here she was, doing the same. Sooner or later, she was going to have to see her husband or make clear her refusal to do so. She couldn't just avoid him for the rest of her life.

As she wasn't going outdoors, then nor officially was I; but in fact Mrs Partridge came regularly to my rescue, inviting me when the weather was fine enough to accompany her to the Queen's Garden. No pretence of posy-picking by that time of year, but we harvested the last of the roses, my bowl always somehow feeling lighter for being full of those petals, and we enjoyed the too-blue early-autumn sky and the shadows cast by its slight winterwards incline. Our own shadows strode out from our feet: big and bold and detailed. What we talked about as we strolled side by side along the paths, I could rarely later recall: nothing much, but such a different kind of nothingness from that which I had to suffer back at the house with Jane. They were happy times for me, those walks in the Queen's Garden: falling in with Mrs Partridge's steady tread, trying and no doubt failing to imitate the stately swing of her hips. What a revelation she was, with none of the gripes and grudges that drove my mother and sisters and which I'd been raised to think were the necessary business of a life. There she was, her life every bit as real as theirs, but

134

lovely: that gently rakish husband of hers, the walled home and royal garden.

And then one perfect late afternoon, the air as bright as a bell-chime, she confided with a lift of her voice, as if granting me a wish, that she had some news: she was expecting a baby. And of course, I thought, of course she was, the only surprise being that I'd not already known it. How had I failed to see it? There amid the rosebushes, the sky heavy-fruited with birdsong, a bumblebee lifted on the breeze, I rushed with congratulations and all the right questions, while feeling foolish because I hadn't already known. Of course she was pregnant, because why wouldn't she be? Young, healthy, not long married but still childless Mrs Partridge: she couldn't possibly be anything but pregnant, if I thought about it. Due at the end of February, she was telling me: four months gone. She'd been pregnant, then, all the time I'd known her. The Mrs Partridge whose shifts I'd worn: all that time, her pregnancy had already been under way. We'd been walking together in these gardens but she'd have been thinking of someone else, someone precious to whom next summer she'd be saying, *Look at this, isn't this pretty?* Someone who would soon be scampering ahead of her on these crushed-shell paths.

But anyway, I'd be long gone by then, I reminded myself: I shouldn't forget that, I'd be gone long before the Partridge baby arrived, the fledgling. By the time he or she was born I'd be no more than a memory in this place, possibly even a nameless one: just the girl who'd roomed upstairs briefly with

Lady Jane Grey. Four months: she hadn't wanted to tell me earlier, she was saying, just in case. Best to be sure, she said, to keep it under wraps for a while, and I was rushing to agree as if that was something that I too did, every day – which was when it hit me. There in the early-autumn, late-afternoon air, so still as to seem spellbound, I realised I had in fact been doing exactly that.

Beside me, Mrs Partridge was picking rose petals, countering their beguiling resistance, extracting them one by one from each bloom. One evening a couple of months back, I'd raised my hand and said 'I'll do it,' and the following day I'd clambered off a wherry on to the Lion Gate steps. It had been as simple as that, and I had so very nearly managed it, had so very nearly stepped up out of my own footsteps into a new life. But the damage had already been done, it had come with me down the river and there could be no walking away from it. As I stood there in a garden so meticulous that it might have been built and stitched rather than grown from soil, my own personal horizon tilted and sank.

'Elizabeth?' Mrs Partridge paused in her petal-picking. 'Are you all right?'

'Yes,' I lied, 'I'm fine, thank you,' but the truth was that I had a problem, a big problem, which was only going to grow bigger until every last person could see it and there was nothing left of the girl who'd been me. I turned, actually physically turned there on the path to look back where just moments ago I'd come sauntering unencumbered, but of course there was no one, that girl was gone and my heart slammed shut because, I knew, I should've taken better care of her.

All the way back to the house with Mrs Partridge, I took not a single breath – not really, not properly – because I didn't dare touch the air, not even with my insides; I had to be sliding clean through the moment when I'd realised and safely into the next, so that something else – anything else – could happen.

At the foot of the stairs, I managed a seemingly cheerful goodbye; then, halfway up, something side-swiped me with the ferocity of sickness but it was rage, sheer rage, although at whom and for what I didn't know and it didn't matter, because what was important was that it pass before it burned me away to nothing. I stopped still to let it go through me, and then I continued on up and opened the door.

Now, a performance was called for: I had to act as if nothing had happened, as if nothing were happening or going to happen. It would have to be flawless, a perfect imitation of everything being exactly the same as when I'd left the room. Not that Jane would be looking, of course. In that respect, I had it easy. I was in the best possible place: I had something to hide, and this was the place – hers the company – in which to do it.

Closing the door behind me, I thought I should sit; it was what I'd normally do. *Go and sit*. I did, and gazed unseeing at the men going about their business down below on the green. Up high, a full moon was stamped on the daytime sky. Across the room was Susanna and, had I not known better, I might have thought that things were looking bad for her: she'd got herself into a bit of a fix with all that lingering naked in her garden. But she was a good woman, a perfect wife and mother, never putting a lily-white foot wrong, and all it would take, for her, was a good man to know it, and although she was as yet unaware, that man was on his way. For Susanna, everything was going to be fine.

I sat there and wondered how I hadn't known what was happening to me. It was that, as much as anything, which astounded me. All this while, the fact of my predicament had been lying low, biding its time in the certainty that eventually — no rush — it would become known. How had it taken me so long to see it? I'd been drifting through the days, the weeks, thinking of myself as sluggardly, as being shut up and out of sorts. Cooped up in a strange place. All of which, I'd supposed, had been taking its toll. I was imprisoned, kind of, and come to a stop: that was how I'd understood it. And perhaps, for a time, that hadn't been so stupid of me. Perhaps I'd been right, for a while, not to leap to conclusions. Because what was the advantage of knowing?

Harry, who knew everything, didn't know this. *Here, Harry, is something you don't know.* One up on Harry. You could see it that way. I shut my eyes. I should get word to him. But then again, no: I didn't want him knowing. I didn't want him coming here. And anyway, what could he do? Nothing. Not even Harry, with his listening ear and deep coffers. Harry, the only person I knew who sent his tenants' sons to school, the only person who could make my mother laugh.

There was nothing he could do about this. And anyway, hadn't he already done enough?

'Come on,' he'd said, that last time, crossing the chapel ahead of me. 'Quick,' impatient with me, as if I were doing something wrong. I'd been asking him what would happen now that the second cousin had been declared Queen over the half-sister. He hadn't answered and I was nervous that he felt there was something better left unsaid. I was wondering if – and how – I dared ask him again, but then, as he opened the door to the alcove, he did answer. 'It's done,' he said, 'done and dusted. The Grey girl is Queen,' unbothered by it, as if this state of affairs were unconnected to us: a natural phenomenon and far away, like a cloud formation.

I didn't quite believe that, but what did I know? Whereas he knew everything; if there was anything to know, he'd know it. But still, I couldn't quite believe it, so, with my hand on his arm to halt him, I checked – 'Will no one try anything?' – but the response was his mouth over mine, right there in chapel, for anyone – should anyone come in – to see. What on earth was he doing? Shutting me up, that was what, as he manoeuvred me with him into the cupboard. But I held back, dug my heels in, because *Not today, Harry*: that was what I'd come to tell him. Back in Hall, he'd given me the look that had said *Chapel* and I'd been at a loss for a look in return that would've said *Wrong time of the month*. He should've known it, but in all the excitement of this deeply peculiar, queen-proclaiming day, he seemed to be forgetting himself.

My resistance hadn't worked, or hadn't been enough, because the door was closing behind us. 'Try anything?' he asked. 'Fight? Oh, there'll be a bit of a stand-off. Fight, though? No, that'd be stupid. They haven't a hope in Hell.'

I needed to get the pair of us back on the other side of that door. 'Harry—'

'And why,' he breathed it into my hair, down my neck, having me shiver, 'would anyone want the Lady Mary on the throne? She'd take us back to Rome.' He took my hand, opened it, pressed it to his codpiece and moved it a little in case I was in any doubt as to what was to be found there.

But we couldn't do what he wanted us to do, and neither did I feel inclined to do anything else: the talk all over Shelley Place was of civil war and I didn't want to be kept in the dark.

'And we're done,' he said, 'with Rome.'

'But,' I whispered, 'it isn't right.'

'Lizzie,' so muted that it was mere rustle of his tongue. 'Come on. Quick.' The rasp of a lace through an eyelet: he was undoing himself.

I'd been too slow to stop him, so now, belatedly, it was my hand on his, to stop it. I had to tell him, 'It's the wrong time.'

'It's a perfect time,' and I heard the smile in the words. 'Everyone taken up with what's going on.' He was getting down on the floor and I was going with him but only to make

140

him listen to me. Crouching there beside him, I said, 'No—'
He'd misunderstood but, oddly, it was me who felt stupid. 'It's
the wrong time *for me*. It's my eleventh day.' *Please understand.*

And he did. He stopped, and gazed at me: that loving gaze
of his; I knew it there in the gloom from the give in his shoulders and the softening of his breath. He was pleased with me,
because I'd saved us from ourselves: one of us had had to do
it, and it had been me. And for that, I got a kiss, so brief and
gentle that it barely counted; it was a goodbye kiss, a blessing,
which was when I realised how hard I'd been holding myself
from him, so I relaxed and drew him close, breathed in the
fragrant warmth of his neck.

'With everything that's going on, though,' his whisper was
so very close as to seem an actual physical entity inside my
ear, 'it's the only chance we'll have for a while.'

I looked at him, despite the darkness: I wanted him looked
at, reckoned with.

'Eleven's fine,' he murmured. 'I promise you.'

I flushed, feeling oddly caught out. 'But you said . . . '

Days eight to eighteen, was what he'd said, back when
we'd started. Best avoided: days eight to eighteen. Best to
play safe. He'd been the one to explain to me the significance
of times of the month because I'd known nothing, I had no
friends to speak of and my sisters were so much older than I
was, and my mother didn't talk to me about things like that,
which was fair enough because it wasn't as if I was married.
There are changes all through the month, he'd said, which
did strike a chord with what I knew of myself: I did indeed

change – and keep changing – all through each month. At certain times, he'd told me, I'd be more ready than others for a baby. That's how you do it, he'd said, that's how it's done: that's how you avoid having a baby. And he'd know: Harry, man of the world, twice-married but only four children. What he'd told me had come as good news and bad news: bad in that it was hard enough to have time together without there being more considerations, but good because there was a way to do what we wanted without consequence. We'd just have to be careful, was what he'd said, which had appealed to me because careful was what we were in any case. It was how we had to be, it was in the very nature of the scant time we spent together. To have time together, we used whatever we could and the new information that Harry gave me was just something more. We'd decided to avoid days eight to eighteen and had been scrupulous in doing so. But now he was saying that day eleven was fine, as if there was some detail that I hadn't grasped and – what did I know? – perhaps that was so.

And his hand was already up inside my shift, his fingers scrabbling at me as if trying to locate something to take from me. 'You're dry,' he observed.

I really couldn't think what to say to that. 'Yes,' I said, hating how it sounded, as if I were owning up to something.

Dry, yes, but still he was pushing fingers inside me, which was exactly how it felt: me and his fingers, and no melding of the two.

'Come on,' he murmured, 'be a good girl.'

Tears smacked the back of my nose and for a moment I couldn't draw breath. It hurt, was all, I told myself: I wasn't ready, so his fingers hurt, hence the tears. But please, please no tears, because they were clogging up my throat when I needed to be saying—

Saying what?

Because who was I to be saying no?

And anyway it was already happening, he'd moved beneath me and was jabbing at me – 'Open your legs a bit wider,' glad to give this tip, as if my legs, their closedness, were the problem – and instinct had me reach down to better position him because I knew it would be worse for me if I didn't.

It wouldn't take long, I told myself. Usually, I'd be racing him but this time I closed my eyes and let him go ahead, concentrated instead on the swing of that foliot above me. One drop of the wheel, one notch, I felt, should do it. But actually it took an age, went on and on, and even he seemed to think so, at one point saying, 'You could at least pretend you're enjoying it,' with an embarrassed half-laugh as if even he couldn't quite believe he'd gone so far. An almost-laugh which, incredibly, hopelessly, I echoed.

It was nothing, though, I told myself: really, it was nothing; it didn't hurt much more than the first time. We had to take our chances, he'd said, which was all he was doing. And shouldn't I, too? Why couldn't I enter into the spirit of it? This was the only chance we'd have for a while, he'd said. My eleventh day was fine, he'd said – not ideal, but fine – and he was no risk taker. No, that was me: I'd been the one to get us started and to keep us going; the clock cupboard had been my idea. I'd started this, so shouldn't I see it through?

I kept my tears balled up in my throat and when at last he did manage to finish, I got off him and stood up as if nothing were amiss, as if I wasn't burning so much that I feared I was bleeding, and busied myself in settling my skirts and straightening my hood.

He said, 'Things will take a couple of days at least to calm down,' and I didn't realise for a moment that he was talking about England, about who was its queen. There we were, continuing our earlier conversation. So I said, 'But the King had a sister.'

'Half-sister.' His focus, I could hear, was on relacing himself and with the same distracted air he said, 'The Lady Mary is a spinster,' and told me how she'd never have an heir whereas Lady Jane Grey probably would. 'Married to a Dudley, true,' he said as we went back through the little doorway into chapel, 'but it's not as if we aren't used to Dudleys,' and he placed a kiss on my forehead, his usual kind of kiss, no-nonsense and fond.

That night, with Jane sleeping beside me, her every breath into the darkness as sweet and smooth as a spoonful of honey, I was sick with envy because she would never have to suffer this: this particular dirty secret was one she'd never have to keep. Married, she was protected from it, she'd been pitched beyond it.

While she slept, I returned to myself little by little: the girl I thought I'd lost out there on the path came creeping back into my veins, curling up close to my heart. Not gone, then, or not entirely, but in hiding, and perhaps there was something in that: perhaps if I stayed still and quiet enough, there was the smallest chance that this calamity might fail to find me. Because what would it want with me anyway, no one and nothing as I was. Perhaps this scandal, this disgrace, would pass over me in a hunt for more satisfying prey.

I'd never known any unmarried girl have a baby. Where would any such girl go? But then, where did any girl go, if, for whatever reason, she couldn't be married off: *A life of contemplation*, as Guildford had said. Which was one way to put it. 'Taken in and walled up' was another. Condemned to a life of penance and servitude. What hit me, that night, was that I'd never now go free. I'd go from stitching Mrs Partridge's odds and ends to wringing blood from a nunnery-load of cloths. Perhaps I should run, while I still could. But where? Because now no one in the world but nuns would take me in.

The days came and went, bearing me towards a future that I knew wasn't there.

I had to trust to luck, of which I knew there was none. There was nothing I could do, nor was there anyone, anywhere, who could help me. No one: not Mrs Partridge, for all her kindness, nor Jane, not even if she'd still been the Queen of England.

I sat at the window and let the hours wash over me as if they might wear me clean; ossifying while all day every day sunlight edged across the floor like a sandbank. On the wall was Susanna, who'd had rather too much her own way in life, and seemed, to me, a little too pleased with herself. Everything was rosy in her garden. But is that ever really true? There she was, having had a touch too much of the sun, having spent a little too long submerged amid the lilies, and I could've smacked her, slapped her face, *Wake up, dozy!* Because there she was, believing her own story, which, it seemed to me, is always fatal.

Sometimes, I almost said something of my predicament to Mrs Partridge, or even to Jane. Or, rather, sometimes the fact of it nearly got told; I was brimming with it and it nearly spilled, the telling about to occur of its own accord. There was so little between not saying and saying; just breath, really. A mere breath. If I let go a breath carelessly, then it would be said.

But I knew that wasn't true, because for it to be told, it would have to go into words, and it didn't fit.

I'm going to have a baby.

I think I'm expecting a baby.

How could I possibly be expecting a baby? That was what anyone would ask first. They'd want to know how on earth I could possibly be expecting a baby, and what could I tell them? That I'd met with a man? Don't make me laugh. That I'd lain with a man? But 'lain' didn't begin to cover it. And that was what it would be about, for anyone else – a middle-aged man, a cupboard, the relentless swipe of a clock mechanism, the kneeling-cushions.

Early one evening, I saw Guildford down on the green, presumably for fresh air after several days of rain, but unfortunately he spotted me in return and began gesticulating. A fly, he brought to mind, buzzing at our window. I knew what he wanted: Jane to be fetched into view.

'Lord Guildford,' I relayed. Needing to be dealt with, I meant.

Which she elected to ignore.

No such luxury for me, ensnared there at the window; no escape unless I actively cast him off, which, under the circumstances, I felt, would be cruel.

'Lord Guildford,' I repeated.

At that, though, she tutted vehemently, as if I'd been going on and on about him and had worn her patience thin. 'And?'

What did she mean, *And*? Wasn't it obvious? He wanted her, at the window. There was also the small matter of his father having recently been murdered in front of the entire population of London but his wife still to offer him her condolences.

'Out there,' I said.

'*And?*' Higher-pitched, this time, doubly irked. 'Can't you see I'm busy?'

Well, no, now that she mentioned it. Whatever she was doing with those books didn't count, for me, as being busy. Busy was what Goose was, wherever she was.

Guildford had stopped the show, but only because he was awaiting my response. I wished he'd go away; I didn't have the energy for him. How could I convey that his wife wasn't interested? I tried a shrug but, expansive though I tried to make it, it obviously failed to travel the distance because there he remained, expectant.

So then I did have to go for a benign, by-the-by gazing elsewhere, which was what I'd been doing anyway before he'd muscled into view, but now it was contrived, not unlike the studied indifference of the Partridges' cat. And in any case it didn't work because, concluding that I hadn't understood him, he was signalling harder. It was no good: I'd have to be brutal, get up and go elsewhere.

What, though, if that too were misconstrued? He might assume we were on our way down – or me, at least, with some explanation or excuse of his wife's. And then, in time, he'd have to acknowledge his mistake, down there under the mordant gaze of that attendant whose dawdling at such a distance, over by the White Tower, was frankly bordering on neglect of duty. There might be others, too, who'd noticed and were watching, ready to gloat. No, I couldn't quite do it to him, I couldn't leave him hanging there. My turn, then, for a flouncy huff, because I was going to have to go down even though I was far from up to it.

I'd barely moved in almost two weeks and it felt as if it took me that long again to get down the stairs. And then there was a shilly-shally with Twig at the door (in? out?), so that when eventually I did step from the house,

Guildford was in a state of agitation which my arrival only worsened.

If I looked bad – and I was quite sure I did – he was no prettier. When I'd first seen him, back in July, he'd been pristine: unsullied, or so it had seemed, by a moment's discomfort or difficulty in his life. Gilded with confidence. Well, now he was stripped of that shine, and pallor lay on him like grime. He looked hungry, too: eyes keen but jaw set in expectation of disappointment. I would've liked to feel more kindly towards him, but merely being there was hard enough.

'Where's my wife?' he was anxious to know even as I was closing the door on the prevaricating dog.

And a good afternoon to you, too. 'Talking with the dead,' I said before I'd given it a thought. *The dead*, and his own father barely cold in his grave, not that he'd actually even been granted so much as a grave. Shamefacedly, I rephrased, 'Reading her books.'

He regarded me coolly, then quibbled, 'Not all those writers are dead, you know. Probably not even most of them.'

'Not the liveliest of company, though, either. Anyway, she's busy.' No excuses, this time, because he knew how it was and any pretence would be an insult. I'd reported her refusal regretfully enough and that would have to do.

It was one of those days that never really get started, a day that had sleep in its eyes. I was about to move off when he said, 'Shame she doesn't spend as much time thinking where we'll end up.' He cocked his head. 'Or does she?'

I hadn't been listening; he'd lost me. 'Does she what?'

His eyes had the flatness of coins. 'Think about how we're going to live our lives when we kiss this place goodbye.'

Well, how would I know? I put him straight: 'She doesn't talk to me.' Did he think I was her confidante?

Not so much as a blink from him. 'Yes, well, that's my job, I suppose, isn't it. As her husband. To worry about what'll happen to us.' Was he being sarcastic? 'And it's the coronation next week.' As if I didn't know that. As if there was anyone, anywhere, who didn't know that. 'After which . . .' he offered up his hands, *that's that*.

Did he think he was going free after the Queen was crowned? Because Jane had been told the trial would have to happen first.

I reminded him: 'There'll be the trial.'

'Oh, well, yes, the *trial*.' Definitely sarcastic, now. 'Yes, we're going to have to be paraded around publicly, my wife and I, in disgrace,' *because certain people can't be denied their fun and games*. 'But that's as far as it'll go. We're just a couple of kids. She daren't butcher us.' No doubt he'd been hoping I'd squirm. 'Then we'll be allowed to run off into the sunset and –' suddenly bleak '– fade away.' He looked away over the bailey and around the towers, the sky concentrated and darkened on his eyes. 'Someone will have to take us in.'

For an instant, I thought he meant me and him – there we were, standing outside, and we'd have to go back indoors. But no, he and Jane, he meant: as traitors, they would have their various means confiscated; they would become dependent on others. He and his wife: well, at least there was the pair of them. They might not have chosen each other's company, but they had it, and neither of them would be braving life alone. And in time they'd probably have a family. Theirs would be a life, it seemed to me as I stood there in that chill wind. A life, even if it would have to be lived for a while in someone else's house.

'And from there, we'll have to move around,' he said, 'reliant on people's good will.'

But at least they'd have it. From some people, anyway. From enough people. There were people who bore them good will even if they were having to be quiet about it: people who thought the pair of them had done nothing wrong, and some people who thought they'd done right.

'But it's there for you,' I said, 'that good will.'

He conceded it. 'But I'm not sure how that puts clothes on our backs.'

Oh, well, you can't have everything, can you. 'It's not forever, though, is it,' I said. 'It'll get better.'

He inclined his head, to size me up.

Which unsettled me, and had me back-track: 'Well, if not for you, then for your children.'

His grandfather had been a traitor – everyone knew that – but his father had made good. Well, for a while, until it had all gone wrong again. 'It's survivable, isn't it,' I said. 'You'll survive it. You might have to live quietly for a few years, but . . .' *is that so bad?*

He turned from me, to pace a circle. 'Yes, how right you are. I mean, here I am, indicted for treason, my father hacked in two on the scaffold, but yes, if you think about it, every-thing's rosy.'

And duly I was shamed. What on earth had got into me? Kicking him like that when he was down.

'Did you get out of the wrong side of bed this morning?' It didn't sound unkind and I glanced up, the better to gauge it. He tried again: 'The wrong side of bed: did you get out of it, this morning?'

I'd barely got out of it at all, as it happened, and, recalling that, suddenly I felt like crying.

'You look awful,' but he said it cheerfully – pleased, perhaps, to come across someone in worse shape than him-self, although with that attendant of his, he didn't lack for choice.

'Thanks.' My own little chance for sarcasm. Then the truth: 'I haven't been feeling too well.'

'I'm sorry to hear that.' Which was what he'd said to his wife, that time, if only via me. 'You had a bleeding?'

My heart contracted.

He frowned, concerned. 'Did they bleed you? Because you're very pale.'

'Oh,' and my heart breathed again. 'No.'

'Well, don't let them. You don't look as if you could take it.'

I nodded my thanks for the advice. 'Well—' *I should go, now.*

'Stay,' he said.

Was that an order?

'The air'll do you good. Being shut away inside's no good for you.'

Whereas standing here in a biting wind with a horribly bereft princeling: that *was*?

Frankly, I just wanted to go and lie down. Well, no, I did and I didn't; I didn't really want to do anything; there was nothing that I wanted to do. But I didn't move, if only because I was too tired. He was lonely; he needed someone, any distraction; anyone would do. Surely, even, at a push, that drippy attendant. He read my glance, 'William?' A hitch of his eyebrows, sceptical. 'Talks of nothing but his darling wife.'

Which had me take a second look at him: Darling wife? Him? 'William'?

'He's newly wed.'

'Like you,' I'd said before I'd realised.

He shook his head, 'That's different,' but didn't elucidate. 'But while he's been stuck in here with me, she's probably run off with someone else.'

I laughed, if dismissively: *Don't*.

'No? You don't think so?' He came close to a smile. 'Bit of a romantic, are you, Elizabeth?'

He'd remembered my name.

'Not me,' I said. 'But some people are.' William's darling bride, perhaps, I meant.

That seemed to throw him; he folded his arms as if to hold himself together. 'Romance is all very well, isn't it.'

Not in my experience, no.

'But it doesn't last. Marriage has to be about the future.'

A future: what a luxury.

His eyes came back to mine. 'Don't you think so?' but before I could answer, even if I'd wanted to, he said, 'My parents' marriage was very strong, they lived for each other,' and there was nothing I could say to that. 'Falling in love, it's just make-believe. Made up,' he said, 'to keep people happy.'

'People': he did like to talk of 'people', but wasn't he a person? And anyway, what was wrong with being happy?

'You ever seen anyone in love after the first couple of months?'

'The Partridges,' I said.

He considered it. 'Oh, well, yes, but once she's had the baby . . . '

Mrs Partridge's condition had become wider-known and Goose had confirmed what I'd suspected from the age difference between the Partridges: there'd been a previous Mrs Partridge, who'd died in childbed. 'Never get married, girls,' she'd added, breezily; then, to Jane, 'Oh, but I forgot, you already are.'

Guildford shrugged. 'I mean, that's all women really care about, isn't it: having babies.'

You really don't know much, do you.

'Did you know Lady Jane,' I asked him, 'before you were married?'

He looked startled, perhaps by the question itself, perhaps by my having asked him something. 'Yes, of course. We'd met.' He revised, 'We'd seen each other around.' He turned curious: 'Doesn't she talk to you?'

About me, he meant, but I answered in general: 'We don't have a lot in common.'

And that, apparently, was funny. 'Oh, well, with her, who does?' But more seriously, 'It's hardly her fault, though. It's understandable enough. Brought up as she was, to be a kind of princess.'

Was it possible to be 'a kind of princess'? But, then, his family had thought it possible for her to be a kind of queen.

'She's been raised to be a scholar. An enlightener, a reformist. Right from the start. If I listed her tutors for you—'

I wouldn't have a clue who they were.

Which he saw, and stopped.

Although I supposed I could've taken his word for it.

'Well, anyway,' he said, 'her tutors told her she was going to change the world. That's how she's grown up: to think of herself like that. That's what you have to remember.'

But I didn't have to remember anything. I wasn't the one who'd be spending the rest of my life with her; she'd be gone in a few months' time and, like it or not, I'd never see her again.

'Problem is, if you think you're busy saving the world, then everything and everyone else just gets in the way.'

He wasn't wrong about that.

He said, 'It's a shame for you that you'll miss the coronation, stuck in here.'

I couldn't have cared less about the coronation. I was missing absolutely everything, stuck in the Tower, and didn't care about any of it.

'The crowning of England's first ever ruling queen. Something to tell the grandchildren.'

Goose had been telling us of the building, painting and draping of platforms and arches in the streets, the regilding of the Cheapside cross and the St Paul's weathercock on which a Dutch acrobat was going to perform.

'Except,' he said, 'in less than no time she won't be. Ruling, I mean. Because she'll be married.'

And wives are ruled by their husbands. If Jane was to be believed, I remembered, her husband would've made a mere consort of her, had he had his way.

I said, 'Who'll marry her, though?'

A certain light came into his eyes. 'Yes, because who'd be fool enough to marry a queen?'

I shrugged: *Have it your way.*

But then he did answer: 'In this particular case, either an idiot or a tyrant.'

Edward Courtenay, he meant, or the Spanish heir. Compared with whom, he wouldn't have been such a dire prospect.

He unfolded his arms, swung them. 'Know what I miss most, being in here?' There was a playful challenge in it but, no, I didn't know and couldn't guess and why did he think I was interested? He corrected himself: 'Not "what". Who.'

His mother?

'My dog, Pip.'

I couldn't help but be amused at that, because I'd always choose the company of a dog, if I could, over a person. And he smiled, too: the first time I'd ever seen him smile. I knew then that I was going to hear all about the wonderful Pip: how there was no one else like him, how in his eyes you could do no wrong, he'd follow you to the ends of the earth and you could trust him with your life. I could've recited it all, saved him the trouble, but actually I was happy enough to stand there and listen to it.

He finished by telling me that Pip had been the runt of the litter, 'Which,' he concluded, 'just goes to show.'

His brothers – all those big brothers of his – had had the pick of the puppies but he, being youngest, had been left with the runt. And it occurred to me that his being youngest made him the runt of the Dudley litter. But those brothers of his were shut in their rooms, while he was free, within the limits of the Tower, to come and go.

I left without trying to tell him of our dogs back at Shelley Place. Ours weren't the sort for eulogising. I had no comparable story of childhood canine companionship; there'd been no endearing, dewy-eyed pup for me. Not that I minded. I didn't doubt Guildford's dog was a delight but ours, coming to Shelley Place as a last resort, to doze away their days, had seen life. There was that to say for them: ours were survivors.

Something that struck me as I hauled myself up the stairs back to the room was that in a way those Shelley Place dogs had given me refuge rather than the other way around. 'Get those mutts out of here,' my mother would shout, and I'd be on hand to do exactly that, and then off we'd slope, me and the dogs, to the privacy of some nook or cranny, some hidey-hole.

Reaching the top of the stairs, I had to concede that Guildford had been right: I did feel much better for having been outside; he'd been right to make me stay a little longer. I felt alive, for the first time in a long while, startlingly conscious of the shift of blood in my veins. I was glowing as I entered that room, as I walked into that miasma of dried lavender: I was silvered with evening air and I didn't see why I should hide it or apologise for it because this could have been her, if she'd wanted; she could have gone out there, if she'd wanted, and she still could. Any time, she could. There was nothing and no one to stop her. Within the walls, she was free to come and go; it was just that she chose not to.

But that hadn't been my choice for myself, and she shouldn't deny me. And it seemed to me that that was what she was trying to do, as she sat there over her books, refusing to look up. Here I was, arriving back, and she didn't so much as raise her eyes. But the fact remained that I'd been out of our room, doing something – talking, and mulling over good times – while she hadn't, and none of her pretending otherwise made it disappear.

Swinging down on to the window seat I said, as if in passing, 'He misses his dog.'

He: as if she and I were already mid-conversation.

I'd been to see her husband and it was only proper that we acknowledged that. And anyway it felt to me that I was dispensing a bit of the conversation that he and I had had; it was

mine to bestow and for once I was in good spirits, I was feeling magnanimous. And if she didn't want to be let in on it?
Well, she should. And anyway, she did, I could tell she did,
even if she wouldn't admit it to herself. Well, I could help her
out with that.

But then she surprised me with, 'Well, it's a nice dog.' And
so the dog was claimed: it was a dog she knew and with
whom she'd spent time. That dog of Guildford's was, suddenly, practically, as good as hers. And then, with a
speculative tilt of her head, gaze unfocused, to make the very
picture of imperfect recollection: 'Chip?'

'Pip,' I said, too quickly.

'Oh, Pip, yes,' and I saw she'd known all along and had
been testing me, and that the test had been something over
and above the mere matter of the dog's name.

The coronation couldn't possibly be sprung on us as the
Queen's initial August arrival had been, because even two
weeks beforehand, in mid-September, the Tower was teem-
ing. Day after day I watched lords and ladies arriving amid
flurries of smartly liveried retainers; they were coming to
make pre-emptive claims on what Mrs Partridge had told us
was a limited number of guest lodgings.

I was always looking for Harry, even as I dreaded spotting
him. Harry, down there in the fray, enjoying better wine than
at home and more of it, and more people with whom to drink
it. Everyone happy, which was how he liked it and why everyone loved him. He would almost certainly have forgotten that

I was near by. The surprise, for me, was how that came as a relief. Something else I'd realised was that even if I told what had happened, no one would believe me. Not even Harry himself, probably – likely not merely to deny it but also to believe himself. And maybe there was something in that, maybe I could understand it, because it was incredible to me, by then, that we'd ever been together.

The Tower might well have been just as overcrowded when the Queen had been in residence back in August, but then the atmosphere had been hushed, reverential, her victory against all odds seeming like a miracle. Now, though, it was business as usual. The impending coronation was something to be got on with, and it was, with gusto, caution thrown to the wind. The place was a mess. Lords and ladies in lodgings needed food prepared, fires lit, furnishings cleaned and in reasonable repair, and closet pits scoured, so the Tower was like a city for those September days, a small, walled, workaday city, and often, under pressure of time, workanight too. Playing fast and loose with the curfew allowed jobs to be done and supplies to arrive for unloading and unpacking at all hours. Jane and I found it hard to sleep, with the courtyards and passageways and the lane behind us ringing with footfalls, the skittering of horses, the whine of wheels and the grunt of the gates.

And even if the workmen didn't keep us awake, there was their knocking off late after a long, hard day. Impromptu revelry was of course forbidden in the Tower but there was only so much that the outnumbered watchmen could do. At all hours beneath our windows, old acquaintances were re-established and celebrated, or old feuds reignited, and no one needed to be especially raucous in order to rattle us because in the smallest hours a single exclamation was enough, amplified inside the vast stone walls or a stairwell. And then would come the calls to pipe down, which usually only made it worse, the watchmen's taking to task of miscreants never failing to give rise to recriminations and back-chat, so that the settling of any dispute was always at least as noisy as the initial affray.

One problem was that the new arrivals acted as if they owned the place whereas actually the majority of them had nowhere to go. Even a lord or lady would have two rooms at most; retainers did their bedding down (and worse) in halls, porches and doorways. One morning, I spotted a couple of men daubing a wall with red paint, and when I made passing mention of it to Jane, she only baffled me further by saying, 'It's to stop the peeing.'

The what?

'They're crosses.'

Which had me look again and so they were: the vertical streaks were being slashed by horizontal ones to make big, red, fairly regularly spaced crosses.

Which still made no sense. 'Peeing?'

She obliged me with the explanation: 'No one dares pee on a cross.'

Was there no end to the things she knew?

Another morning, when we pointed out to Goose that we

were running low on firewood, her response was a mere 'There isn't any left,' and 'Maybe later or tomorrow.' As if it didn't matter. As if we didn't matter. We were, it seemed, low-priority. Well, we were prisoners, that was true; or Jane was, and, by association, me. We were being held, kicking our heels, biding our time before Jane's inevitable release but the Tower, pissed all over though it now was, had suddenly become all about the future, the new, steady reign. We played no part in that; we had no claim on it. It belonged to all those workers and officials, busy with their jobs, and the nobles with their optimism. The Tower, that late September, was a place for those who were building England's future.

Had we mentioned the lack of firewood to the Partridges, they probably wouldn't have been all that much more recep-tive because they too, it seemed to me, had become a little devil-may-care; they too sported a new, festive air. The day before the coronation, Mrs Partridge told us that the Earl of Arundel would be standing in for the Queen, that evening, in the creation of the new Knights of the Bath, 'Because imag-ine,' she laughed, 'if it was the Queen who had to be clambering into the bath to kiss those men on their shoulders.' And so it was good, clean fun, the coming coronation, and the Queen in her femininity was endearing.

Jane and I were united in our disdain for the palaver. We didn't much discuss it, but during those trying days we acted put-upon, scowling, huffing and muttering at the various inconveniences, and drawing in on ourselves, a little less con-vivial with Mrs Partridge, a little more disapproving of

Goose, and I closed the shutters earlier than necessary in the evenings.

One afternoon about a week before the coronation, something had me pause at the chamberpot and swivel inside my shift, wrenching it around my hips and craning to check the back of it. And there on the linen was a blotch of the blood on which I'd given up hope. There, on the back of my shift, as unequivocal as a thumbprint. My heart hammered to see it and even though I was the one who'd uncovered it, I felt wonderfully sprung. It had crept up on me. Unbeknown to me, something had got going, staking its claim, taking root in the fabric of my shift.

Brash and bold, that poppy-bright bloom was unlike the start of my usual monthly bleed, which would have been a trace, a smudge, a half-hearted stirring. This blood had a confidence to it, proclaiming its own arrival. There was jubilation in it, and flourish: *See?*

What I saw, written there on that linen, was my reprieve, my own blood come to save me.

Let it come, let it come, and I vowed then and there to God, the heavens, the Devil, whoever else might be listening, that I would never, ever do again what I'd done in that clock cupboard, I would never so much as look at a boy or a man. I would be faultless, unimpeachable, a shining light, a fucking saint, *if you please please please just give me this.* There I stood, staring at that stain, not daring to relinquish it because nothing was more precious to me than that blood and there could never be enough of it. But at the same time I was afraid that, if I kept looking, I might scare it off, this steady, stealthy animal creep of my insides. I should pretend to look the other way, and leave it to do its work.

Preparations, first, though: I would need to cover its tracks. Well, I'd do whatever I could, I'd be the perfect handmaiden, I couldn't do enough for it if only it would just keep on coming. Practicalities: I was going to have to go back next door and bide my time, keep this to myself, live out the rest of the day as if nothing were happening, although I didn't know how I was going to do that with elation rising indecently off me like steam.

And I almost laughed aloud to think of it – me here, leaking and matted, my blood-fouled linen hoiked around my waist while on the other side of that door was the girl whom the whole world considered to be the errant one. There she was, head bowed over a book, quill poised; I was surprised and pleased by how clearly I pictured her – the precise incline of her neck, the exact configuration of rings on her inky fingers – and even more surprised how pleased I was to know I'd find her there. And I felt for her, all of a sudden, because she immersed herself in books but what, really, did she know of anything that mattered? She would never know the glory of having taken a wrong step and got yourself lost but then, by a sheer accident of nature, being handed back, intact, your life.

Off to bed, that night, padded up, I anticipated nothing but a steady bleeding, and fell asleep easily. Some time later, though, in deep darkness, my consciousness began to make its presence felt, and eventually I came properly awake to find myself already on all fours in a kind of surfacing, pain having bowled me over and up. Another cramp was closing on me, taking me back down, and so there I was, wide-eyed in the dark and busy before I knew it: rocking back and forth, breathing deeply to get myself through.

The fist-sized, fist-tight pain was familiar enough from my usual monthly bleeding; what was new was its viciousness. And perhaps I should've been scared but instead I was awestruck because it was extraordinary in its intensity, it was a creature come to reside in me, impressive in its strength and purpose, vital and kind of beautiful, big and hot and bright as it was. It had work to do and I knew I shouldn't hinder it; all I had to do, I knew, was breathe, to keep myself alive until it was done. And I didn't doubt I could do that; I was more than able to do my bit. I had the help of a darkness, too, that was quite different from any I'd ever known: not bearing down on me but bearing me up, making itself my refuge, my lair.

And so I rocked and breathed, endured and survived while my body ground out its insides. How much time was passing, I had no idea, because there was only ever the coming contraction, and then, when it loosened, the following one on its way. And each and every one of them, I welcomed: braced and ready to ride it forward, *Don't stop, don't stop.*

At the very edge of my mind, though, was the mess of blood that I imagined to be in the bed: blood printed liberally across the bedclothes, I suspected, florid and indelible. I was going to have to deal with that. And I would, I told myself, I certainly would, but later.

And something else of which I couldn't be completely unaware – or, rather, some*one*: Jane, as persistent a presence in the bed as that blood. Then again, I didn't have to worry about her, because she was asleep, shut tight into her diligent dreams until her early rise-and-shine. Except that she wasn't, because just as I'd found myself awake in the darkness, eventually I grew conscious of her watchfulness.

Not that it touched me: I was way beyond it, bowing back and forth, and anyway, she'd soon be sinking away again, like a child lifted and carried somewhere, suddenly wide-eyed, apparently all-seeing, fleetingly lucid but just as quickly back asleep.

But then, 'Elizabeth?' Whispered, but coming like a call despite our being together in the bed. 'Elizabeth? What's wrong?' A peculiar lightness to it, as if she were in a cart cresting a bridge.

I managed an unconvincing 'Nothing.'

Which earned me a pointed lack of response. What was obvious, though, in the darkness, was her scrutiny, which was the very last thing I wanted. I'd been doing fine. I needed her off my back, I wanted her gone, which would happen soon enough, I knew, because she wasn't much interested in people and especially not in me.

I dredged up the energy to give her just a little more, to send her on her way: 'A pain,' I said. 'I get it.' Sometimes, I meant. Which wasn't wholly a lie.

There was a small silence, the very sound of disbelief, before she voiced a sceptical 'You do?'

But she'd distracted me and the next fist came before I was prepared; my focus had slipped, I'd lost ground and had to scrabble for a toehold.

She said, 'I'm going to get someone,' a flex of the mattress confirming it.

'*No.*' I'd never spoken to her like that before and it gave her pause, during which I heard a humming and realised it was coming from me, and that it was helping. I rode that long hum over the clench and it was quite a find, it was quite possibly the answer, the key, because suddenly this was easy, or almost, or soon would be.

But Jane was trying again, if less surely: 'I should get someone.' Seeking my permission was how it sounded, which struck an odd note.

She'd shifted – she was sitting up – which had the advantage of putting space between us; I had space, at last, and breathed it in.

The disadvantage was that from her distance she could better regard me, and I really didn't want to be a spectacle.

Her being there beside me was holding me back and dragging me down; I didn't want to have to take account of her. If she weren't there, if only she weren't there, I could do this, I knew I could. I could hum my way right through this pain to the other side.

Who knew what she thought she was witnessing? But that wasn't my problem and, anyway, if I could ignore her for long enough, if I could just do that, I was sure she'd give up and go back to sleep.

Not yet, though, because, 'What's happening?' and loud and clear in this demand for an explanation was her certainty that I had one.

'Nothing.'

Wrong answer, because, *Right*, 'I'm going to get someone.'

'*No!*' and for an instant I was so much bigger than the pain, shooting above it to sit squarely back on my heels and confront her, forbid her. '*No.*'

An admission, though, that this was something: not nothing, but something, and to be kept between us.

And she got it: I felt it hit her that whatever she went on to do, she was, whether she liked it or not, my secret-keeper.

She backed down, reluctantly asking, 'Well, then, do you need anything? Can I do anything?' and it was softer-voiced, but I didn't trust to that because it was gentle not from kindness, but stealth: she was still after an explanation, and despite everything I almost laughed because even if I told her, how could she possibly understand?

Because what did she know of life? Superior as she was, with her velvet-covered, gilt-worked books. And what the fuck was I doing, cooped up like this with her? I should be at home in my own bed and suddenly I felt like screaming and couldn't even be sure I hadn't, because why wouldn't she just *go away*? The palm of a hand – hers – was pressed to my forehead and I'd have knocked it away if I could, because now she was acting the nursemaid, as if fever was the problem. Fever: that was all she could imagine, fever was all it could be, visited upon poor sweet little innocent me.

Fever nothing. Fever fucking nothing.

But then the hand wasn't there, and its absence had a sting of its own.

I opened my eyes, and the darkness was undifferentiated – no sign of her. She'd gone somewhere and I strained to catch sound of her return.

Soon there was the punching of knees into nightdress as she clambered back across the bed, and then on my forehead was no palm but a wad of cool, damp linen, and I trawled the depths of it, drank it down, letting the pain go on a long breath that I hadn't known I was holding. And only when that cold pad was lifted away, leaving me in the lurch, did I realise I'd been lulled. The pain still burned but somehow I'd drifted from it into a kind of sleep.

She said something I didn't catch but I understood she was going to refresh the cloth, and this time I was avid for her return. The pain was more of a scalding now, if still deep and raw and wild. Back came the tingly-cold, fresh-smelling linen which was everything to me and when after a while she shifted, stiffly, I realised I'd been leaning on her – I'd given myself over to her and she'd had to hold me up. I heard myself mutter an apology and similarly she dismissed it. I intended to draw back, to make it easier on her, but then wasn't sure that I had.

Just as the pain had had to be reckoned with earlier, now it was the drenched, inflexible mass of padding between my legs: I was going to have to do something about that. Stating an intention might, I hoped, get me started, so I summoned the wherewithal to sound a warning: 'I need to . . .'

. . . *do something.*

I need you to move.

Which she did, so that although she was still beside me, I was on my own and on my way.

Slipping through the hangings from the bed into the wick-lit room came unexpectedly easily, so much so that I slid beyond my feet and down on to the floor. Well, I could crawl. But the blood-slicked nightdress made that difficult and in no time was frozen to me by an icy sweat. I couldn't manage to ruck it up when I reached the chamberpot, so I rummaged underneath to try to untie the wadding but several times, depleted and sickened, I slumped back on to my haunches, which only made everything worse.

I didn't know where to put the soiled padding, nor had I any replacement ready. There were cloths inside my oak chest, but, peculiarly, I couldn't think where that was and didn't seem able to raise my head to look around for it. The loosened wadding dropped between my knees to the floor with the abandon and stink of dead flesh, to be fol-lowed by the protracted slither of a clot. Jane chose that moment to peek through the bed-hangings and recoiled as if wounded.

Squeamish, I observed, which didn't surprise me.

'Elizabeth?' She sounded scared even to say my name. 'What's happening? What *is* this?'

Practicalities, I told myself, keep to practicalities: nothing else mattered. 'I need a fresh pad.'

Before she could stop herself, she'd answered absently, 'I have some,' but then, catching herself, 'I'm going for help.'

'Pad,' I repeated.

She came from the bed, her own nightdress dazzling in the room's night-light, to crouch in front of me, to remonstrate. 'This ... blood,' but she could barely say it, as if it were an obscenity, 'all this ... blood.'

Blood is blood, I thought; it just looks bad. And, anyway, the more the merrier, in this case, to flush me clean, not that she knew it. But if only she'd look at me, if she'd look properly at me rather than staring at the mess on the floor, she'd know. Because if I wasn't worried, then why should she be? She needed to trust me. 'I'm fine,' I said.

But that did it: she was outraged – 'Stop saying that!' – and the whisper came with the force of a roar. 'This goes on and you'll be dead by morning.'

I wasn't dying, but I was too tired to argue. 'If I am, I am.'

The pattern worked in black thread on the bib of her nightdress was of peapods; I'd not noticed them before, but there they were, staring me in the face, elegant elongations like smiles and the regularly spaced peas inside them like good teeth.

'I'm fetching Mrs Partridge.' Her words were tangled in her throat, as if she were crying. 'She'll be a comfort to you.'

What, and you're not? I almost said it; I nearly joked, *You'll do*, but then, instead, I accused her: 'You think I'm dying but you wouldn't get me a priest.'

'You want a priest?' Guilelessly, 'Why wouldn't I get you a priest?'

I shouldn't have said it, I'd been harsh to say it, and anyway the truth was 'I'm not going to die. This is almost over, I think,' and she could make of that what she would; I didn't care. I just needed her to be useful, to bring that padding for me.

'Elizabeth,' she implored, 'Elizabeth,' *look at me*, and she was so perfect, her parting like a bloodless incision in her scalp. 'Elizabeth, did someone hurt you?' Whispered, not in caution, because there was no one to overhear, nor because she didn't like to voice it, but more, I suspected, because she hated even having to think it.

I knew exactly what she was asking me; what I didn't know was how to answer. Because, yes, he'd hurt me, that last time: he definitely had. This was his fault, and nothing would be better than dumping it all on him: all this blood on his hands, where it belonged. My eleventh day hadn't been safe by his initial reckoning but then he'd said it was, just because he'd wanted it to be.

I could have told her yes, he'd hurt me, and been done with it. No need, even, perhaps, to bother with the actual word: a dismal little shrug would do, *Yes, someone did this to me, but it's over now, and I don't want to talk about it, I'd like to put it behind me and get on with my life*. Evasive, martyred, but ultimately a survivor, facing it down and seeing it through with only my nightdress ruined. Unwittingly, she was offering me the chance to walk away with my reputation intact. She alone had seen me in this state, and for her it would be explained clean away if I said yes. But it wasn't quite the truth, it wasn't the whole truth, which she wouldn't know unless I told her and I had no intention of doing that. How could I? I couldn't tell her that I'd left my room one night to go to a man – a man asleep behind his closed door – and insist he take me into his bed. I couldn't tell her that he'd been content with kissing but that for weeks on end I'd badgered him for more, for everything, to which he'd always said, 'That wouldn't be right,' and I'd always laughed because really, honestly, Harry, what was right about any of it?

Jane wanted to know whatever it was that her books held; but I'd wanted to know what it would be like to have everything of Harry in the way that a wife would. I couldn't imagine myself as anyone's wife, try as I might, and I certainly couldn't be his but I didn't see why that should deny me. For as long as we stayed at kissing, then something was being kept from me. There was something to experience and I had had to pursue it because I was sixteen and anything else – a turning away, a leaving be – would have been a kind of death.

If I said yes to Jane, then none of that had happened. But it had, and I'd made sure it did. To say that a man had hurt me – to say only that a man had hurt me – would be a kind of lie and I didn't want to lie to her so I said, 'No.'

And for a moment she said nothing, then, 'Do you need him?' *Here, now.*

I almost laughed: it was laughable that she thought she

could go and find him for me, and laughable to think that I'd ever again want him anywhere near me.

That, I could answer: 'No,' I said, with as much derision as I could muster, which, I hoped, would tell her all she needed to know. 'But thank you,' I remembered to say. 'What I do need is that padding.'

And this time it worked: off she tripped like an obedient child, to return with a handful of clean, neatly folded cloths. Gesturing at the sodden, reeking wadding, she said, 'Put that in the chamberpot and we'll deal with it in the morning.'

I so badly needed to be back in bed but first she was going to have to leave me so I could secure the clean padding in place. When she'd gone, though, I discovered my hands were useless and what should have been the simplest of tasks was beyond me. I didn't know I was crying until she was back from the bed and again kneeling with me, handing me a handkerchief. She took the clean cloth from me and I levered myself up on her just enough for her to be able to get to work, folding it around and beneath me, her head inadvertently butting my stomach and one of her rings glancing the inside of my thigh. 'Come on,' she said when she'd finished, 'back to sleep,' and so we climbed into bed, me first and then her, and I knew nothing more until I woke in the morning.

I hadn't expected to feel so bad for so long. Well, I hadn't expected to feel bad at all beyond that one dreadful night; I'd presumed that, come morning, it would be over, which was in fact true of the worst of it in that the blood-flow was steady

174

and the pain diffused to an ache. The shock came, though, when I tried to stand: my legs at a loss, and my heart lashing out like something cornered and doomed.

For the next couple of days, shuffling between our two rooms took everything I had. Even sitting or lying down was too much, with daylight carping at me, demanding to be seen, and to shut my eyes only left me wider open to noise, which came at me through the floorboards, closed windows and doors. I lay on the bed, day after day, pitted with the various sounds of the household, of which Twig's barks were the worst: before, they'd seemed well judged but now were inane and maddeningly, inconceivably, mercilessly unanswered.

Someone tell him to stop. Can someone, anyone, just get that dog to stop.

And then of course there was Goose, in our rooms each morning and countless other times during the day: Goose, unable to put down the head of her broom without bashing it on the floor; incapable of pushing it away across the boards without taking it that bit too far and smashing it into the panelling. In my mind, I chased every single one of those broom-strokes of hers in the vain hope that I could somehow snatch it up, stop it short, and by the time she left us each morning I was outraged and exhausted, sending her on her way down the stairs with every possible calamity wished on her head.

It would have been obvious to her that I wasn't feeling well but, to be fair, all she knew was that I was bleeding. For all she knew, it was a usual monthly bleed, just taken badly, and naturally enough she'd have had scant sympathy because, had she been in my place, she wouldn't have been able to lie around.

The initial bleeding could never have been passed off as anything normal but Jane had destroyed those incriminating cloths, along with my unsalvageable nightdress. That first day, she'd somehow managed to hide them from Goose, which had been no mean feat in itself – presumably she'd packed them sodden and rank down among my clothes, although I didn't dare ask and didn't want to think about it – until she'd burned them all on our hearth. The blood that continued to come for the next week or so confounded me: blackened as if cooked, and clot-coiled, tying up any cloth with which I attempted to clean myself.

Jane and I spoke not a word of any of it, not the awful night itself nor the aftermath. Her only acknowledgement of anything having happened at all was a tiresomely repeated exhortation for me to rest – *You need to rest, You should rest* – which infuriated me, because what did she think I was doing? What else could I possibly do? And the confidence and calmness with which she said it: that, too, enraged me. As if what had happened to me was something she came across every day. *Nurse Jane*, I'd think, nastily, although probably nothing she could've said to me at that time would have been anything less than galling, because there she sat, day after day, squeaky-clean and purposeful while I languished, dizzied, draining away into a pad.

And then one day when she dispensed the usual nugget of wisdom, I countered, 'Why don't *you* rest?'

Mid-turn of a page, she paused exaggeratedly but expressionlessly: a show of patience, an invitation for me to explain myself. Which, of course, I couldn't, because it had been a pointless little rejoinder. Backed into a corner of my own making, I whined, 'You never stop.' Why, though, would I want her to stop? So that we could talk? We had nothing to say to each other. Not that it had mattered on the night when I'd bled so badly: we hadn't talked much then, but she'd been company for me in a way that she hadn't before or, frustratingly, since. She'd managed it then, so why not now? Why were we straight back where we'd started?

She asked, 'Are you sick? Do you need anything?' but this dutiful placing of herself at my disposal only further riled me.

'No!' I was so sick of being the patient.

'Elizabeth,' she came over all indulgent, 'listen: I don't stop because I don't have the time. Because we're being ruled by a queen,' and this was gently related, in the manner of a bedtime story, 'who's about to hand England over to the Pope.'

Oh, that again: about as original as a bedtime story, and as boring. And as untrue, was my suspicion. And anyway, I should've asked, and would have if I'd had the strength: what did it matter if the Queen wanted to take us back to Rome? For all the fuss Jane made of thinking everything through, it seemed to me that she was overlooking something very simple: England had been fine for all the hundreds and hundreds of years before *The Book of Common Prayer*. If someone had to be head of the Church, then why not the Pope? King, queen, president, pope: all much of a muchness, as far as I could see, or certainly as far as I could see on that particular dismal day. How had it been any better, I wondered, when we'd had the boy-King, and all the men of the Council – not least her father-in-law – making up his mind for him?

But I said none of that and instead asked her, 'And how are you doing anything about it?'

'You're just like Guildford,' she said, pleasantly, and before I could knock that right back at her – *I am absolutely nothing like Guildford* – 'Books are our only chance, because they can't be silenced.'

'They can be burned,' I objected, 'and a lot easier than people can.'

'A *copy* can be burned.' There was something of a self-satisfied stretch in her sitting back in her chair. 'Or a whole pile of copies. But they are copies, and there are always more. Someone's always made a copy, and someone else is already copying that one.' She was so sure of herself. 'Ideas are inde-structible. Word spreads. You can, if you need to, get a book across a border beneath your skirts.'

Yes, and I bet she dreamed of doing exactly that. I bit down an urge to lunge at her, knock her off that chair of hers, because did she really not see? I said, 'They're just *words*. Books and ideas are *just words*.'

She shook her head, her throat a flurry of pearl-wink. 'Words make ideas, and ideas change everything. Priests insist you believe what they tell you and nothing else, but books let you find out for yourself.'

So very sure of herself.

'Yes, but books just tell you other things,' I said. 'They're still telling you what to think, it's still men – just different men – telling you what to think.'

For some reason, she almost smiled at that. 'Yes, but some men have your interests at heart more than others do, and if you read books, you can choose who to listen to.'

Some of those men, I thought, are dead, a lot of them are dead, and quite why that mattered, I couldn't say. But it did matter, or at that precise moment it did. I said, 'It's all just words.'

'Yes, well, the alternative,' she said calmly, definitively, returning to the book that was open in front of her, 'is silence.'

On coronation day, I woke to the absence of Goose, which had an immensity all of its own. Usually, her thumping around – either on the stairs or already inside our room – would be what woke me. Lying there in the surprising silence, I wondered how early she'd had to leave in the hope of a good place at a roadside. And why I was surprised that she'd gone at all. I mean, she was only human. *Something to tell the grandchildren.*

And I knew the Partridges had gone, so her ministrations weren't required.

No Goose meant no breakfast: although when I said so to Jane, she said, 'She's probably out there now with that tray, foisting it on to the good people of London.' I got myself to our door, opened it, leaned over the stairs: not only no

Partridges or even Twig, as far as I could ascertain, but crucially no aroma of baking bread or roasting meat. 'No lunch, either,' I reported back. My kitchen friends too, then, were gone, and who could blame them? Rumour had it that the water fountains in the city would be running with wine. We'd have to help ourselves, which, as long as I could get myself down there, wasn't too dismaying a prospect because I'd spent a fair bit of time on the kitchen threshold during the past couple of months and even without knowing what it was that I'd be looking for, I quite fancied a root-around in there.

That was for later, though; for the time being, I slouched as usual in the window. This particular October day was dank and cloud-stuffed, not fit for a queen. Not fit for anyone or anything, really, and indeed there was nobody about. Absolutely nobody. It dawned on me that this was something I'd never seen: a complete and utter absence of people in the inner bailey. Intrigued, I began to look harder: kneeling up on the window seat and craning to check from corner to corner. But no: no one. The Tower, deserted. No doubt there'd be guards on the main gates, but here the only sign of life was a solitary, lapdog-sized raven.

When had everyone gone? Had they all left at once, when the gates were opened at dawn, or – enticed by tales of wine fountains – had they been slipping away earlier? Leaving perhaps during the night, with a nod and a wink and a handful of coins to a porter. I stayed alert at the window, because it was like an optical illusion, and, like an optical illusion, would somehow, sooner or later, I felt, give itself away. But time moved on – perhaps a quarter of an hour – and still I'd seen no one. I felt as if I'd chanced upon something that I shouldn't have: the Tower of London, vacated and defenceless. Not that it looked in the least compromised; it stared back at me, unabashed, bare-faced. Bedraggled, maybe, but it was hardly as if it hadn't seen rain before, which anyway didn't really touch it, just coursing off its hefty cobbles. It wasn't as if it hadn't seen queens before, either, and of plenty of kinds. This one, though, this new one, there'd never before been a queen like her and perhaps that was why her fortress now lay empty. She had no one to fear; her own subjects had put her on her throne. Her people had been ordered to accept one queen but had simply shut the town gates all over England and declared for another. And of course, because after everything that England had had to endure in the years since my birth – the queen-mad King, the power-crazed duke – who could possibly object to being ruled by a staid, rock-steady, sweet-tempered lady?

So now everyone from Goose to Princess Elizabeth was lining up to celebrate her procession to Westminster. England was a different country and perhaps that was it, now, for the Tower; from now on, maybe it didn't really even have to be the Tower any more but could retire to become nothing more than a monarch's riverside retreat. When people in the future would say of it that it used to be a fortress, those who were younger would be incredulous: *Fortress?*

Because why would London ever have needed a fortress?

The emptiness of the bailey lay there below me like an

expanse of virgin snow but in very little time they would return and it would be back to normal, nothing special. I needed to get down there while I could. Now was my chance, my one and only chance after so long spent watching everyone else down there, to walk entirely alone right through the centre of the Tower of London. England was busy crowning its queen and I was in the eye of the storm. I could walk out there into the middle of the green and stand there; claim it, just briefly: me, alone, at the heart of the kingdom. Something to tell the grandchildren indeed.

Then I thought of Jane, sitting behind me at the table, and why not her, too? Why not the pair of us, together? She was allowed outside as long as I kept her in view, and there was nowhere down there for her to hide. And she was just a girl, she was just like me; she was no one, or not any more, and certainly no danger to the Queen.

I didn't quite know how to put it. 'Look,' and I heard the wonder in my voice, but she didn't look – or rather she did, but barely, minimally and uncomprehendingly. She glanced across the room at me, whereas I wanted her to look at the window.

'Down there.'

No, not at the window but through it. There she was, though, staring at the greenish glass. I was getting nowhere, so I had to tell her: 'There's no one around, down there; no one, not a soul, they've all gone.' Still nothing, so I said, 'We could go down there.'

Nothing.

'And ... walk around.' Realising, even as I said it, how unexciting that sounded.

And then she did ask, 'What for?' and it was genuine, the question, I could hear that, and I understood why she had to ask, but also it pained me that she didn't somehow just know.

I was alone, in the end, when I stood on the threshold. Apprehensive, too, because for somewhere with so many towers, stairs, roofs and chimneys, a proliferation of gates and porches and passageways, there was also so much nothingness, around which the wind hurled itself. This was a place to make or break a queen, and if it was for now in a doleful slumber, it was nevertheless malign, like a dragon, and those cobbles stretching ahead of me were like spines crammed into the ground.

I wanted to go home, and wished I had a home to go to.

Press on, I urged myself. Nearly there. I'd been to the far side of the inner bailey plenty of times, but always with Mrs Partridge — she'd undertaken a kind of smuggling of me, which had had a certain deliciousness to it, and we'd kept to the edges, moving speedily and unobtrusively among the men, our eyes down, making every pretence of being on business and getting away with it. Other times, I'd stood in that fussy herb garden, mired in ankle-high, tiny-flowered plants; and sometimes I'd been far above it all, up on the wall, confined to a strip of walkway, but on each and every one of those occasions I'd been in attendance or, latterly, on someone's errand. Always, before, I'd been minding my place.

When I stepped from the doorstep, the wind rushed at me,

merciless and only a squeak the dry side of a downpour. I'd imagined the cobbles would bear me up, bounce me along, but they seemed determined to floor me, hobbling me, brutal on my insteps. Do it, I urged myself. Head up. Walk. You can do it. Eyes up, look around, take it in. Here you are, this is yours.

But who was I kidding? I was nothing, inside those vast walls, no more than the rats I glimpsed sometimes whipping along the gutters. No, I was less than a rat, worse than that, because I was ridiculous: my skirts buffeting around my shins, my breathing still clumsy after the blood loss.

The hush over the whole place bore down on me, booming between the towers and echoing inside my ribs, and I'd never felt so alone. I could die here, I thought: this was a place you could die.

But just then a fresh gust caught and somehow lifted the edges of me so that inside I snapped tight into a single tough strand and suddenly there I was, all that I ever had been and ever would be, and I knew myself right down to the blood and the bone and the breath that were singing there loud and clear and wild in the wind.

III

Not long after the coronation, I came through from the bedroom one morning to find Jane reading something which evidently didn't please her. She was drawn tall in the chair, affronted by whatever it was and subjecting it to unfavourable inspection. It wasn't a book but a single leaf of paper, which she folded and slapped back down on to the table, her hand pressed to it as if to keep it down.

She never folded any of her own writing, or not that I'd ever seen. Was that a letter that she had, there? How on earth would a letter have found its way in here? She glanced up and caught me nosing.

'I need to talk with Guildford,' she said, as ever giving nothing away. 'Arrange that for me, would you, please.'

Well, that was a first. Clearly something was wrong. *Could* it be a letter? Not bearing good news, obviously. Something family-related? I dithered by the door in case she wanted to tell me but of course she didn't.

I took the request to Mrs Partridge, who didn't question it nor even look surprised, but asked me where Jane would like them to meet. I didn't know; I hadn't thought to ask.

'Because it's raining,' she said.

I was barely up and knew nothing, so far, of the day.

The doorway, then, we decided – the jetty would provide a modicum of shelter – and she went to dispatch word to Guildford via her own husband while I returned back upstairs to find Jane already fastening her cloak.

On his way across the inner bailey towards us, Guildford looked dazed, which, given the rush and the rain, was understandable. William seemed to have developed a limp. Guildford nodded first to me – no doubt dreadful-looking me – before turning his attention to his wife on an intake of breath, preparing to launch into the appropriate courtesies, but she was already demanding, 'Have you heard?'

The content of the letter was about to be revealed.

He knew nothing of any letter though, and turned wary. 'Heard?' He was probably worried that he was in trouble with her, which was certainly how it looked, although that was nothing new. He took his place beneath the jetty, standing alongside her, and so there we all were, all four of us, shoulder to shoulder and backs to the house, staring into the tipping rain.

'Five days,' Jane complained. 'It's taken her just five days to repeal everything. Five days into her reign and that's the last seven years' work destroyed,' and then she broke away, stomping nowhere in particular, just out into the rain, leaving Guildford and me next to each other but with her absence between us. 'Everything,' she regaled Guildford, 'everything he did, gone.' *He*: the King, the boy-King, her great friend, her supposed soulmate. Which was all very well but she should come beneath the jetty, I thought, or her cloak would get soaked and our room would smell of wet dog. 'Can you believe it? And how exactly will that work? Priests can't now be married – so what are the married ones going to do?' She glared at him as if it was his fault. '*Un*marry? Is that what she wants?'

I appreciated that it was going to be awkward for those priests, and their wives and children, but I'd been thinking that someone had died. Letting go a breath I hadn't known I was holding, I began thinking of lunch. I was enjoying my food again and charmerchande was my hope for today, it would be ideal on a day like this and the Partridges' cook did it so well.

Jane whirled back into her place in our line, looking accusingly into the distance.

Guildford sounded casual: 'She won't last.'

My thoughts of lunch skidded to a halt, and even Jane was taken aback, truly so, turning to him but rearing back so that I feared for my toes and almost copped a faceful of hood. *Treason*: treason even to make mention of the monarch's death, let alone predict it as he seemed to have done, although of course he was already indicted, so perhaps he was thinking that a little more wouldn't harm. I tried and failed to catch his eye, to see what he was up to. Was he trying to shock? Or impress?

On the far side of him, William coughed, so it seemed to be him with whom Guildford took issue when he said, 'Oh, but come on, the chances are she won't.' Either he didn't care who heard him or he considered himself among friends. 'She's always been ill, always had everything wrong with her, and she's old——'

'She's not old,' Jane spoke up. She was missing the point, though, surely, because if the Queen had done what Jane had said she'd done in a mere five days, then time was hardly of the essence. 'And she's not even that ill, it's just chills, headaches, toothache. She could still have a child.'

I was with Guildford on that: I couldn't imagine it of the lady I'd seen below us on the green.

'Yes,' Jane insisted, 'yes, she could.'

'Well, I for one don't think she'll get that far.' He almost sounded bored. 'I think we'll end up with the princess.'

He was probably right. If the Queen were to die with no heir, then the throne would almost certainly pass to her half-sister, because who else was there? And having vaunted her own legitimacy, it would be difficult for the Queen to disallow her half-sister's. Not impossible, per-haps, given their different mothers, but difficult. She was her father's daughter, in her subjects' eyes, and that was why she was Queen. Well, the other sister was also her father's daughter, and he'd left them equal under the terms of his will.

Jane said, 'The princess is no better.'

There was an incredulous pause from her husband before he reminded her, 'She's *Protestant*.' How, in their eyes, could the princess not be better?

Jane was unmoved. 'Not enough of one.'

He could barely bring himself to say, 'I don't think we're in a position to be choosers.'

But as if she hadn't heard him, Jane said: 'The princess only ever has her own interests at heart.'

Guildford said, 'Well, perhaps this isn't very noble of me, but at the moment, with us where we are, as long as those interests of hers coincide with my own, I don't think I care.'

And fair enough, I thought, but Jane still wasn't having it. 'This is a girl who is contemplating marrying Edward Courtenay.'

'No,' he corrected her patiently, 'that's the Queen.'

'*No*,' she was straight back at him, 'not now. Now it's Elizabeth.' She folded her arms, hard. 'That's what my sources say, and they're reliable.' So, she had sources. But of course she did. Who was it that had delivered that letter, and how? 'There's no substance to that girl. She doesn't know her own mind.'

Guildford was struggling now, I sensed, to maintain his air of lofty amusement. 'She won't marry Courtenay, she's just throwing people off the scent. And if you don't mind me saying,' and he did say it gently, 'it's been quite a while since you spent any time with her.'

She shook her head, emphatic. 'She's not going to save this country. You've seen her: toadying to her sister. She'll never stand up and say what she believes in. She cares too much about saving her own skin.'

Guildford tried, 'Well, you know, as she's all we've got, perhaps that's no bad thing.'

'But if I wasn't stuck in here—'

'Don't,' he said, which had me tense without quite knowing why.

Jane could barely contain herself, but she did.

Guildford, though, didn't. 'And, anyway, *what*?' His patience was suddenly, spectacularly gone. 'What could you be doing, if you were out there in the big wide world?'

And now she was the one in retreat, muttering so that I could barely hear the response: 'More than I can do in here. I can't get the right books, in here. I can't talk with anyone—'

Well, anyone who mattered.

'*Listen*,' which she couldn't fail to do because he'd raised his voice, 'I didn't want you shut in here, believe me. But you *are*, and honestly, I don't know any more ways to say I'm sorry.'

This was an echo, I was sure, of some earlier, intimate exchange they'd had, in the days before I'd arrived, and I was desperately curious even as I knew I shouldn't be.

Jane stepped away again into the wet. 'Well, I can't stand it.'

He was almost shouting: 'And you think it's what I want? You think I want this?'

I felt I should stop them, do something to stop them, but then suddenly they had stopped, had already stopped before they'd even really started, and she was sighing – short and sharp – and saying, 'Well . . .'

Well, I suppose I should be going.

And, 'Yes,' he was only too ready to oblige, so that it became the sum total of her leave-taking, that one little word, *Well,* which was no real word at all, and then she was gone, back through the door, leaving me on the wrong side of it. William was remarkably quick off the mark, too, for someone with a limp: already on his way back towards the White Tower.

Guildford and I stood staring after him.

And Guildford said, 'I saw you.'

When I turned to him, he seemed just as startled by what he'd said as I was.

'What?'

He took a moment but then could only repeat, 'I saw you.'

'Saw me *what?*'

And now it was he who was lost for words. He indicated the green. 'Walking.' But he knew that was inadequate. 'On coronation day.'

He'd seen me on the green, all alone; seen me stripped to my bare bones by the wind and more alive than I'd ever been.

'What were you doing?'

I paused in the doorway with the open door before me. 'Walking.' *You said so yourself.*

Not until I had that door closed behind me did I take a breath. He was perfectly entitled to look out of his own window. And, yes, I'd been there, right in the middle of the green, for anyone to see. But I hadn't been just walking and he knew it, although quite what there had been of me for him to see, I honestly didn't know.

Incredibly, Guildford took Jane's railing at him about the Queen's retrograde measures as a sign that she was keen to resume their meetings. The very next day, an anxious-looking Mrs Partridge brought word that he was outside and would welcome a little of his wife's time.

Jane checked: 'For anything in particular?'

Mrs Partridge didn't think so.

'Well, then,' she concluded, 'I think we've said all we need to say to each other for the time being,' and she said it so nicely, as if it were the best of all possible responses. As if other married couples were burdened with things to say to each other but by good fortune she and Guildford had now moved beyond that.

Mrs Partridge glanced at me; I rolled my eyes and said I'd let him know. She demurred, as she probably felt she should, but I assured her I was happy to do it. And she knew how I liked an excuse to get outside. But really I'd volunteered because I had a bone to pick with Guildford.

In the middle of the Partridges' herb patch was a trough planted with thyme to make a seat which, as far as I knew, no one ever used. But there was Guildford, now, sitting on it in hope of a fragrant half-hour or so with his wife. William was keeping well back, crouched on the steps to Beauchamp Tower, playing himself at cards.

I strode up to Guildford saying 'Don't,' as he got to

his feet but too late because he already had, so I plonked myself down in his place on that scrubby, springy, scented cushion. If it had been good to tell him to sit, it was even better watching him not quite dare to sit back down so close to me.

There he stood, in front of me, and the sheen of his velvet jacket was substantial enough in itself to be a distinct, additional layer. Everywhere over him were buckles and toggles and buttons, an armoury fending off the sharp-angled October sunlight. Dressing and undressing him must take some doing: no wonder William was permanently enervated. I relayed the message: 'She's said all she needs to say for the time being.'

He absorbed that. Then, 'You never address me properly, do you. Anyone else would say, "She's not coming out, *my lord.*"'

I gave him a tight little smile that was no smile at all, which might've said, *I'm not 'anyone else'*, and possibly even, *You're not my lord.* And it occurred to me, 'You don't call me Mistress Elizabeth.'

Surprisingly, he mulled that over. 'True.' Then folded his arms, defensively. 'I should. And *you* should address me as my lord, or' – his turn for the unsmiley smile – 'I could report you for insubordination.'

'Well, I'm already in the right place for that.'

With a sigh, he gave in and joined me on the herbaceous seat, which made for quite a squeeze. The air around us held the scent of thyme but, closer, he smelled of mud. 'You know,

Mistress Elizabeth, being rude isn't how to go about making friends.'

'And you're the expert on that.'

He stared resolutely ahead at the Lord Lieutenant's shuttered house. 'And anyway, why don't you? Why don't you address me properly? Is it because I'm in here?'

Held in the Tower, disgraced, reduced. I was about to say no, of course not, *What do you take me for, kicking you when you're down*, but I realised that it was precisely the reason. He was in here and so was I: both of us in the Tower and, in that respect, equal.

'I mean, do you call other lords "lord"?'

'Depends.'

He protested, 'It does *not* "depend". They're *lords*. They're what they *are*. It's not for *you* to decide.'

I was enjoying myself, for the first time in a long time. 'Who does, then? Who does decide?'

For a second, he was stumped. Then, 'The monarch.'

'And it wouldn't do to go disobeying one of those, would it.'

For a moment, he said nothing; together we watched a particularly corpulent raven going about its obscure business.

'What about my wife, then? Do you call her "my lady"?'

No. Same reason. And anyway, 'A month or so ago, you'd've been having me call her Your Majesty.' I stood to leave.

Up came those eyes, after me. 'You don't go to Mass,' he said.

'Don't I?'

He bit his lip. 'I've never seen you.'

I started back towards the house.

'If you said you were going to Mass,' he called behind me, 'you could come outside every day.'

I could go wherever I wanted any time I wanted, but I called back, 'What's there to come outside for?'

And when I glanced round, at the door, he half smiled and said, as I knew he would, 'Me.'

'You're on your way to Mass,' he said the following day, when I took my place beside him on that bed of thyme.

'I am.'

He was looking better – his hair had been washed – and even William, too, on the Beauchamp Tower steps, seemed in surprisingly good spirits, delighting in the presence of the Partridges' supercilious cat. All well and good, it all made for a good start, but immediately we ran aground because I couldn't think why I'd come, nor what to say, and I didn't want to be reduced to commenting on the weather, spectacular though it was. He sat pensively, forearms laid along his thighs, hands clasped, fingers interlaced, and earnestly broke our silence with 'Tell me, then: as a Catholic, do you really believe that the bread is the body of Christ?'

Oh, give me strength. And anyway, 'What do you care what I believe?'

He denied it, fast, 'I don't,' but back-tracked just as

quickly: 'Well, no, I do, if you're—' then flinched from his own unspoken words.

I was intrigued. 'If I'm what?'

'If you . . .' A flex or two of his joined fists, to pass the moment.

'If I what?'

'. . . believe something that's . . .'

I too was leaning forward, now, but in pursuit, because I had an inkling of where this was going, and I wouldn't let him get away with it. 'Something that's what?'

And so he gave it up, with bad grace: 'Stupid.'

I made as if to give that some thought. 'Stupid.'

'You know what I mean.'

I shrugged hugely. *Do I? I'm just a stupid Catholic, right?*

'Because you're not stupid,' he insisted crossly.

I tilted my head, mock-solicitous. 'You sure about that?'

He spread his hands, *All I'm saying is,* 'It'd be a shame for you to be believing something stupid.'

'Well, thank you for your concern.'

Silence. *Let him stew.* But eventually I said, 'I suppose a Catholic would say it's a kind of miracle.' And I asked him, 'Don't you believe in miracles?' before answering for him: 'Just some of them. The less miraculous ones. You decide which ones to believe. Multiplying fishes and loaves, fine; but *being* a loaf, a step too far.' I sank my hands behind me into the scratchy thyme, and luxuriated in a backwards stretch. 'Do you believe there's a God?'

'What?' He sounded nervous. 'Of course I do.' And

dismayed: 'Are you saying there isn't a God? Are you saying that's a stupid belief?'

I bounced my heels on the base of the trough. 'I'm saying it's a belief.'

To that, nothing, for a moment. Then, coolly, 'That's heretical, Elizabeth. You could die for saying that.'

I grinned. 'Only if you tell.'

He didn't reciprocate.

'You weren't listening,' I said. 'I didn't say there wasn't a God; I said I didn't know if there was. I said you have to *believe*.'

Still nothing.

'And anyway, if your wife's right about the way things are going, people are going to be dying soon for saying what you just said about the bread.'

'I didn't *say*, I *asked*.' He was despondent. 'Everyone thinks they know what I believe. Everyone thinks they know everything about me.'

After a moment, I said, 'But you're not just your father's son.'

'No, but I am just my wife's husband.' *And that's why I'm here.*

'Not to me,' I said, as I stood up.

He looked up at me. 'Where are you going?'

'Mass.'

He was startled. 'What, really?'

'Yes, really,' I said, although actually it was a lie. And I thought, You've never had to slip by, have you: you and your kind never have to cover your tracks and go unnoticed. Well, you should start learning, I thought, and you can do worse than learn from me.

Despite her agitation at the content of that letter, Jane was generally easier company after the coronation. Perhaps she considered herself on the home stretch, although, in view of what Guildford had said about the practical difficulties of their future life together, I wondered what kind of home she envisaged. Funnily enough, around that time she became quite the little housewife, procuring linen and silks from Mrs Partridge for the stitching of two purses as New Year presents for her sisters. A honeysuckle pattern for Katherine, and gillyflowers for Mary. Occasionally she'd stop reading and would stitch for a while instead. The Partridges could of course send those purses on but I couldn't help feeling that Jane was hoping to be able to hand them over in person. And indeed, a couple of days into her stitching, she broached it: 'It would be odd to be here for Christmas, wouldn't it.'

Would it? Odder than at any other time?

She didn't look up from her work with a pink silk. 'I wonder what it's like here at Christmas; I wonder who stays around. The Partridges, do you think?'

I reminded her that Mrs Partridge would be heavily pregnant by then: hardly in a fit state to travel.

'Oh, yes,' as if she'd forgotten, and then, 'I do so love Christmas at home at Bradgate,' and I'd have tried to get her to say more had Goose not come crashing in.

Later that afternoon, I related it to Guildford, flatly, for comic effect: 'Jane does so love Christmas at Bradgate.'

We were sheltering from drizzle in the entrance to the White Tower; William was nowhere to be seen although he had to be somewhere, watching.

It was mean of me, I knew, to be reporting what Jane had confided and in a manner to make light of it, but then, I was beginning to realise that if I looked at her in a certain way, which meant through someone else's eyes, she did sometimes rather lend herself to being a figure of fun. And anyway, it was too valuable to pass up. It was something of a coup: Jane having expressed a sentiment, and such an unlikely one.

None of which was wasted on Guildford: '*Does* she now?' Something about Jane that we hadn't known and, better still, something we could never have guessed. He was keen for more: 'Well, what? What is it that she so loves about Christmas?'

There, though, I was going to have to disappoint him. 'We didn't get that far,' I admitted.

'She didn't say?'

Suddenly I was weary. 'Does she ever?'

In the distance, a roost of starlings rose like a puff of cinders.

'And you?' he asked me. 'Are you a lover of Christmas?'

Last Christmas was when Harry had kissed me. It seemed to me now that not only had he forgotten himself but, drunk in the darkness, had quite possibly forgotten me, too:

forgotten who I was, even mistaken me for someone else.

'I bet you like a party,' Guildford was saying, 'and I bet there are parties back in Suffolk. I imagine you're quite a dancer. Or would be, if you let yourself go, which you probably don't. Everyone worries too much about what everyone else thinks. But I mean, that's what Twelfthtide's there for, isn't it – out with the old, in with the new.'

'Yes, but then life just goes on, doesn't it,' I said and, giving up on any pretence of going to Mass, got up and headed back instead to the house.

I was never gone from the room long enough to have attended a Mass but on this occasion there couldn't be even the most bare-faced pretence. Jane, though, didn't seem bothered; I was barely through the doorway before she said, 'You can be back home by Christmas, if you like,' in a reasonable, cheerful tone which I rarely heard from her unless we were in the company of the Partridges.

I didn't follow, not least because I was busy catching my breath from the climb up the stairs. She was standing at the window, her back to it as if hiding something although there was nothing behind her but sky. 'You could leave now, if you like.'

What was she talking about?

'I mean, you don't have to stay, especially now that you're all right . . .'

That, I did grasp, although I couldn't believe she'd said it. 'That wasn't why I came here!' I was appalled. 'Is that what you think? That I came here because of that?' Because, apart from anything else, how short-sighted would that have been? I was furious with her. 'What? Would I have had you' – I didn't know how else to put it – 'delivering the baby?'

She rushed in with 'I'm sorry, I wasn't thinking.'

Jane, not thinking? *Jane?* Well, maybe that was what too much sewing did for a person. I flung my cloak at the hook. Behind me, she tried again, but cautiously: 'All I mean is that you can go any time,' *as you know*, despite neither of us ever before having spoken of it. 'It's just that with Christmas coming . . .'

One of us needed to say what we meant, so I turned around and put it to her: 'Is that what you want?'

But she still wouldn't have it, turning away and saying only, 'It's for you to decide.'

Not until that night, when I thought she was already asleep, did she answer me: 'Since you ask, I'd prefer if you didn't leave until this is all over.'

I waited in case she had any more to say, but she didn't.

'Well, then,' I said, 'I won't.' Because it was no hardship. It wasn't as if I had other plans.

When I told Guildford that Mrs Partridge had taken me on more than several occasions to pick flowers from the Queen's Garden, he was disgruntled that Mr Partridge hadn't favoured him with some similar privilege. He mused, 'What would be the equivalent, for me?' We were in the mouth of a passageway at the side of the Lord Lieutenant's house; it was William's turn for the White Tower's entrance. 'Shouldn't Mr Partridge be taking me across the river to a brothel? Isn't that what Bishop Gardiner used to do for Edward Courtenay?'

Very funny. 'No, that was what he *didn't* do, although it's what Edward Courtenay did as soon as he was free of him.'

'Ah, well, bishops,' he was mock-rueful, 'what are they good for?' Then, 'For running the country, if this queen has her way.'

Who would you have instead? I didn't say it but it was there in the air between us, halting any conversation until he salvaged it with a deliberately anodyne enquiry as to the progress of Jane's embroidery. Then, 'Do *I* get a Christmas present?' He was back to being mischievous. 'Has she mentioned anything?' He knew she hadn't.

'Do you want one?'

He dropped back to rest against the wall, in a show of contemplation. 'Well, if it's made by the hand of my own fair lady wife, then maybe I do.'

'In which case, I'll put in a good word for you.'

Sharper, he said, 'I do need some stitching done.'

I gave him a look.

And got one in return. 'What? She *is* my *wife.*'

'She's busy changing the world, remember.'

He sighed, hugely. 'Well, what about you, then? It's only a lining that's coming away.'

'William would be your better bet.'

'No one you're stitching presents for, then?'

I wasn't getting into that.

'Well, if you're not stitching, and you're not praying – and I know you're not doing that – then what are you doing all day every day in there?'

'Looking out.'

'And thinking.'

No, actually, not thinking: not thinking was what I was emphatically doing. 'And what do *you* do, all day?'

'Pester William to play cards, mostly. But he's always writing to his wife. A letter every day: a long, long letter.'

I was incredulous. 'What does he find to say?'

'Ah, well, that's for us lesser mortals to wonder.' He heaved himself off the wall to press one foot hard on to the ground: cramp, or pins and needles. 'Then again, perhaps not. Because perhaps you've been in love, Elizabeth; have you?' He cocked his head, appraising me. 'Anyone you have your eye on? Any suitable Suffolk sorts? Or,' he smirked, 'anyone *un*suitable? Any – I don't know – stablehands?'

'No, but how about you? Any stablehands *you* have *your* eye on?'

'Elizabeth,' he warned. *You could die for that.* He peered into the distance as if to check on William. 'Well, anyway, you've got all that to come,' he said, 'because you'll be marrying for love, won't you.'

'Which is a stupid thing to do, according to you.'

'No, *for me*.' He turned back around. 'For someone such as me, coming from a family such as mine.'

I couldn't let that pass. 'And what do you know about *my* family?'

Hands up. 'Good Catholic family, and well connected: must be, to have got you here.'

I put him straight: 'I volunteered, and let me tell you that I didn't have a lot of competition.'

He was surprised. 'You volunteered for this? Why?'

Questions, questions, questions. 'Because I thought I might meet my prince.'

Another of those searching looks of his. 'You want a prince?'

'No, Guildford,' I said, moving off past him. 'Actually, what I want is some peace and quiet.'

I didn't see him every day, nor even most days, because sometimes the cold was too much for me or he himself was too much, and the day after we'd stood discussing Jane's embroidery was one of those times, although it was my mistake to think it would be easier to stay put. Jane was pleased with her progress on the honeysuckle bag, and that afternoon she pressed on with it. I wasn't bothered when she was reading or writing but, inexplicably, her embroidering drove me to distraction. I could never have joined her in her reading and writing, but I could well have joined her in the needlework. She'd offered – several times – to share her silks with me, but the silks weren't the half of it because I also lacked her eye for detail, her steady hand, her patience. I didn't want to show myself up. Not that I said so. I just declined politely, and she could think what she liked.

That particular November afternoon was when she nodded towards the Susanna tapestry and, apropos of nothing, pronounced, 'Apocryphal.'

I got the impression this was supposed to be helpful.

What?

'Means it didn't really happen. It's just a story.'

Oh, what, unlike the rest?

Anyway, how did she – or anyone – know? They'd read it somewhere in a book, but who'd written the book and how had the writer known? And the funny thing was – and I nearly said it to her – that Susanna was one story that I could believe. Those two old men, the respected elders: *You either let us do whatever we want to you or we tell everyone you have a lover, and just who, girly, do you think they'll listen to?*

And, actually, while we were on the subject, there was something I'd often wondered: 'Why don't you ever try to convert me?'

I'd thrown it at her from nowhere but she didn't so much as glance up to reply, 'Well, if I took the time to try to convert everyone ...'

But I wasn't everyone. And I was right there under her nose. Right there, day after day, week after week. 'But I've started going to Mass again,' I said, at which she did glance up, but sceptical, which infuriated me. 'I have!'

She was already back at her stitching. 'Did I say you haven't?'

'Well, why don't you ever try to stop me?'

She said nothing, just sat there stitching.

'Why don't you ever really talk to me?'

'We're in prison,' she said. 'Not at a party.'

'But isn't that all the more reason we should talk? Stuck in here like this, just the two of us?'

'Talk about what?' A pulling tight of a thread gave her an instant in which to frown up at me, but I couldn't read it: puzzlement? Disapproval? Challenge?

How could we ever know what we might have in common if we didn't talk? And anyway, I thought, what does anyone ever talk about? What did Guildford and I talk about? 'Just . . . anything,' I ended up saying, pathetically.

Suddenly she surprised me, laying her embroidery down in her lap and saying in the manner of offering me something, 'Katherine Parr would've converted you.'

As a conversation opener, it left me at a loss. Katherine Parr? The one who'd survived the old King.

She warmed to her theme, literally: sitting back, stretching her legs, her feet closer to the fire. 'I lived with her for a while at Chelsea and, I tell you, she would've converted you. She wrote and published a whole book but she still managed to win everyone over, convert everyone she came across.'

'How?'

That had her shrugging, although taking some pleasure in it, making light of her own cluelessness: if she knew, said that shrug, then she'd be doing it, wouldn't she. 'She was just . . .' she came back with, 'lovely.'

'She won *you* over,' I said.

'Oh, no,' she crossed her ankles. 'She didn't have to; I was raised Protestant, remember. My father likes to think of himself as a man of ideas,' it was obvious she didn't concur, 'although my mother's more of a horsewoman. In her view, life's for living,' which she pronounced to make clear that she was quoting, and raised her eyebrows as if we agreed that was self-evidently absurd. 'So, no,' she said, 'the Dowager Queen didn't have to win me over.'

'Actually,' I had to tell her, 'I didn't mean it that way.'

And she got it, 'Oh,' and turned shy. 'Well, yes, I was very fond of her, yes.'

Fond. I almost smiled: it struck me as a most Jane-like word.

She remembered, '*We* used to talk, the two of us. She used to sit me down morning and night to comb my hair and that was when we had our best talks. About what—' another shrug, for what was lost. 'But I remember the feeling of it. She'd ask me to think, really, and then think a little more and then a little more, and there was always further to go, and I loved that.'

'What was she like?' I didn't know quite what I could expect as an answer.

Jane didn't hesitate: 'Tall,' before reflecting, 'but I was nine, so everyone was tall,' and then, with the twitch of a smile in her eyes, 'Mind you, everyone still is.' She decided, 'She was good: that was what she was,' but then, to prevent my taking 'good' to mean 'pious and sanctimonious', 'No, she was clever and kind and funny and forgiving.' Unlike her own mother, was my guess. Suddenly I felt the lack of

Katherine Parr. We were in need of her, I felt: we could've done with her here with us.

'*She* was a queen,' I said, although I didn't know why I'd said it and then worried that I shouldn't have.

But Jane, back at her stitching, was unperturbed. 'By then,' she corrected me, 'she was just a wife.'

I recalled the story as I knew it: only very briefly a widow, a dowager queen, then once again a wife. I had a sense it hadn't gone well, that latter marriage, but if I'd ever known the details, I couldn't remember them.

'She was sure I was going to be both,' said Jane evenly, absorbed in a stitch. 'She was sure I'd marry the King.' The boy-King, the Dowager Queen's little stepson. Jane sounded vaguely interested in the idea, as if discussing someone other than herself. If she had married him, she'd probably have been no better off. She'd already be his widow, his dowager queen, and with Mary Tudor on the throne, she might well have ended up in here anyway.

I thought I might as well ask: 'Why didn't you? Marry him.'

'Oh, I don't know.' She didn't look up. 'She died and I got sent back home and everything changed.'

'I thought you'd suffered a loss of faith,' Guildford said when I turned up several days later.

'I've been busy,' I said, sitting down beside him on the thyme, 'listening to your wife talking.'

The speed with which he turned to me was a joy to behold

210

and I'd have loved to have strung him along further, unset-tled him a bit more, but actually I just told him straight: 'Not about *you*,' refraining from adding, *You should be so lucky.* 'She was telling me about when she lived with the Dowager Queen.'

'Oh.' He was reassured, and uninterested.

Nevertheless, he was going to hear about it, because 'She was happy there,' which, surely, was worthy of note.

'Well, yes, until that husband disgraced himself.' And then, seeing my incomprehension: 'You didn't know? The Dowager Queen's new husband and the princess? You don't know about that?'

Was he having me on? 'Which princess?'

'Well, not Mary, obviously,' he said brutally. 'But Elizabeth. She was there too, at Chelsea – gone there to live with her stepmother. She was –' he took a guess '– fourteen?'

'And?' I was agog.

'And the husband was ...' he considered how to put it, '"over-familiar" with her.'

Over-familiar: a borrowed expression behind which he'd taken refuge, but he still looked uncomfortable.

Which was nothing, I suspected, to how I looked.

Over-familiar: was that what people would say Harry had been with me, if ever they got to know?

'Not that anyone knows exactly, of course – it's all rumour – but whatever happened was bad enough for the princess to be sent to friends and Jane taken back home.'

'But hadn't they just married?' The new husband, the

Dowager Queen: married for love, far too soon, mere weeks into her widowhood. She'd been left in a position to be able to choose for herself. 'So, why would he do that?'

Guildford shrugged. 'He was a chancer. A dowager queen is a dowager queen but a princess is a princess. Too good a chance to miss, I suppose.'

A chancer: was that what Harry was?

'And afterwards,' he said, 'they made the best of it, I think, for appearances' sake, but then she had a baby and died, and once she'd gone, Council moved in for the kill, because no one's going to behave like that with a princess and get away with it.'

I'd given Harry the chance. He hadn't been looking for it, he was too lazy to be bothered. Opportunities had to be handed to him, and I'd done that.

I said, 'Jane didn't tell me any of that.'

He gave me a look.

It occurred to me: 'What did she know of it all, at the time?' She'd been nine, she'd said.

He sighed. 'It's never what she knows, is it. She knows an awful lot. It's what she understands of anything.'

Well, yes. Poor Jane: 'There she was, to have that wonderful upbringing with the Dowager Queen, and then that happens.'

He looked surprised. 'Oh, but that wasn't why she was there. Did she tell you that?' He allowed, 'Well, perhaps there was something of that, perhaps that was what the Dowager Queen wanted. But she was there because her parents sold her to that chancer. He'd said he'd marry her to the King. He was the King's uncle, remember.'

'*Sold* her?'

'Wardship. Sold her wardship. Seymour paid her parents and then he'd get to keep whatever more he could make from her.' He said, 'You know how it works.'

I'd never thought of wardships in that way. He was right, though, I supposed. 'Did Jane know that?'

He pulled a face: 'As I say . . .' Even if she did, who knew what she understood of it, either at the time or since.

Poor Jane: first that, and then the betrothal to another Seymour, and then her Dudley marriage. Always associated with the wrong men. But then perhaps all men are the wrong men, I thought: perhaps there's no other kind.

And that was when Guildford said, quietly, 'I know what you think of me.'

Well, I was glad one of us did. Heart in mouth I listened for what he might say.

'Yes,' he said, 'I could probably do it, I could probably walk away from my marriage. I could probably get this marriage annulled, but then what becomes of her? She's back where she started and they'll just marry her off to someone else.' He said, 'I know you think I'm stupid, because she's never going to thank me for standing by her. You think I don't know that, but I do. The way I see it, though, is that someone has to do right by her, for once, whether she likes it or not.'

*

The decision about whether or not to go and meet Guildford was there to be made every day, after the breakfast I never ate and before the Mass I never attended, and I resented it because my life here in the Tower was supposed to be easy. Wasn't that why I'd come? Not to have to think. Not to have to see anyone.

What weighed on me was the thought of him waiting for me, which he never failed to do, perhaps even in the worst of weathers, because he was always there whenever I did turn up. The times when I hadn't appeared were never mentioned; I came trailing them but they weren't acknowledged, which only made them more conspicuous.

But why was it sometimes so hard – too hard – to go and spend a little time with him? Why so difficult to sit and talk about nothing very much? I'd never expected to like him, but I did; or on the whole, I did. There were still times when he was high-handed and self-righteous and then I'd have loved to set Goose on him. That was how I got through the times when he was less than likeable: by pondering what Goose would make of him.

Generally, though, my reluctance had nothing to do with what he did or didn't say. What made me want to run was how he looked at me whenever I did turn up: the looking up at me – he never, after that first time, got to his feet – as if he were handing himself over to me. As if I could save him. But from what?

And if on the days when I didn't see him I still kept company with him inside my head, that was only because it was empty of everything else.

One day in late October he told me he was worried that his exercise was going to be curtailed or even stopped. That was what it was, for him, officially, our sitting side by side: exercise. That was how he put it to William and to anyone else who needed to know. For me it was Mass, but for him it was exercise. 'Honeymoon's over,' he raised his eyebrows, 'for our new queen. She's getting a harder time of it. People are asking questions. About how far she's going to go. Waking up a bit, now, they are. Too bloody late, the dozy bastards, but they wouldn't be told, would they.' He coughed. 'Easy for her to be magnanimous when everything's rosy, but when things turn iffy, it's easier to have us under lock and key.' He revised, 'Or more locks, more keys.'

Thrown, unsure what to say, I fell back on the worst possible thing: 'Well, you'll need to start going to Mass, then,' realising even as I said it that he of all people wouldn't appreciate flippancy about expedient conversion. Flustered, I tried to make light of it – 'I mean, *I* have to' – but he didn't look at me and sounded tired when he said, simply, 'Well, you'll get your place in Heaven, won't you.'

And after that, understandably, he was poor company, so before long I gave up on him and resigned myself to a long afternoon back in our room.

When the Partridges invited us down to dine, one evening in early November, it was because they had news for Jane: there was a date for the trial, the 13th, a mere week away. Jane gave no sign of how she felt to hear it, and perhaps she felt nothing at all. She'd been living with the threat of the trial for a long time, and, as Mr Partridge had been quick to reiterate, it was of no real consequence, whatever the verdict: it had to be done; it was just something to be gone through.

Me, though, suddenly I found I had all kinds of questions. I'd understood all along that the trial would be a formality but only now did I wonder what form it would take. For a start, how long would it last? Hours or days? And where would it be?

As if he'd read my mind, Mr Partridge said, 'It'll be at Guildhall.'

At that, though, Jane's demeanour changed. 'Guildhall?' Apparently this was of some significance to her. Her sights were firmly on Mr Partridge and I had a sense that she was refusing to let him off a hook. Holding him in that unnerving gaze of hers, she then cocked her head as if listening hard for something. 'Not Westminster?'

He took a breath, audibly, to fortify himself before confirming, 'No.'

And Jane drew back in on herself, as if to consider.

I looked to Mrs Partridge, but she was staring down at her hands. Nothing particularly unusual in that, but still, something was going on. 'What?' I piped up, but no one responded. Instead, Jane asked the Partridges, 'How will we get there?'

'Barge, first,' said Mr Partridge, 'then a walk.'

A walk, as if it were a stroll. But if I was fooled, Jane wasn't; she pinned him down: 'How much of a walk?'

He lost his nerve, referred the question to his wife, who was notably reluctant to take it up. 'Half an hour?' Said diffidently, to disown it.

To me, this presented a practical problem. 'You'll need boots,' I said to Jane. 'Half an hour through London streets in November. You'll need boots.' It was my job, after all, to think of such things. She'd been detained in July and then the only walks she'd been expected to be taking would be brief and at her choosing, on the finer days; she had no boots with her, she hadn't come equipped and in four months neither we nor anyone else had remedied that. I said to the Partridges, 'She'll need some boots,' but it seemed that no one was listening to me, so I said to Jane, 'Or I suppose you could try mine.'

'Elizabeth,' Mrs Partridge touched my hand, as if to return me to my senses, 'you'll be going too.'

'Oh, yes, of course,' as if I'd just remembered, but in truth I was thinking, *Will I?* And how far? How far would I be going with Jane? And into what? Was it a room, a normal room, with benches and tables? Or was it more like the throne room that I'd once seen?

And Jane was saying to me, 'I can't walk in boots,' and sounding definite about it, but what on earth did she mean, *can't walk in boots?* I countered with 'Well, you can't walk in little velvet slippers, can you. It's November and it's half an hour.' Then it struck me and I put my bright idea to the Partridges: 'Can't she ride?'

The silence implied I'd said something wrong.

Then, gently, Mr Partridge said, 'Walk is what we've been told.' And to Jane, 'You, your husband, and the archbishop.'

Which was when Jane turned to me and explained, 'Like penitents,' and finally, belatedly, I understood that it was important that the walk was a walk. A long walk, no less, for everyone to see. The walking was as important as the judgement, or even more so, seeing as the verdict, whichever way it went, was neither here nor there. The real work of the trial was to have Jane and her husband and the archbishop paraded past everyone in London.

Jane was asking the Partridges, 'Who will try us?'

Mr Partridge's set of his jaw, defensive, pretended that the choice of whoever was to be in charge was nothing much, was all in a day's treason-trialling: 'The Lord Mayor and the Duke of Norfolk.'

This did get a response from Jane: a despairing, sceptical exhalation, at which the Partridges both looked shamed.

But again, I had to ask, 'What?'

Matter-of-fact, Jane told me, 'Traditionalists. Papists.'

'Yes, but,' Mrs Partridge was animated, 'we've been told to make very clear that your case has to be heard; this is your opportunity to be heard. Whatever can be said in your favour, the Queen wants it said.'

'Oh, I bet she does,' Jane responded, 'because that'll make it so much easier. Poor little me, horribly misled. But,' she relaxed back in her chair as if this were her last word on it, 'they should find me guilty as charged.'

*

'We've a date for the trial,' were Guildford's first words to me when I next saw him. I hadn't expected him to be gloomy at the news; he'd always been sanguine on the subject: it was, he'd always said, something to be endured before he could move on into his future, inglorious though that might well be.

We were sitting on the Lord Lieutenant's front step and he was fussing Twig, who'd come along with me, but there was something assiduous in his fondling of the dog's ears, just as there was in his refusal to meet my eye. 'And a place, too,' he added.

He smelled a bit: too long since a wash, or the last wash hadn't been thorough enough.

'It's low,' he said, 'it's really low, to have us paraded through the streets like that.'

This was similar to Jane's talk of penitents, but penitents, I felt, were demonstrating contrition whereas to be paraded was to be turned over to a crowd.

Twig was intent on his touch, taking the utmost he could from it.

'You saw what they did to my father.' *They*: the crowd, the onlookers who'd lined the way into London; presumably he was referring to the egg-throwing. 'And he was riding, so they actually had to put a bit of effort into it. Whereas we're just going to be offered up to them.' He sighed. 'I don't know why she doesn't just have done with it and stick us in the stocks.'

'You're not your father,' I reminded him.

But he misunderstood. 'Exactly,' and now he did look at

me but his eyes were unseeing, his focus inwards. 'My father could walk through anything. Nothing ever put him off. He could rise above anything. He was never cowed. If he believed in something, he'd see it through. But,' and his voice splintered, which had me catch my breath, 'you know me: I can't, I just can't,' and suddenly his eyes had a sheen of tears.

'You'll be fine,' I said, quickly, with a confidence I didn't have, because it scared me to see him like that. He had to be fine, he just did, because what was the alternative? *I can't*: what would that entail? My stomach lurched at the thought of him out there in the London streets, with everything going wrong for him.

'I'm hopeless at crowds,' he said. 'I hate being in front of people.'

I knew I should hear him out and offer comfort, but instead I distracted him with a change of subject: 'What will you plead?'

'Guilty,' and there was no hesitation, he was back on sure ground. 'It's pointless to turn it into a fight; we lost that fight back in July.' He was stroking Twig's bony head with his thumb, as if working something into or beneath the fur. 'We need to hold up our hands' – which, for an instant, he actually did – 'and get our wrists slapped, then we get out of there, get it behind us.'

I kept him talking: 'And you think you will?' We had to keep talking: this was how it should be, this was how it was best between us.

'Well, yes, me and Jane, yes, because we don't matter: we're just kids who got pushed through the wrong door into the wrong room.'

The throne room, presumably.

'But the archbishop, no, I don't think so.' He turned circumspect. 'She blames him for the last twenty years.' The ruining of her mother, the wrecking of the Church. 'She'll want him to recant long and loud enough for everyone in England to hear it, but I doubt even that'll save him.' And then suddenly he was up, sending Twig scampering shy of him. 'The problem is, I get nervous when I'm in front of people and then I get angry and then' – his hands raised again but this time in helplessness – 'I make an idiot of myself.'

Well, yes, that I'd seen, but not for a while and I'd assumed we were beyond all that. *Guildford*, I had the urge to say, to plead, *Guildford*, a calling him back, the Guildford I'd come to know in recent weeks.

'And when I get nervous, I get cramps, and it's a long walk, all that way in front of all those people, and if I start to get cramps, what am I going to do? Where am I going to go?'

But I didn't know, did I? Why was he asking me? 'I don't know,' I said, alarmed by the pitch of my own voice and the scalding of tears at the back of my nose. Goose was coming out of the house and I was pretty sure there was something I needed to ask her about our laundry. 'I don't know,' I said again as I got up, giddied, and it was unfair of him to ask me, he shouldn't ask me because what did I know about any of this? About treason trials and pretenders and public parading and abject disgrace. What could I possibly know about caring what happened to some noble-born pretty-boy?

Come the morning of the trial, it was clear that Jane saw herself, not as any child who'd been pushed through a wrong door with Guildford, but as someone standing shoulder to shoulder with the archbishop, even if he was being kept at a distance by a handful of guards. That was him, I guessed, behind us in the gatehouse: that slight, black-clad, heavily bearded figure. Of Guildford, there was no sign: he was late.

It was atrociously early, hours before dawn; I was steeped in sleep and insensible with cold, and lacked the presence of mind to be able to utter a single word, but Jane's silence, like that of the distant archbishop's, was different from mine, was eloquent. The pair of them hadn't spoken, but in the hubbub, amid the self-important men who were organising our departure, their affinity was striking. Held apart though they were, it was obvious that they were drawing strength from each other's presence.

For four months I'd lived hard by the Thames, but this was the first time I'd seen it since I'd been helped off the wherry in July. Not that I could see anything much of it now, other than the patchy, fractured gleam of torchlight on its surface. I sensed it, though, racing against itself, bullying its way between the banks, king of its own world of fish and fish-guzzling birds and flotsam. All around us were men who knew enough to be able to ride it, but still it had them in its grip: there was plenty of raucous phlegm-clearing, the ejecting of sodden river air from throats. The faces, tightened against the chill, I didn't recognise. They'd come from somewhere specifically for the job of transporting such important prisoners to trial. They seemed to know what they were doing, and were a lot livelier than I was, but they didn't seem any happier.

How I envied Guildford even those few more minutes of indoor warmth. Just detectable on the air were the first breaths of the earliest morning fires; perhaps one of them was his. We'd had no fire. Goose had been entrusted with rousing us and had made no bones about how onerous a duty it was. She'd come banging in with the single command, 'Up!' then banged back out again with force enough to extinguish our night-light. She'd have had us both summarily executed, I reckoned, if it could've gained her an hour longer in bed; or minutes even. Had she been even half equipped, she'd have probably done it herself.

As ever, I'd been slower than Jane to get up, I'd been no use to her, and she'd largely dressed herself in the dark, occasionally issuing the briefest of instructions, 'Pin this.'

She'd been dressed before I'd even begun struggling into my kirtle. I was still only half fastened into my gown, hoping it would hold if I didn't move too fast.

All that rush, only for us to have to stand for ages in the freezing cold on the riverside steps, before at long last came the first lumbering barge, butting the bottom step, the oarsmen slacking off, their formation frayed, disintegrating, oars drawn in.

And that was when Guildford arrived, dashing through the gatehouse but then keeping coming, in a run of rapid steps beyond where he probably should've stopped, and several strides past his own halted guards into the midst of ours. His breath freighted with breakfast ale, he demanded of me, 'Why did you let her do this?'

What?

Jane was quick: '*Guildford*.'

Her. Jane. He'd said *her*, but he was shouting at me. *Let her do this*. But do what? One of our guards muscled in, trying to bar his way, but Guildford just stepped around him and although I drew back he was still coming for me: 'Why,' he yelled, 'did you let her dress like this?'

Like what? What was it to do with me how she dressed? To my horror, everyone was looking at me – all those men, their raw faces – and who could blame them?: Lord Guildford broken free from his guards to tear a strip off his wife's attendant.

Jane was livid. 'Guildford, how dare you!'

But dress like what?

He was back at her, 'No, how dare *you*. Because have you *any* idea how this looks?' *This*: a hand flung down the length of her.

'*This*,' she blazed back at him, 'is who I am,' and there couldn't have been a person in the whole of the Tower precinct who didn't hear it, and her hands, too, both of them, and much more so, made an extravagant, sweeping gesture: *This, here, me*.

He whirled back to me. 'Look!'

And I did. I was, I really was looking, but I still had no idea what it was that I was supposed to be seeing. She looked to me as she always looked, and anyway, *anyway*, what had that got to do with me? Why was he taking it out on me? It was too early in the morning, I couldn't stand it, I was too near tears and shaking so much I feared I'd be sick and where was William? Shouldn't William be doing something to stop this? '*What?*' I screamed back as best I could, taking Jane's example, and who cared who looked. I wouldn't have him shout at me and especially not when I didn't even know what I'd done wrong.

But he wasn't cowed: 'Look at her! Dressed like a Protestant martyr!'

He turned back to her: 'How is this going to help us? How is this going to help us walk out of here and get on with our lives? You, dressed like the fucking archbishop.'

Did he just say that?

And now I could see it: black, yes. But she always wore black. Even her hood, though, I saw now – even the jewels on its band were black. Pieces of jet. She'd gone to considerable trouble to dress entirely in black.

She was scathing: 'I don't pretend, Guildford, not for anyone.'

He kept up the volume: 'No one's asking you to pretend! No one's *ever* asked you to pretend, but if you could just for once think of someone other than yourself, because how do you think this looks?'

She was icy. 'I imagine it looks as if I read the Bible in English,' and she proffered a book, which until then I'd failed to notice, but there it was, on a golden chain, a girdle, around her middle. 'Which I do. As everyone should.'

At that, though, the heart went out of him, and he turned away from us both. 'You know what?' He sounded hopeless. 'You're no use to anyone if you're dead.'

She'd rolled her eyes at that, and she rolled them again, minutes later, when an axeman stumbled through the gate-house. My own eyes must've widened before she told me he was just for show. 'Holds his blade away from us when we're innocent,' she said, demonstrating with a deft switch of her hand, 'and turns it towards us when we're guilty.'

When. Not *if.*

And had she not enlightened me, I should have guessed anyway because he was no actual executioner – unless executioners are tubby, wheezy, put-upon little men. Her contempt for him hadn't been misplaced, because he failed even in his ceremonial role. Standing in the barge, that axe was too much for him, cumbersome in his grip so that the blade rarely had any recognisable orientation.

Neither was the crowd anything to be feared. We disembarked, not to an ugly crowd as Guildford had dreaded, but rather, to judge from the expressions on the faces, a largely uncomprehending one. A long way from forgiving and forgetting his outburst though I was, I hoped Guildford could see, as I did, that the crowd bore him no malice. Not many people looked as if they knew who it was that had been landed among them to be humiliated. And perhaps that was understandable, because ours had been a topsy-turvy world not merely lately but for a long time: the six queens, the boy-king, the banished half-sister, the rapacious duke, the girl-pretender and the victorious, pious spinster. This, whatever it was, this parade, was just one more turn. People gawped, but anyone being escorted through the streets would be a source of curiosity, and as far as I could tell, they didn't distinguish between Jane and me, two well-dressed girls as we were. Their stares were as much for me as they were for Jane, if not more so because I was wearing the brighter dress. Finer distinctions as to who we were or why we were there seemed to be beyond those Londoners and however much I resented their mistakenly directed attention, however much I might have liked to have put them straight, there was nothing I could do about it.

Jane's Bible-reading was most likely lost on them, too. A pretty little Latin-written book of hours, they'd be thinking if they were thinking anything of it at all: prayers and psalms, beautifully illuminated for the succour of a lady; a jewel box of incomprehensible words. Walking ahead of me, she appeared properly absorbed in its pages, and maybe she was; Guildford might have been wrong to suggest that her ostentatious reading was a performance. It looked real enough to me. She read for much of every day and perhaps she wasn't going to allow a treason trial to distract her. Our processional pace could only have helped: ideal for reading, if not quite so conducive to the simpler act of getting anywhere. Behind a phalanx of guards, we tottered on consciously foreshortened steps, which made for a literal dragging out of our journey. I could have walked more than twice as fast, even four months out of practice as I was, and a brisker pace would have helped see off the chill that dogged us.

The morning was unremittingly grey, from the sky right down to the ground. No rain, but only because the air was already saturated. Jane's cloak, in front of me, was damp-spangled and I itched to run a fingertip down the length of it, draw a channel in it. The bottom of her gown would be less picturesque, because with each step she was hauling the dead weight of it behind her through the London mud and muck. I could've retrieved it, lifted it clear, but then what? A long walk lay ahead of us and I couldn't possibly lug it all that way.

I was tired, cold, and still unsettled by the motion of the barge. For all London's tall, timbered houses and halls, for all its spired stone churches and walled gardens, this city, I felt, was nothing against the river which lay at the foot of it. London was cobbled together on its bank and barely tolerated. As we progressed further from the water, I never lost the sense of the Thames at our backs with the feigned indifference of a predator. It might suddenly rise up and into the streets after us, I felt, and wash our grave little procession away.

Something else I couldn't shake off was Guildford's fury. Rather than walking away from it, I seemed to be driving it deeper into my bones with each and every step: I was rattled, literally; I was in bits. But although I'd hated what he'd done, yelling at me, more than anything I was perplexed by it: the gusto with which he'd gone for me, not caring who witnessed it. He was scared, of course, and probably tired – I doubted he'd slept much – and therefore perhaps not quite in his right mind. But still.

When we reached Guildhall, Jane and I were ushered straight ahead into a chamber. Guildford and the archbishop either had their own anterooms or shared one. Ours was a room for nothing but waiting: the hearth clean-swept, the walls lime-washed. A pair of guards stood in the doorway, affecting not to look at us but with nothing else to take their interest, which left them with a blankness which in other circumstances might have been comical.

The only furniture was a bench, on which Jane sat down with a sigh, the bible shutting in her lap, and she closed her eyes, either to rest or to pray. There was nothing in the room for her to eat or drink despite the long morning she'd had, and the afternoon wasn't going to be a picnic. I wasn't bothered for myself, sickened as I was by the barge, but I was thinking of her, which was my job, my purpose, it was why I was there. No offer of sustenance looked to be forthcoming, so I was going to have to pursue it. With whom, though? Those deliberately gormless guards? The younger – taller, leaner – of the two was dramatically cold-eyed, intent on acting the big man. Well, let him; I couldn't be bothered with him. His considerably rounder colleague, though, reminded me of our stable manager back home at Shelley Place, which was how I knew his eyes would crinkle when he smiled. We weren't going to get as far as a smile, I knew, but still, he was my man. He could stare all he liked but I could see he was a push-over. He'd pitched up in the wrong job and that was something we had in common. 'Lady Jane should have something to eat and drink,' I said to him, and then he was flummoxed and contrite as I'd known he would be, even though Jane had roused herself to contradict me, claiming she was fine.

Her being fine or not was beside the point; the point was that she should be offered something, and I made very sure to sound incredulous at the blatant neglect of common courtesy: 'She needs *something*.'

The kindly, cuddly man muttered nervously about a buttery and stepped aside, clearing the way for me, but Jane renewed her protest: 'Really, I don't want anything.'

No, but you'll damn well have it.

'Well, I can't go, can I,' I complained to the guard. I couldn't leave her alone in here with two men.

Both men, now, looked concerned. 'But,' said the younger one, 'it's just—' and he gestured, *down there*. From the doorway, I peered into the passageway.

'Just—' he said again. *Down there.*

It was further away than he'd implied, though, and around a corner, and despite my being quick, I came back to an empty room: a vacated bench, no guards, no one. Vanished, all three of them, as if they were playing a trick on me.

There I stood in that doorway, stupidly, with a trencher and cup, casting around for clues as to where they'd taken her. She was taking her place somewhere in front of all the peers of the realm. Those noblemen would be filing into a room, shuffling on to benches, scrunching their toes inside their boots against the chill of the flagstones and dreaming of a speedy return to their suites at court or their London residences, to a fulsome fire and a bird pie. Jane would have to stand for those men, all of whom had been happy to kneel at her feet during the days when she was Queen. Their doing of this particular duty today was earning them the privilege of never having to think of her again. Only if asked would they ever remember her: *The Grey girl? Oh, the Grey girl! Odd little thing she was, terribly serious about it all.* As they'd tell it, in the years to come, a mistake had been made but mistakes happen and they're for learning from, and anyway it had all been over in the blink of an eye and no harm done. I knew exactly how she'd be standing there for them: that straight little back of hers. I knew that back, I realised, bone by bone. And what I wanted more than anything in the world was to be standing right there behind her.

Jane being judged guilty of treason brought just the one practical change to our daily lives. Mr Partridge received an order that she and Guildford were to be confined, for the time being, to their respective rooms. This, he intimated, was the full extent of the Queen's censure: just for a while, Jane and Guildford were obliged to be proper prisoners. He was suitably grave and apologetic when breaking the news to Jane but he'd have been under no illusion that his charge would much miss either standing around in the November drear or consorting with her husband.

Myself, I barely took it in; we were only an hour or so back after a very long day, and, having at last had something to eat, I was desperate for bed. I could have lain on the floor then and there, and given in to oblivion. I ached from the only recently assuaged chill and hunger, and the barge still held me in its sway. All I felt when Mr Partridge told us that we'd not see Guildford for a while was that I'd been expecting it, I'd known it was coming. *So be it.* Honeymoon's over, as Guildford himself had said. The Queen was settling to the proper business of ruling, and Jane and Guildford were to begin the proper business of being her prisoners. And anyway, I still stung from his lashing out at me. If I felt anything, that first night after the trial, it was relief, because, with no Guildford to deal with, there was less to think about, and I was always in favour of that.

In the following days, I had a more pressing concern, because something was seriously amiss with Jane. No fault of the verdict itself, surely, because by her own account, if for reasons I didn't understand, it was what she'd wanted, and indeed on the return journey it had been all too clear from her high-held head and the shine of her eyes that she took it as a victory. And of course she knew it made no difference to her prospects: she'd be released just as soon as the Queen and her advisers decided it was safe to do so, which would be when she was forgotten. Judging from the faces we'd walked past in London, that wasn't too far off.

If anything, the trial and its predictable verdict should have been liberating for her, because everything that needed to be done had been done and she'd got through it. She'd publicly done her penance, been paraded through London in disgrace, pleaded her guilt before every last peer of the realm, and received due judgement. It was done. She was, in all but actual fact, free to go.

Yet the trial seemed to have depleted her beyond any physical weariness. She did as she'd always done, every day – the reading, praying, stitching – but whereas before she'd been absorbed, now there was an emptiness to it.

I'd been wrong to think that whenever she'd had her head in a book or over her embroidery, she'd been ignoring me. I realised now that she'd always had half an eye on me, or if not so much as half, then at least a sliver. She'd always been heeding my presence, if, admittedly, with a degree of antagonism. But even if that indifference of hers had held a mild antipathy, I found I missed it. And however much I told myself that her withdrawal had nothing to do with me, I didn't always manage to stop myself from meeting it with an abruptness of my own, from retaliating with snappiness, a kind of *See how you like it*, which was pointless because, as I knew, she didn't see it at all.

I imagined the mood would pass; I supposed she'd pick up. A few days of rest – a week perhaps – would be enough for her to regain her composure, I felt, and get back to being Jane, busy at her books and sometimes tackling her sewing.

In the meantime came interminable days of coaxing the fire

and fussing with wicks as the late-autumn wind thrummed in the chimney and Susanna's luscious garden drooped, stupefied by the weight of its own swollen blooms. Often, I'd look across at the White Tower, its vast walls and sheer windows. Inside there, incredibly, was someone I'd spent time with on most days, whose company I'd sought, but now never saw at all. During those weeks, his absence from my daily life was a purely physical sensation, like water in my ears. And as if there was water in my ears, I lived my days hampered and hindered.

For that month, life was just the four panelled walls and Susanna in full flush, eternally trusting, and Jane's little bags that were only ever incrementally more completed and in any case belonged to an unimaginable world, not just one in which there were fey wisps of honeysuckle or perky pinks but one in which people were well enough disposed to one another to give gifts.

We were near the end, was what I suspected: those December days would probably be among our last. The Tower was almost done with us. There we were, down at the bottom of the year when the only daylight came from darkness turning over in its sleep, and soon we'd simply slip from this room into another. Shelley Place, for me, and I might as well be there as anywhere. What difference did it make which fireside I sat at and whose hems I stitched? My only hope was that Christmas was over before I got there: Christmas, with its forced jollity and Harry even more drunk than usual.

But if I wanted to stay at the Partridges' until after

Christmas, I was keen to go before the end of January, when Mrs Partridge's confinement would begin, because if I was lonely now, I'd suffer worse when she shut herself away. Perhaps she knew it and was making up in advance for lost time, although it was at least as likely that she was worried by Jane's poor spirits, but whatever her reasons, she came several times a day to see us and stayed longer, often bringing her own needlework. She was sewing items for the baby, and I wished I could have joined her in her endeavours, but frankly, anything I could've produced would've been an insult. And I'd almost certainly left it too late, I realised, to ask my parents' steward to bring something in for her. The weather was probably too bad, now, for him to travel. I hadn't even thought to ask him for a box of dates which I could have given her for New Year.

Unlike us girls, she was on good form, with the early, tiring days of her pregnancy behind her but the debilitating heaviness yet to come. One day, though, she told me, 'Look,' and the object of curiosity was her own hand, the back of it offered up for my inspection, its fingers splayed. *Look*, as if there were something to see of the knuckles, which were nothing compared to mine. 'No ring,' she prompted, and so it was indeed an absence that I was supposed to see, but her cheery tone suggested it hadn't been lost. 'Took some doing,' she said appreciatively, flexing her fingers at the memory in a kind of wince, but then, seeing my bafflement, 'to get it off.' Which left me none the wiser, so she had to enlighten me: 'I'm swelling,' and she sounded surprised at how much I didn't know. 'It happens,' she said, happily enough, 'when you're carrying a baby.'

Does it? Hands, as well as bellies? And her acceptance of it – of her physical distortion – stunned me at least as much as the fact of it.

Whenever I waved her off down our stairs, I felt as if I were doing an impression of a cheerful enough girl, when in truth exhaustion was clanging in my skull and the chambers of my heart, making a relentless, blaring, obliterating silence.

Not only was Mrs Partridge making sure to spend time in our room, but most evenings she invited us down to dine. And surprisingly, given her lassitude, Jane usually accepted. It was easier, I found, to be on their territory and in wider company, if only wider in that it held Mr Partridge and Twig, although Goose's ostensibly servile presence was disconcerting: Goose, keeping to the background and not speaking unless spoken to. Jane, too, was muted, but always polite and at least minimally attentive. The Partridges were scrupulous in avoiding contentious subjects, Mrs Partridge dutifully progressing through topics so safe that I suspected she'd spent time beforehand compiling a list: family, extended and even including pets; food and weather; Christmas traditions.

But then one evening, when perhaps we'd grown complacent, Jane evidently felt she'd paid her dues and decided it was time to raise something of importance, something that, according to Goose, was currently preoccupying the whole country.

'So,' she said, breaking into her bread roll, 'the Spanish marriage is going to happen.'

Mr Partridge put down his knife, taking time to decide how to pitch it. 'As far as we understand it, yes,' holding too much eye contact with Jane and discovering too late for comfort that she was more than a match for him. 'There are, as far as we know, negotiations under way.'

I wondered at Jane's true feeling about it. Like just about everyone else in England, she wouldn't want a Spaniard on the throne, but the marriage, as a bolstering of the Queen's position, would move her closer to freedom.

'Negotiations,' chipped in Mrs Partridge, 'to limit his influence.'

'But what about when she dies?' Seemingly oblivious to everyone else's instinctive recoil, Jane rewrapped what remained of her roll to keep it warm. 'Is her husband simply going to pack up his trunk and go back to Spain? Leave England to the Protestant half-sister? "Thanks for having me and it was nice while it lasted"?'

Mr Partridge looked helplessly to his wife.

But Mrs Partridge rose to it: 'What else can she do, though?' she anguished, 'because she has to marry, doesn't she. She has to. She needs an heir. But when she marries, she becomes a wife, and a wife—' She despaired, because we knew the rest, it didn't need saying: *A wife is subordinate to her husband.*

And not any old husband: this particular husband just happened to be the heir to the Holy Roman Empire. I recalled the day I'd come to the Tower, the thousands of Londoners dancing in the streets. Had no one foreseen this? What on earth had we been thinking would happen?

Mr Partridge gloved his wife's ringless hand with his own in a gesture of comfort but also restraint. 'I don't think we can talk about this here.' He was addressing not only Jane but the room as a whole, including Goose. 'There's a lot of work going on in the background; the best brains in England are engaged on the problem and I doubt we can throw any better light on it.'

Goose hadn't been so measured; for her, best brains didn't come into it. The Spaniards would soon be here, she'd told us while banging her broom around our room as if to drive them off. 'And along with that prince,' she'd said, 'come thousands of others,' starting, she said, with his staff and their own servants, but then there'd be wives and children swarming off the ships, and, she claimed, every Spaniard had several wives each, which had Jane rouse herself sufficiently to counter that we didn't know that. Goose roared, 'But what *do* we know about them? Except they think they know it all. But all they know is what their Pope-worshipping priests tell them.' And then she'd called them ignorant and bloodthirsty, and said England would end up like everywhere else in the world, beneath their boots. 'And let me tell you this,' she finished, 'they veil their women,' her parting words being, 'No one will ever put a veil on me.'

To the closing door, Jane murmured, 'How about a gag?'

Looking for the smallest smile, though, even of the most

rueful kind, I was hoping for too much. What I got instead was 'She didn't mention how Spaniards don't just burn people for being Protestant, but for not being good enough Catholics.' She raised her eyebrows. 'So, you'll want to be careful, with your on-off Mass attendance.' And now she did smile, but unpleasantly. 'Because they'll sniff *you* out.'

Every day when I returned the lunch tray to the kitchen, I took my cloak and braved outdoors for a breath of fresh air; and so fresh was it that I never needed much more than a breath. Head down, I'd scurry around the inner bailey; should anyone have looked, all they'd have seen was a hooded cloak, while for me the view seldom stretched beyond the toes of my boots.

But one of those lifeless mid-December days, I glanced up and there on the wall behind the Partridges' house was a lone figure, shrouded in a cloak and facing away in the direction of the city. Guildford was supposed to be confined to his room but that was definitely a Guildford-dawdle up there, Guildford-dejection against that leaden sky, and despite everything I nearly laughed aloud to see it.

When he turned, he seemed as struck by the sight of me as I had been by him, and then the very slightest inclination of his head spoke loud and clear, *Look*. Duly following the direction of that nod, I saw at a distance a guard; Guildford was being supervised, if laxly. No sign of William but a guard instead, and I, too, stood there stealthily still to confirm that I understood we couldn't be seen to have spotted each other.

Then he began strolling, with a well-feigned casualness; it was quite a performance, enacted for the guard, of going nowhere in particular. He meandered to the end of that section of walkway, up to one of the intermittent, low partition walls, over which, with incomparable languor, he leaned.

He could've clambered over it, had he wished, and I watched the guard consider the possibility but reject it because there was no way it could be done without clamour, and, anyway, where would it take him? To a further staircase, which only went down, as did they all, into the inner bailey. Should Guildford try it, he'd simply be back where he'd started.

I understood what I was being shown. If I were to crouch on the far side of that partition wall, in the lee of it, I'd be hidden at quite a remove from the guard, but Guildford and I would be close enough to be able to talk.

I didn't give it a second thought, not least because there wasn't time, and when I emerged from the top of the staircase into the doorway there he was, across that expanse of stone and behind that wall, waiting for me with a wan smile. He'd had a haircut and the sight of the newly exposed, pallid skin snatched at my heart, or perhaps it was just the cutting itself, something having been done to him when I'd not known.

He raised one hand minimally and lowered it, *Get down*, and yes, of course, I needed to stay unspotted by that guard, had to keep below that interrogative line of sight. Giving him a look – he'd have expected nothing less – I squatted, gathering what I could of my cloak and gown off the filthy flagstones into my lap, then began the shuffle towards the wall, fearful for the state of my clothing and trusting him to avert his gaze, not merely to keep me covered but to preserve my dignity.

Reaching the wall, I huddled back against it, facing the way I'd come. He'd have to talk over my head and I'd have to talk to the doorway; we'd be disembodied voices, carefully low. But, still, we'd be talking. I'd never been so happy to crouch on a wet, cold floor. It was as if there'd never been anything difficult between us, as if I'd never got up and walked away from him when he'd needed me and he'd never shouted at me in front of everyone on the riverside steps.

He murmured, 'I've not been well,' because he knew I'd be wondering. 'Nothing bad, but they say I need some air.' Then, 'How's my wife?' because he had to ask. After all, that was what we did, that was what we were there for, both of us, in our different ways: to look after his wife, whether she liked it or not.

I had to think, before I decided, 'Garnering her strength, planning her strategy.' An optimistic view, but the one I'd favour until I knew otherwise.

'And you?'

Well, that was harder to answer. I'd been getting through the days; the days had kept on coming and I'd been getting through them. How was I? I just *was*. 'Not bad. But you?' Because he'd said he'd been ill. Nothing too bad, he'd said, but still.

No reply.

'Guildford?'

'Yes, fine, just . . . '

'Just what?'

'Thinking all the time about what we're going to do – where we're going to go – when we get out of here.'

He and Jane: how they would live their married life. I said nothing because there was nothing I could say to that; I was no part of that, and anyway I had problems of my own.

High above us, the birds seemed to be skating across the sky as if it were sheet ice.

He said, 'I'm thinking we'll have to go abroad,' and, 'I can speak to some people for you, if you like, to see what—'

'No,' and I only just remembered to add, 'thank you.' My life was nothing like his and Jane's. A word in an ear, a help-ing hand, a leg-up: none of those figured in my future. I didn't live in that kind of world. That wasn't how it was ever going to be, for me.

'Oh, well, then,' he was offended, 'back into your old life, for you.'

But he knew nothing of my life, never had and never would. Once he and I left the Tower, our paths would never cross. It hurt to be hunkered on the balls of my feet, and I shifted, hedging cramp.

'Back to your Suffolk people,' and he sounded as if he were the one being left behind. 'Nice Catholic girl that you are.'

I hadn't come up here for one of his scenes. 'Stop it, Guildford.'

'And life'll go on for you as it always has. You'll get mar-ried to some nice Catholic boy—'

'Stop it, Guildford,' *I'm warning you.*

'—and have nice Catholic children. He's probably waiting for you even now, isn't he, whoever he is.'

'Guildford . . .' I twisted to look up at him, to look him in the eye, but he wouldn't have it, staring away over my head so that all I got was a view of his nostrils and some icy, spitting rain on my upturned face.

He said, 'You'll have done them proud, your people. You've more than done your bit, haven't you, by being here. I imagine they'll welcome you back with some fanfare.'

'I can't go back,' I said and, in the instant it was voiced, I knew it to be true, and what a relief it was. 'I won't be going back.'

Back to a house that so often had Harry in it. Harry, who was quite possibly so stupid as to expect us to resume where we'd left off. Coming to the Tower, I'd been walking away from Harry: I saw it now. That was what I'd done when I'd raised my hand at the Fitzalans': I'd got myself clear of Harry. Why had I ever believed him when he'd said my eleventh day was safe? But I hadn't, had I. Why, then, had I let him go ahead? I hadn't. I'd tried to stop him but he'd gone ahead regardless.

Guildford did now glance down at me, if pointedly and infuriatingly expressionless. 'Well, no, come to think of it, because why would you go back? Because you're quite a prize, now, aren't you, after this? You can have your pick of nice Catholic boys.'

'Guildford,' I seethed, 'you know nothing about me.'

'To be fair,' he shot back, 'you don't tell me much.'

'Why would I?' and for a whisper, it came perilously close to a wail. 'You're going off and I'll never see you again.'

He hissed, 'You know I have to do that. You know I do.'

We were going round in circles. I was sick of it, and so tired, and gave up, sinking back against the wall and drawing myself in. It was horrible up there; my mother's favoured threat was 'You'll feel the flat of my hand,' and what I was being subjected to, up there on that wall, was the flat of the wind's hand.

'What I'm saying,' he spoke with exaggerated patience, 'is that you should come with us.'

What on earth did that mean?

Suddenly frantic, he said, 'Elizabeth, please come with me,' the words catching in his throat, which had my own tighten.

But how could I? What did he mean? 'How *can* I? I *can't*, can I.'

'Well, in that case,' he was stung, 'you'll just have to go back, won't you.'

'*No.*' He wasn't going to send me back on my way like that. '*Listen,*' because he should know, 'I had an affair, back home.' *You do not know me. You like to think you do but you don't.* Had it been an affair? No, worse than that and, worse still, with my father's best friend, and of course there was even worse but he didn't need to know that, about what had happened as a result and how I'd nearly bled to death one night in the presence of his wife. He wasn't going to know any of that. My heart was intent on flushing me out but I was refusing to go

244

along with it, folding my arms to hold firm, a lump in my throat and my nails in my palms. All he needed to know was the truth of me as far as I understood it, which was that I was not some nice Suffolk girl on my way back into some nice Suffolk life.

I was sure he'd sloped off, leaving me crouching there, but then came 'He was married?' His tone, cool: the word 'affair', I supposed, having led him to that conclusion.

'No, not really,' and at least there was the relief of being able to say that.

He was quick to deride it, though, sighing exasperatedly.

Did he think I was an idiot? 'No, *really* not really. Separated. Years ago. She's –' how to explain? '– off with someone else.' That was the long and the short of it. That would do.

From a distance came 'Lord Guildford.' *It's time*: the guard.

'But, still,' said Guildford, 'you can't marry him.' Stating the obvious, but, I felt, with a notable lack of generosity.

And anyway he'd misunderstood: 'I don't want to.'

'But you did.' Not letting me off the hook.

'No—' but I faltered, could merely reiterate, 'No.' Perhaps yes, if I was absolutely honest, I'd thought of it once or twice but only because I'd had no other prospects and, anyway, show me the girl who could do what I'd done in that clock cupboard and not occasionally wonder if something more respectable might come of it. But also I hadn't, and that too was just as true. A likely story, I knew – that I had and I hadn't – but it struck me as the truth of it. I just couldn't explain it any better.

'But you loved him,' and this came with a startling lack of selfconsciousness, the word 'loved'. As if love – that kind of love – were for Guildford unquestionably real.

'No,' and I knew that as the truth, now, even if in a way I wished it were otherwise because then at least what I'd done in the clock cupboard would have been more understandable. 'I think I thought I did, sometimes, but I didn't.'

'There's a difference?' Amused, almost, was how he sounded, and not really questioning me so much as picking me up on a point. And he had one, I could see it; he did definitely have a point. I could see what he meant: *I think I thought I did—*

I could see that it was funny, if you stopped to think about it.

There's a difference?

Not really a question, but it occurred to me that I might just have an answer. Well, didn't I?

But I couldn't quite think, or not fast enough because there was the guard again, 'Lord Guildford, sir,' his patience dwindled, observing the formalities but barely, brusquely. And footsteps: just-doing-my-job footsteps but coming none the less, to fetch Guildford. Above me, behind me, Guildford was being taken away, and I heard the intake of breath on which he turned to try to placate that guard, fend him off, *I'm coming, I'm coming*, and leave me undiscovered to make my own way back. *There's a difference?* Didn't I have the answer to that? Shouldn't I tell him? But turning around, I caught the last of him, a blur of wool sheened with damp and a flash of stitch-heavy silks, leaving nothing above me except the sky.

I came reeling down the stairs, that day, unsure quite what had and hadn't been said, and, stopping to catch my breath in the dank stairwell, I began to lose heart. The words themselves, I kept close – *come with me* – but the tone had flown on that merciless wind. Barely sheltered by that ancient doorway, I felt dreadfully alone. What had I been thinking, scrabbling up there to whisper with Guildford? Was I going to spend my life in hidey-holes with married noblemen? After everything that had happened to me, did I really know no better? Stop it, I told myself, you need to stop it, it's nothing, it's hidey-holes and whispers and that's all it is. *It's nothing and you need to stop it.*

I'd been in no mood for Goose hot-footing it up the stairs behind me on my way back to the room and regaling us before she was even through the doorway. 'Those New Year presents?' This was for Jane, maker of New Year presents as she was. 'Got someone to deliver them for you? You're going nowhere while there's dead dogs being chucked around.'

Jane merely closed her eyes, admirably composed in the face of such an extraordinary claim, but I was unable to be quite so big about it. 'Dead dogs?' *Chucked around?*

And so Goose told us, as she was clearly bursting to do. The previous day, she said, at the close of Parliament, a dead dog had been thrown into the Queen's Great Watching Chamber, its fur shaved into a tonsure. I wished I hadn't asked. That poor dog, mutilated in death into a mock-monk: everything that it had been in life reduced to a hideous gesture, a pitiless, gruesome thud on the Queen's marble tiles.

'We won't take this Spanish marriage,' Goose trilled, 'and she's going to have to listen to us. Just because everyone wanted her on the throne doesn't mean she can do whatever she chooses.'

Except that she was Queen, I thought, so actually she probably could.

Goose seemed to have been right, though, that Jane was going nowhere. As we edged daily closer to Christmas, no word came of her imminent release nor even of her being allowed, should she wish, to leave her room. Nor was Guildford outside again, that I saw. Not that I was looking.

A week before Christmas came a letter; Mr Partridge jovially dropping it off for Jane as if this were something he did every day, all part of the service, before turning busily on his heel and leaving her to it. Her family, I presumed: they'd written to her — had been permitted to write — because it was Christmas; there had been a relaxing of the rules, the turning of a blind eye. Jane's expression quickened at the sight of the handwriting: the writer was definitely someone from whom she was pleased to hear. And how nice for her, was all I thought as I returned my attention to our sullen fire — the colder the mornings, the meaner Goose was with firewood — but when I'd got as far as I could with it and straightened up, I saw how Jane was struck. The letter — whomever it was

248

from — had delivered her a body blow, yet still she was sitting there, reading it, taking it. She sat there undefended, letting it befall her.

Then, suddenly, before I had a chance to do or say anything, she laid the letter on the table and stood, although it was more a recoiling, as if wounded.

'Jane?'

She glanced at me as if she'd forgotten I was there and I saw that she meant to respond, or perhaps even thought she had, but the impetus had already deserted her and she retreated to the window, sitting there as if put.

I stood adrift, poker in hand.

'Dr Harding—' She gestured at the letter. 'He was our chaplain when I was growing up,' and her eyes came to mine when she said, with feeling, 'A sweet man.' It took her a moment to be able to tell me, 'He's recanted,' and then I felt something of it, too, the betrayal and the loss. Her own childhood chaplain. 'He thinks I should, too.' Hence the letter, she meant, but it was said with none of the contempt I would've expected.

I had no idea what to say; what could I possibly offer that would be any comfort?

'Is it easy for me, do you think?' She frowned; she was thinking. 'Is it easy for me, in here, to stick to my guns? Because how would it be, to be out there all alone with the whole of England turning the other way?'

I hadn't thought of it like that; I'd considered her to be the one, shut in here, who was all alone.

'He writes as if he believes it, but you can't believe something you know to be untrue, can you?'

And fleetingly it was him for whom I felt.

'He does know.' She spoke slowly, as if she needed to spell it for herself. 'Or he did know,' and she was wide-eyed, wondering, 'and you can't *un*know, can you?'

I wanted to say I was sorry, but it would be so inadequate that I didn't, and just stood there, uselessly, poker absurdly in hand.

'He was the one who taught me,' she said. 'And all the learning I've done since ...' A quick shake of her head. 'Well, you can do all the learning you like, you can dress it up in all the theology you like, but when I was six he walked me up to a rood screen and had me touch it, and he said, "Here, see? Wood."'

Carefully, I laid the poker back down on the hearth.

'"Wood, is all it is. Just wood. Carved and painted and gilded, all very beautiful, so much work gone into it but still," he said, "it's wood, it's a barrier there to keep you on this side of it. And on the other side," he said, "are the priests, dressed to the nines and swigging the wine and keeping God to themselves."'

I sat down on the stool.

She said, 'I don't remember whose chapel it was – some family we were visiting, might even have been the Fitzalans – but at the foot of the screen were all these ...' and she was entranced to recall them, 'these *dolls*, really.'

She smiled at me as if she felt I might've liked the dolls.

'The prettiest little faces. Bright blue eyes, upturned noses, red lips. Dr Harding asked me, "Who's this one, do you know?" And I did, because we might not have had saints in our chapel but we knew people who did and anyway you can never stop servants talking about saints, can you? So I said to him, "That's Saint Barbara, holding her tower. And that's Saint Ursula, with her ship, and there's Saint Catherine with her wheel." I knew them all; there must've been twelve. And he said to me, "Aren't they lovely? All lined up with their bits and bobs and smiling away at us. But why are they here?" That, I didn't know, but I took a guess: "So we can learn from them."'

I knew what she was going to say.

'And he asked me, "What do we learn from them?" and I said, "How to love God," and he said, "But you already know how to do that, don't you?" I said I did and he said, "You don't need these saints to show you. You don't need their lightning and fireworks. You have to love God every minute of every ordinary day, and, in a way, that's harder to do." And he said to me, "All you need is this,"' at which she placed a hand to her heart, '"and this,"' fingertips to her forehead, '"and the Bible." Dr Harding said to me, "These ladies are nowhere in the Bible. They're just stories, but we don't need stories because in the Bible we have the truth."'

She sighed. 'But now he's gone back on all that. Priests do matter, he's saying. And statues.' She said, 'I wonder where they put them, the Fitzalans or whoever they were: I wonder if they still have those little lady-saints.' She looked at me. 'Did you see them, when you were there?'

No, I said, I hadn't.

In the direction of the window, she said, 'They've made a liar of a good man, is what they've done, and how can that be what they want?' Turning back to me, she wondered, 'Can that be something that anyone would really ever want?' She stood. 'What's happened to him, Elizabeth? How did they do it? Get him to write to me like that. Is he scared? Is he confused?' Then she resolved, 'I'm going to write to him. I won't abandon him to them. He's written to me and I'm going to write back to him.'

Day after day, she wrote that letter to Dr Harding. I'd never have imagined there could be so much to say; sometimes I wondered if she was coming up with her own version of the Bible. Whenever she wasn't actually composing that letter, she was reading for it, leafing through several books in succession, scrutinising certain pages and leaving volumes open all around her as she worked. During that time, she was all bitten lip and blotted fingers, her neck and shoulders stiff, and I was so relieved to see her restored to herself that I didn't mind that she rarely had a word to spare for me.

The letter-writing occupied her right up until the first day of Christmas and then even took the day itself, which, when we got to it, seemed to me as good a way as any to spend it. During those last days of Advent and on Christmas Eve and Christmas Day, we declined invitation after invitation from the anxious and dutiful Partridges. Or I did, because that was my job. She was ill, was our excuse, and I wanted to keep her company, which, surprisingly, turned out to be the truth. She needed me, I told them. I had to remind her time and time again, 'You're ill.' Because although the business of keeping the Partridges at bay fell to me, I needed her help. The sound of anyone on the stairs was her cue to sit forlornly at the fireside or rush through to lie on the bed. 'You're ill, remember? Too ill even for Christmas. And you need me. But you're not ill enough to need a doctor.' I hated worrying the Partridges and did my best to pitch it so as to spare them as much as I could. It was tricky, it kept me on my toes.

Not that the Partridges themselves could come up in person to check on us. Mrs Partridge, in her condition, couldn't risk catching whatever was supposed to be ailing Jane, and nor should Mr Partridge be in any position to pass it on to her. So, no Partridges for us, for a whole week, not even on Christmas Eve or Christmas Day – for which they sent up various thoughtful treats – by which time mercifully we were also free of Goose and her rampant scepticism because she was allowed off to her sister's for the season.

Goose's replacement, lugubrious old Mrs Dunch, was the one relaying those frequent enquiries from the Partridges but she was relatively easy to placate and send back on her way. She seemed to believe anything we said, unlike Goose.

When I'd asked Jane why she didn't try to convert me, she'd said it would be a waste of her time to work on one person alone. For Dr Harding, though, she more than made the time. Or perhaps her efforts weren't strictly for Dr Harding alone, because who knew how many hands that letter might have to pass through to reach him. Because what had Jane once said to me about books? There are always copies. *Words spread*, was what she'd said. And what had Guildford said about her changing the world? Well, maybe that was what she was trying to do, during those dead-end December days, while I stood guard.

See? I'd have loved to be able to say to Guildford, *see?* We two girls, here, in our little room, changing the world, *and you'd better believe it*. It was during those dead-to-the-world late December days that I started to care, and I wished Guildford could've known it. Jane's battle wasn't mine – it didn't mean much to me and probably never would – but I was glad she was fighting it. That was what was different: I was glad, at last, that Jane was Jane.

But then we really were ill, as if we'd wished it upon ourselves; it came for us as if to serve us right for our lie and to show us what being ill really meant. Jane first, then, a day or so later, me. Head, throat, chest: everywhere that should have been filled with breath was instead a slough of snot or phlegm. Everything ached, even my scalp. And now I was laid low, Guildford's absence badly bothered me. While the remaining days of Christmas passed us by, I kept compulsive, surreptitious and pointless company with his absence as I would with the socket of a recently pulled tooth.

The year turned, and after Twelfth Night Goose was back. 'Thirteenth day,' as Jane put it when we heard her advancing up the stairs. She burst into our room pink to the gills with one of her stories. The high-and-mighties, she said, had arrived from Spain to sign the royal marriage contract but, riding up to their London lodgings, they'd been pelted with snowballs. And how she'd have loved to see that, she said as she set about Susanna, wiping her down because we didn't know how to manage a fire, and look at the smoke-smuts that had accrued while she'd been away! 'Them on their oh-so-fine horses scrambling for cover, and everyone laughing.' She slapped at the elders. 'Thinking they can come here and we'll just roll over. Well, that might be *her* idea of a good time . . .' The Queen, presumably. 'And you know what?' She stopped, veered alarmingly close to me, her face revealing too much of its various rims and linings. 'I reckon they could've thrown just that little bit harder, those boys, and closer, and icier, and driven those Spaniards back down to the docks.' She grinned. 'It would've worked, because the Queen can hardly pitch an army against schoolboys, can she.' The exertion with the cloth had brought on a raucous sniff, and I feared that in her distracted, excitable state she was going to wipe her nose with it. 'She can send an army down west but not into a crowd of schoolboys.'

Groggily, Jane queried, 'An army's gone west?'

'Yesterday.' Never one for details, she was bored already. 'Trouble down west.' Stepping back to appraise Susanna, she straightened her on her rail, yanked her into shape. 'But isn't there always.'

Goose was our only source of information, with her partly comprehensible tales of dead dogs, snowballs and permanently agitated West Country-men, but then within days we didn't even have her because she too fell ill. She had seemed so robust, that Susanna-drubbing morning, but our illness had washed through those raw, open seams of her nose and eyes and she went down hard with it. We wouldn't see her again until she returned from a month's recuperation with her sister, for whom it had no doubt been a considerable surprise to see her back again so soon.

Mrs Dunch was the one to bring us word – brief and barely audible – of Goose's indisposition, and that was pretty much her last word on anything. From then on, we were on our own.

Mrs Partridge's two sisters were due to arrive in mid-January to help prepare and then accompany her into her confinement. Two older sisters, she told us she had: Sarah and Lucy, who had families of their own. Mrs Partridge was the baby of her family then, just as I was, but whereas she spoke of her sisters with awe, and I made sure to look suitably impressed, life as a younger sister was, in my experience, one of put-downs and hand-me-downs. But her sisters didn't have to be like mine, I supposed. There was a good chance they'd be like Mrs Partridge – Mrs Partridge writ large – although I found that unimaginable: a houseful of Mrs Partridges, so much self-effacement in a single household, like a trick done with mirrors.

You'll like them, Mrs Partridge assured me on more than several occasions, which only raised my suspicions, and once she went so far as to describe them as 'fun', which, to my mind, boded even less well. Then, one afternoon, the stairwell echoed the self-importance of men proving themselves happy to help, and the scraping of boxes in passing against doorframes. The sisters, I guessed, were moving in. But when the boxes had been manhandled inside and the men were gone to make themselves useful elsewhere, the house didn't return to its usual peaceful state. Those sisters downstairs, I discovered, were given to explosive laughter. I took a tip from Jane: I couldn't close my ears but I could close my eyes, and I kept them closed for most of that afternoon.

That evening, returning our tray to the kitchen, I bumped into one of the sisters as she came barrelling into the passage from the parlour. She made a show of being startled, exclaiming and slapping a hand to her heart. In the shadowy stairwell, I couldn't discern much beyond her being big, but in a different way from Mrs Partridge. Substantial, this sister: well built. She'd carried with her into the passageway the intriguing scents of her journey: a haze of horse and varied woodsmokes.

I began mumbling apologies despite my not having been at fault, but then the other sister was there, the door flying open and her demanding, 'Who's *this*?'

Which of course her sister didn't know, so I had to be the one to answer: 'I'm—' Starting again, more to the point: 'I stay upstairs with Lady Jane.'

At that, they closed in on me, cornered me: more alien fragrances, of a darker ale, a sweeter flower-water. 'Oh, of *course* you do.' The first sister placed a hand on my arm to claim me, saying unnecessarily to the other, 'She's the girl who's upstairs,' prompting, '*You* know,' even as that sister was confiding, 'Oh, Ellen's told us all about you.'

Really? Ellen, Mrs Partridge. Whatever it was that she'd told them, it seemed to have gone down well enough.

The second sister asked, 'What's she *like?* Missy up there,' which almost had me laugh.

'She's . . .' but what, really, could I say? How to convey Missy-up-there? Casting around, I looked down on the tray in my hands, the littering of dishes that had barely been touched. 'She's not hungry.'

And they laughed.

They introduced themselves – Lucy, Sarah – and when in turn I said my own name, they choroused, 'We know,' and that too, somehow, was funny.

'Can you escape?' Lucy indicated the parlour door. 'Can you come in for a drink? Is that allowed?' Implying that if it wasn't, then perhaps we shouldn't let it unduly trouble us. Well, I was willing to give it a go. I said I'd be pleased to, just as soon as I'd been to the kitchen.

Off I went, heart beating high and bright, blood singing in my ears. They weren't so bad, those sisters, it seemed to me; perhaps it wouldn't be so hard after all to have them in the house and why had I assumed it would be? Why had I assumed the worst? Dumping the plates with minimal ceremony ('That was lovely, thank you'), I sped off back to my new friends. Well, no, Jane first, of course. To make my excuses. Not that she'd care.

My uncharacteristically speedy descent of the stairs had Twig alerted, so that when it was me and not a stranger who opened the parlour door, he cringed, mortified at his mistake. His being there, sprawled on the hearth, implied that the cat wasn't, which was an excellent start. Mrs Partridge made an effort to rise for me, or at least to sit forward in a kind of welcome, but the more freckled of the sisters – Lucy – lunged, to shove her back on to her cushions – 'Will you rest!' – at which Mrs Partridge looked bashful but pleased.

'Isn't she dreadful?' crowed Lucy. 'Never takes a moment's rest.'

'Oh, she's impossible,' said Sarah, and to Mrs Partridge herself, 'What are you? Impossible, that's what.'

'Yes, but *we're* here, now,' Lucy was all raised eyebrows, 'to make sure she doesn't dare ever move.'

To me, Mrs Partridge raised her own eyebrows, while Sarah, heaving herself from her own pile of cushions towards a jug of something and a fascinating array of sweets, wanted to know from me, 'What can I get you?'

And that was how it was, every evening that week. Gratifyingly, even thrillingly, if I hadn't presented myself in the parlour by what they deemed a suitable hour, which arrived earlier every day, one or other sister would bustle into the stairwell and yell up, 'Liz-beth?'

At which, Jane would look expectantly across at me: *Off you go.*

You bet I will.

Jane wouldn't have wanted to join us, even if she'd been

allowed. Guildford would've, though. If Jane was Missy-up-there, then what, I wondered, would Guildford be? *Him-over-there*, perhaps. Or *Dukey*, or *Dukey-boy*, I imagined they might call him; *Little Lord Whatnot*. I could almost hear it; we were always, I felt, on the brink of a mention of him and I couldn't help but listen for it, be ready for it, ready to take it up and chance my luck. They'd love him, I knew – well, as long as he was behaving himself, which, given the chance of company and drink and sweets, I knew he would.

But even Mr Partridge rarely looked in on our parlour evenings, and in his notably frequent absences the sisters treated Twig as the man of the house. He'd never had it so good: they spoiled him rotten, having him swoon and drool.

'Oh, you're a mad dog, aren't you, Twigster?' one or other sister would cajole and flatter. 'Twiggle Partridge, what are you? A mad dog, is what you are. A roaring beast. A wolf. Oh and it's such hard work being a wolf, isn't it . . .'

They plied him with titbits, against which Mrs Partridge would occasionally voice caution ('Lucy, I don't think—' 'Sarah, I'm not sure that—') but which only, apparently, showed her as the fusspot – the killjoy – she was.

Whenever Mr Partridge did brave our company – 'Nate', the sisters called him, eschewing the 'Nathaniel' favoured by his wife – he was pint-sized in comparison to them, and easy game. Affectionately, they pushed and pulled him about: 'Look at you! That girl you've got doing your laundry? Give me those shirts, I'll sort you out.'

What a good job, I felt, that Goose was away. They spoke

with similar derision of their own husbands, unaccountably called, as far as I was able to distinguish, Dip and Ted-man. Ted-man was an idiot, Dip a dimwit – and they revelled in the chaos they imagined they'd left behind. The profusion of children confused me – certainly there was a Poppy-Beth, a Mims, a Pom – although their mothers' complaints about them were the same ('But *does* she listen? *Does* she?'). None of it seemed to matter, though: Ted-man being a 'lazy b' or Betsy-Mop's back-chat. On the contrary, their shortcomings were to be celebrated, their households were happy riots. I wondered whether they might need any help, back home: could I possibly be of any service? Why, I despaired, had I never learned to be of any use to anyone?

They were suitably sympathetic to my plight. Once, when Lucy remarked how miserable it must be for me up in the room, Sarah probed, 'Just Bible-reading, is it, that she does up there, all the time?'

'Most of the time, yes,' and it was such a relief to have it acknowledged for the strain that it was that I turned tearful.

Sarah saw it, 'Oh, you poor darling!' but Lucy said, 'Listen, you do a marvellous job up there, with her – you know that? Ellen says you've been terrific with that little miss up there. And it can't have been easy, all this time. She doesn't know how lucky she is, getting everything her own way.'

At that, I felt the faintest stirring of a defence. 'We get on all right,' I said. 'It was hard at first but it's a bit better now.'

Sarah asked, 'Do you have sisters near your age back home, sweetie?' and when I said no, Lucy said, 'That must be very lonely for you,' and then it came, what I'd been longing for: 'You should stay on here, when we've gone. We can't stay for ever, but ...'

'She'll need help,' Sarah finished. *Mrs Partridge*, 'She'll need company.'

And, yes, this was such a little household: what lady of any substance lived like this? I didn't dare breathe, let alone look up, but I could hear Mrs Partridge murmuring in agreement.

'Because,' Lucy blared over her, 'you're going to be free of your duties up there, soon. Can't be much longer now.'

'Unless,' teased Sarah, 'you've got some young man waiting for you,' and I burned as she grabbed my wrist, her rings more than a match for my bones. 'Promise me,' she said, 'that you'll think long and hard before you hand yourself over to any man. Promise me you'll do that.'

Yes, I told myself: look her in the eye and do it, say it. And I did. *And believe it.* All that was odd about it was how easy it was. There I was, at that fireside, for all the world a girl with an unblemished life ahead of her.

Abruptly, a week later, the good times were over, when Mrs Partridge withdrew with her sisters into her room. No unmarried ladies allowed. I'd assumed that particular rule applied to the actual labour, but that didn't seem to be their view and who was I to question it. If they wanted me enough, I decided, they'd make an exception, and so I lived in hope but no word came.

Unmarried meant virginal: everyone knew it, if no one ever actually dared say it. Jane, married, could've gone into that room with Mrs Partridge and her sisters if she'd wanted, if they'd wanted her, if she had been permitted to go any- where other than her own room. Jane could have gone into that room, despite being almost certainly unqualified to do so. Whereas me, if only they'd known: I could've taken my place in there with honour.

Shut out, left alone, I fell prey to fears for Mrs Partridge. *Ellen.* Well, and for the baby, although in truth I couldn't quite imagine the baby. All too precarious, it seemed, now: too much to hope for, that the birthing of that baby would go well. I reminded myself that her sisters – like mine – had managed the seemingly impossible physical event time and time again and not only had they lived to tell the tale but so too had their countless children, the Billy-bobs and Kitty- kats. But possibly there had been others who hadn't, and certainly my own sisters had each had a baby who'd died. And anyway, Mrs Partridge was nothing like her hulking, hardened sisters. But for anyone, what a horror to have to endure; for anybody, the rending of the soft core, the most tender part. I'd recall the pain when I'd passed whatever I'd passed, which, really, had only been blood. A baby? It was an unbearable prospect and sometimes, thinking of it, I had to pace to quell my panic.

Once, Jane asked me, 'What's the matter with you?'

'Nothing,' I said, which had her return to her book with something of a flourish, *Have it your way*. 'It's Mrs Partridge,' I hurried; but the best I could do was, 'I'm worried,' and then her infuriating sigh had me snap, 'And don't say it.'

She frowned, puzzled. 'Say what?'

'That I should have faith in God.'

She didn't flinch. 'I wasn't going to,' she replied, matter-of-fact. 'Because having faith in God doesn't stop something being scary, does it.'

IV

One morning less than a week after Mrs Partridge's retreat into confinement there was a commotion above us, probably coming from up on the wall behind the house. Grinding, scraping: some heavy objects being shifted would've been my guess. Something was happening up there, but so what? Maybe this was normal: some routine early-February Tower activity. And anyway, we took anything, pretty much, those days: guilty verdicts of no consequence, snowball wars between schoolboys and foreign dignitaries. Whatever was going on up on the wall, we barely registered it; and didn't so much as remark on it.

Or not until the first gunshot, which brought us to our senses because there's no ignoring a gun-blast, distant though this one was. The thud of it – ungracious and truncated, no preamble, no niceties – bounced our gazes into each other's. Twig, below us in the house, had fewer qualms about sounding his dismay. Curiosity took me from the fireside to the window and although Jane didn't move, her eyes followed me and she was the one of us to speak: 'What was that?'

I didn't know, but, 'Something.' Something that we should probably know about. Something, perhaps, that we were up against.

There was nothing to see from the window, so I went downstairs. Not a peep more from Twig but I had a distinct sense of him having been quietened, of someone having gone to him, to hush him. Of whoever that might be, though, there was no sight or sound, nor of anyone else. When I opened the front door on to the stupefying chill, someone unseen – a man – somewhere outside, yelled at me, 'Get back! Get inside!' and I ducked back as ordered, even as I bridled at it.

I stepped back into the kitchen boy, which was a shock of its own because I'd never come across him anywhere other than the kitchen, but there he was, unruffled and benign, and telling me much the same: 'Stay inside.'

'What is it? What's happening?' I hadn't intended to sound incensed, and fortunately he didn't seem to take it badly.

'They've reached Southwark,' he sounded almost contemplative, 'but the drawbridge's up.'

None of which meant anything to me. 'Who? Who's reached Southwark?' Rooftop men lambasting me, kitchen boys spouting nonsense. There was another blast, brutal and primitive, which I was now somehow certain was gunfire.

Deeper inside the house, Twig went berserk, as if he'd personally taken a hit, and someone was shouting him down, which served only to increase the racket. Other dogs, too, all around the Tower, were expressing their outrage.

The kitchen boy was quick to hide his surprise that I didn't know. 'Wyatt's men.'

My heart was thwacking against my ribs. I had no idea who Wyatt was, but whoever he was, he had men. Something else I knew, with excruciating clarity: we'd been sleeping, Jane and I; dreaming, for days, or even weeks, while all around us everyone else had taken cover, and it was breathtaking, my sense of being far beyond shelter and laid wide open. The kitchen boy was so close to me that I could see flecks in his irises but he was across a divide, on the safe side, because he was informed, he knew what he needed to know. *Help me*, I wanted to say: we were adrift, Jane and I, the pair of us up there in our little room. Take us in, I thought, although of course we were already in.

The kitchen boy said, 'There's thousands of them,' *Wyatt's men*, but there was nothing alarmist in it. It was accepting, almost, the way he'd said it.

Thousands: I tried and failed to picture them. How long had this – whatever it was – been going on? Bewitched: Jane and I, sleeping enchanted. Another blast heralded more dog-hysteria and I almost screamed, *Someone shut those dogs up!* Did all those men have guns? 'Where?' I asked the kitchen boy.

'Southwark.'

Oh, yes, Southwark: he'd said. For a heartbeat, I couldn't think, and then I remembered it was across the river. Directly opposite. But the drawbridge, he'd said, was up. 'What do they want?'

'The Queen.'

Yes, of course, the Queen, because who else? They wanted the Queen to join them: those thousands of Wyatt's men, clamouring for the Queen to come and lead them, because hadn't I seen it just six months before? The Queen riding triumphantly to her people. But even as I was thinking it, the kitchen boy said, 'Wyatt's calling for her surrender.' As if in battle. As if the Queen too were an army, all by herself, against them. Which was when I realised I'd got it wrong. Whoever they were, they weren't calling for her to lead them. No, instead they were coming for her.

Another crack of the sky and I couldn't stand it; it had to stop. And why were they doing it? She wasn't even here. Would the drawbridge hold? Could they come across in boats? But, anyway, why would they? *She's not here!*

The kitchen boy told me: 'They're . . . anyone. Everyone. Just . . . Englishmen.'

Englishmen, which meant, as he'd said, anyone, everyone, but also, I knew, this was about the marriage to the Spaniard. The marriage of our half-Spanish queen to the Spanish heir. The handing over of England to Spain. This was it: England saying no. And hadn't Goose warned us? *She'll have to listen.* Well, this was certainly loud enough.

'But she's not here,' I protested, then checked, 'Is she?' because evidently I didn't know much.

He shook his head. 'Whitehall.'

'Then why—?'

He shrugged. 'It's the Tower.' The heart of the kingdom.

The Tower was where she'd come as victor, six months ago, when Jane had surrendered. It had been so simple, back then: Jane tipping the coins from her purse and her father taking down her canopy. That had been the end of it. Usurper escorted off the throne and order restored. Righting that wrong had been a mere matter of walking a pretender across a green.

But now this queen, too, was being told to surrender – this rightful queen, the one we'd all taken to be rightful – and where would that leave us? I didn't understand, I didn't follow, because if Jane's vanquisher were vanquished ... Well, would both of them be held here?

In a rush, I asked him, as if he'd know: 'What'll happen?'

'They've turned the guns,' was all he said.

So that was what we'd heard earlier, then, above us.

'Not firing them, though,' he added. 'Those aren't ours,' the guns that were blasting. 'No cannonfire, says the Queen, because of the people over there.' In Southwark. 'Homes. Children.'

Only when I was halfway back up the stairs did it dawn on me that I had no idea of what to tell Jane. Thousands of men were coming for the Queen, but what about Jane? She was their enemy's enemy. She was in the fortress that they wanted to take, but as its prisoner.

She, though, knew exactly what to make of it. As soon as I'd regurgitated the bare bones, she concluded, 'This is in favour of the princess.'

I'd forgotten about the princess. The princess, radiant on

271

the occasion of her half-sister's victory. Could that princess possibly step past her frumpy half-sister to the throne, even with thousands of men to help her on her way?

'Who are they, though,' Jane wondered, 'these men,' these pro-princess men.

I quoted the kitchen boy, 'There's thousands of them.'

'Yes, but whose are they?'

'Wyatt's,' whoever he was.

She considered. 'And?'

And what?

'Who else?'

Who *else*? She wanted more? No one else had been mentioned. Why would there be anyone else?

Several more booms, a run of them, had us halt before she resumed: 'What do you think we should do?'

We had to do something, this was to be got through and how should we do that?

But, well, how difficult could it be? We were in the Tower. We couldn't be safer, and anyway none of this was to do with us. We were going to have to hear it, have to have our ears boxed, have an uncomfortable time of it for as long as it lasted, but even if by remotest chance the gates did end up being opened for Wyatt and his men, then so what? She was their enemy's enemy: surely they'd just set her free.

'Where's Mr Partridge?' and that, too, she was right to ask, seeing as she was his charge and she was in the middle of a battle, although I couldn't see what he could do for us and he had his wife to worry about. As far as I understood it, his non-appearance told us all we needed to know: if he wasn't here, then he wasn't worried.

And so we resolved to stay put, as if we had any choice in the matter, and the decision, such as it was, had us feeling all the better for having made it. We were staying put: from then onwards, that was what we were busy doing, sitting it out, and it was a relief to be doing something even if it was nothing at all. While everyone else lay low, we two sat to attention, doing our best, doing our bit, as if our vigilance alone were sufficient to repel the attack. And it did feel oddly strenuous, that bearing up of ours; it demanded a certain stance of us, and despite my barely moving a muscle, the blood was rushing in my veins. The gunfire was sporadic throughout the morning but whenever it came, we were ready for it, we were no longer rattled by it. Twig, though, succumbed every time, and his cacophony, so much closer and angrier than those desultory, lofty blasts, was hard to bear.

What mattered was that it was coming no closer, and of course it wasn't because there were walls, there was a river, a drawbridge. The Tower was unbreachable and anyway the Queen wasn't in it. And a queen doesn't surrender, not a proper queen, a real one, as this one was, however many men demand it and however noisily. A queen rules and eventually those men would remember it and give up and go home.

During the long hours of that peculiar morning, I'd think often of Mrs Partridge, of how unfair that for the brief time that she tried to shut out the world, it had come banging at her window. And of course I thought of Guildford: I couldn't help but do that. He was having to endure each blast as we did; and so, for once, I knew exactly what he was doing. What I didn't know was what he made of it. *Not so little now, are they, your 'little people', now that they have guns.*

At the usual time, I headed downstairs to fetch lunch – because if that was odd, it would've been odder not to. I didn't know what – who – I'd find in the kitchen, but they were there, the cook and his boy, although with none of their characteristic ease. Perfunctory preparations, that lunchtime, and no smiles. No reference, either, to what was happening outside. Like us, up in our room, they were refusing to give it credence. Nor did the boy acknowledge our earlier exchange, for which I was grateful. That looked likely to stay our little secret: me, flailing in the front doorway, under fire.

Back upstairs, when there came a renewed onslaught, Jane put down her spoon and declared, 'This is ridiculous.'

That we were picking our way through lunch while under siege? That England was rising against its own crowned queen? I took the chance to say what I was thinking: 'If they get the princess on the throne, you'll go free.'

But that, she dismissed out of hand. 'Makes no difference who's Queen. I'm the Queen's prisoner; I'd just be Elizabeth's instead.'

Oh, come on! 'What would she want with you?'

'No queen, whoever she is, leaves a pretender at large.' She retrieved her spoon. 'And anyway, you don't know Elizabeth.'

That again.

'Mary's muddly.' Raising the spoon to her lips, she said, 'I'm safer with Mary.'

There was no sign of the cook or his boy when I returned our tray; the kitchen hummed with their absence. Back in our room, I asked Jane, 'D'you think Guildford's still over there?' Because the White Tower was head and shoulders above all others, the rough-cut jewel in this vast, rough-hewn crown. The easiest target.

She didn't look up. 'Well, where else would he be?'

Well, I don't know, do I, which was why I was asking. 'Perhaps we should—'

'What?' and now she did look up, very much so.

I didn't know, but try, perhaps, somehow, to go and see if he was still there? It seemed to me that, in the peculiar circumstances, it might well be possible for us to do that.

'Elizabeth.' She was staring at me.

'*What?*'

'No.'

Not even with what was going on? The way she'd said it, that one word, *No*: what it said was that Guildford was too much for us, hard work, a liability. To be avoided. And, yes, I could understand why she'd feel like that, but shouldn't she give him another chance? If she did, she might find he wasn't so bad. And, anyway, everything was changing, fast, and this was no time nor place for grudges. Bygones might just have to be bygones, whether she liked it or not.

But, 'No,' she decreed, and I had the clear sense that at least for now there was nothing I was going to be able to do about it.

The green had a deserted look to it; discarded, even, as if dumped when everyone had run for cover. But mid-afternoon, from the doorway beneath our window nudged a presence which took me a moment to see as a cloaked head and shoulders. Someone. I'd seen no one outside all day, but now here was someone leaving the house. I knelt up for a better view. There were more cloaked figures, a huddle, a knot becoming discernible as a trio. Dark-dyed cloth unfolded unevenly across the threshold, each individual holding back for another to take the lead and all three of them cowering not only from potential gunfire but also from sleet.

And then from inside all that heavy cloth came a flash of white. A nightdress? Was that Mrs Partridge, down there, being moved from her sanctuary? Yes: Mrs Partridge and her sisters, hounded from their lair, befuddled and wind-harried, tripping over cloak hems, their conferring and recoiling meaning they inched caterpillar-style across the green. There Mrs Partridge was, struggling in her nightdress through a gale in the vicinity of gunfire, and my heart clenched to see it.

I was in too much of a rush to be able to answer when Jane asked where I was going, and although at the foot of the stairs I ran into a muddle of men and boxes and heaps of bedding, I was quickly past them. Stepping through the doorway was like leaping into cold water. The wind rose up to smack me in the eyes but I pursued the blurred figures, only to find that when I drew alongside them, hooded and huddled as they were, I couldn't get their attention. My breath had been snatched by the cold and all I could do was grab the nearest one. The touch to her arm had Sarah turn to me but not only was there no welcome in her eyes, there was no recognition either. Before I could explain myself, offer my help, Lucy too had turned, and her face was stark and pinched by the wind as she yelled at me to 'Get back indoors.' In between the sisters was the cloak-coddled figure I knew to be Mrs Partridge, picking her way through the mud, her hands full of her skirts, her head down and face obscured by her hood, intent on getting herself and her unborn baby to refuge. If I just held on, if I could just hold on, she'd look up – catch her breath, get her bearings – and she'd see me, know I was there and take me in.

But she didn't, and step by step she still didn't, and then by default I was doing as Lucy had insisted. One step back, then another, and soon I was alone in that courtyard as they moved off and the only place for me to go was back.

But it was nothing, I told myself as I climbed the stairs: Lucy's ferocity had come from the stresses and strains of the awful circumstances and I knew much better than to take it to heart. And, anyway, it had been for my benefit because here I was, safe and sound, back inside, and only shaking so horribly because I was cold.

*

Odder even than going to the kitchen for lunch was heading there again at suppertime, but I wanted to discover who was still in the house. All day long, no one had been up to our room and from the time I'd seen Mrs Partridge and her sisters leaving, there'd been no sound of Twig.

The air beyond our door had an ashy sourness to it, and darkness reared up the staircase. If I'd been hoping against hope that the kitchen might be back in use, that was increasingly hard to envisage as I went downstairs, and when I reached the end of the passageway, the room gaped: nobody, no fire nor lights. If the kitchen was abandoned then so too, I reckoned, was the rest of the house. Most likely, everyone had followed Mrs Partridge's example and retreated deeper into the Tower.

My little light was tremulous in that cavern and my nose so cold that it seeped. There'd been no gunfire for a couple of hours and I willed the peace to hold for as long as I was alone in there. What I heard instead, though, were footsteps, the light scratching of soles across stone, and I half sobbed with relief when into the doorway came Sarah, although I hadn't forgotten our earlier encounter. Her light, borne before her, like a pulsing heart, cast the rest of her cadaverous in its shadow. My standing there, motionless, in the sickly lit darkness seemed to give her a fright but she was quick to recover and go about her business, and of course she did, because it was far too cold for any hanging around.

She hadn't said a word, so I pitched in, grave but hopeful: 'How's Mrs Partridge?'

'Tired.' She turned her back to me, became busy at one of the benches.

Tired, yes, of course, after the upheaval.

As she carved slices from something – I couldn't see what – she said, 'This is terrible for her, in her condition,' and I heard that she was livid. 'You really wouldn't think it so much to ask: a couple of weeks' rest before the baby.'

I was quick to agree.

'But there are people,' she hissed over the rasping of the blade, 'who don't stop to think about anyone else. People who are so caught up in their own—' But here she halted, as if it were offensive to name.

Who were these people who didn't stop to think? The men in Southwark? I hadn't even known they existed until the kitchen boy had told me, so why did I feel that Sarah was blaming me for their insurrection?

'People who are so very sure they know what's best for the rest of us,' and then she did turn to me, the knife sleek and honed at her side. 'Because most of us would've given it a chance, this Spanish marriage; it's not perfect, but what is?' She glared at me as if I might have an actual answer. And, indeed, whatever it was that was so wrong between us, my standing meekly mute certainly wasn't helping to put it right. Pathetically, all I could come up with was 'Is there anything I can do for you?'

That, though, was a red rag to a bull. 'You'll be pleased to tell your Lady Jane,' she seethed, 'that Nate says no one's mustering. They're giving up, in the city. When Wyatt gets to the gate tomorrow, they'll just open it and in he'll come.'

And sweeping up a laden tray, she was gone back through the doorway.

I suffered a whiplash of tears, because what on earth did she mean by *pleased to tell your Lady Jane?* Then came a flash of fury because how dare she, that cow, how fucking dare she presume and pronounce on us like that.

Storming back into our room, I blared, 'What if people think it's for you? What if people think Wyatt wants you?'

Jane, though, wasn't troubled for an instant. 'Oh, no one wants me.' She seemed cheerful. 'I've already lost, remember. I'm the kiss of death.'

And so impressed was I by her breezy confidence that I forgot what I'd actually asked: *What if people* think *it's for you?*

The firing stopped not long after dusk and the silence lay everywhere like snowfall. No bells, even, I realised after some time: the clocks hadn't been wound. Should we, I wondered, go to bed? Would we sleep? We did, and it was waking that came as the surprise, as if we'd forgotten the existence of mornings.

We were woken by the sound of Goose, but of course it couldn't be Goose because she was at her sister's. But that, in our room, was definitely Goose. I shifted on my pillow to look at Jane and found her staring back at me. 'And to think,' she breathed sleepily, 'that it was Wyatt we were fearing.'

I got up and went through. Goose was seeing to the fire.

'Sorry I'm late,' she trilled, obviously not sorry at all; on the contrary, hugely pleased with herself.

I crept towards her as if I still didn't quite know what, up close, I'd find. 'How did you get here?'

She flapped a hand behind her. 'Stairs, door, the usual.'

'Goose,' I stressed, 'we're under siege.'

'Lady Lip,' she answered back, rising, and striking her hands down her apron, 'you're behind the times.' With evident pleasure, she said, 'I've just walked from my sister's, all through fair-ol'-London-town and right through Lion Gate.'

It was inconceivable. 'Just now?'

'Give or take.'

Not Wyatt through the gate, then, but Goose. And looking good on it, too.

'And *guess*,' she bobbed with the excitement of it, almost made a jig of it, 'who I saw?'

Jane blundered in, wrapped in our coverlet.

'No less,' crowed Goose, 'than our own lady Queen!'

Jane staggered to the fireside stool.

'At Guildhall. Come from the palace, where all her ladies have been screaming and crying and barricading themselves in, so says my sister, and she'd know.

'And all of them armed, those ladies,' she brandished our poker in demonstration, 'and all the servants, too,' accompanied by a provocative hitch of her eyebrows. 'But there she was, our Queen, at Guildhall, with the doors wide open to all of us. Got up in her robes and crown and on her throne and –' to Jane '– isn't she weeny!'

Jane looked blank.

'But what a voice!' She was chucking cloths and brushes into her pail; it seemed that she wouldn't be staying. 'Everyone could hear her. All of us hundreds and hundreds of Londoners, packed in the hall or on the steps outside. And she's our Queen, was what she said, and loves us all like we're her children, and everything she's doing, it's for us. It's all, always for us, is what she said.' She hefted the pail on to her arm. 'And those men coming? Well, she said, we can see 'em off; "I'm not scared of them," she said, and, I'm telling you, that was no word of a lie.' From the door, she said, 'Everything had been all shut up, doors bolted, but then suddenly everyone was everywhere again, and when ol' Mister Wyatt got to Ludgate – he'd crossed at Kingston – he was thinking they'd open up but they didn't.' She shrugged: done and dusted. 'And of course he couldn't go back, because of the lords on his tail.

'I mean, they couldn't stop him coming, could they,' a roll of her eyes, 'but they could just about manage to stop him getting away.'

Jane asked, 'Where is he?'

'On his way. Bell Tower. So, if you'll excuse me,' and she made a lot of it, the full Goosey force of her in that one word 'excuse', 'I've got work to do.'

And then nothing more, all day long; nothing out of the ordinary; no trace of the previous day's turmoil. Everything back to normal. Men busy in the inner bailey, the cook and his boy in the kitchen putting good food on our tray for lunch and supper, Twig downstairs and Goose from time to time in our room despite her much-vaunted duties tending to Wyatt. And we read and stitched our way through the day; and Guildford, presumably, in his tower, was back to badgering William to play him at cards. It was as if nothing had ever happened, although surely no one trusted to that.

During the night, sometime in the small hours, we were woken by Mr Partridge in our bedroom doorway, apologetic but firm: 'Lady Jane, if you could come with me,' and it was softly said only because of the hour. It wasn't a request, but an order.

I shot up but he shook his head at me, quick and secretive, *Not you*, as if I'd understand, as if there was an understanding between us. But this was lunacy: Mr Partridge had gone mad, cut loose and turning up here in our bedroom in the dead of night, asking for Jane to go alone with him. I had to get help. But he *was* our help. And he was blocking our doorway.

Jane was startled too, but she focused on the practicality: 'But I'm not dressed.'

Of that, he was dismissive. 'Well, just—' *throw something on*, and he sounded sad and exhausted, not mad; and so, in my confusion, in my half-woken daze, her state of undress became the issue. Scrabbling from the bed to her chests, I pulled out a gown and held it aloft. 'This?'

Was she going outside? Who, exactly, would be seeing her?

'Fine.' He was spectacularly uninterested.

There we were, in front of him in our nightdresses, the

guileless white of them, their good-natured stitching. I was frantic to object because this was outrageous, she simply couldn't leave this room in the middle of the night, not without me and certainly not with any man, even if that man was Mr Partridge. But the words stopped in my throat and Jane was the one of us who asked, 'What's wrong, Mr Partridge?' She didn't sound scared, but, if anything, sympathetic.

He didn't answer; said, 'You need to come with me,' but soothingly now, as if that were a reassurance.

And she did. She got up, shrugged the gown loosely over her nightdress, and pattered from the room without a backwards glance.

I'd never been alone before in those rooms of ours. Jane had, often enough, although never at night. I lay there tracking the scuttle of mice in the roof but, incredibly, must have dozed eventually, because then it was morning and she was back there beside me in the bed.

I presumed she'd tell me what had happened, but she didn't. We were both slow to rise, bone-tired from the difficult few days and nights, but still she said nothing and I didn't dare ask for fear of bad news. And then came a knock at our door. She was ahead of me to it, which was odd because it was my job to answer it. What was going on? First I was excluded from an extraordinary night-time excursion which was ominously unexplained, and now she was answering our door as if I didn't exist. Perhaps it was all somehow to do with me: perhaps, I worried, this was it, for me, and I was about to be told that my services were no longer required.

She opened the door to an old priest. Or perhaps he was an old man impersonating a priest, so impeccably in character was he: a priest as I remembered them from my childhood, when they'd pinch my cheek and call me Jesus's little lamb. Life had treated him well: he was broader than he was tall – although that wasn't very – with cheeks ruddied by ale and sugar-shrunken teeth, not that he stinted on his smile. He stood there in our doorway, bouncing on the balls of his feet, and Jane welcomed him in. She'd been expecting him, was how it looked, and in he came, burbling greetings, his tiny jellied eyes everywhere at once as if unable to imagine any finer earthly place to be.

If he was doing well in playing the priest, Jane did at least as well as the gracious hostess. 'Father Feckenham, this is my friend Mistress Elizabeth Tilney; and Elizabeth, Father Feckenham,' as she ushered him towards the fireside and into the chair that habitually she took as her own. For herself, she drew up the stool, and doing so, passing the table, made a minor adjustment to her pile of books. It was the merest touch and to no obvious end but perhaps more a taking of comfort from them. The priest was talking ceaselessly – 'So good of you to see me, I do appreciate it, and I'm hoping we'll make real progress, I'm sure we'll discover lots of common ground' – but spotting her reach for those books, his pitch rose as if in competition with them, to assert his own physical presence over theirs.

Jane turned pleasantly from him to me: 'Elizabeth, I wonder if you'd be so kind as to fetch Father Feckenham some refreshments.'

The tray with which I returned was given a rapturous reception: 'Oh, look at that, how very generous, how lovely, what an impressive spread, this looks absolutely delicious and you really shouldn't leave it all to me because it won't do me any good at all.'

Jane, though, persisted with what was presumably an ongoing conversation. 'He also said, "I'm a vine," father, and, "I'm a door," but he was neither of those, was He; I mean, surely you don't think—' She gestured towards the door, which I'd just closed behind me: *Is that Jesus?* She awaited the priest's considered response, with which, wisely, he declined to furnish her. He turned his attention instead to the quince paste. 'Doesn't this look magnificent?' and, incredulous, to both of us, 'Are you sure you won't have some?' He spoke through a mouthful: 'You wonder, don't you, what spices your man has used, here, to give it such a delicate flavour.'

Jane kept a smile on her face but, I saw, it didn't reach her eyes, which was where her tiredness was pooled.

Then the priest did come up with an answer, if only after a fashion: 'Oh, but it's all just words, Lady Jane, in the end, isn't it, just words; and we can quibble for ever about words but I doubt we're so very far apart on the important matters.'

Hers was such a sweet smile, despite her obvious weariness, and I felt for that priest because he'd be beguiled. He wasn't to know that whatever he said wouldn't touch her. She'd heard it all before, countless times, since she was a small child. That poor man, he had no idea what he was up against. He'd have been better off, I thought, spending his time on me. I was the sinner in the room, if he wanted one. Except that I was no more interested in listening to him than she was.

And then, mercifully, I didn't have to, because Goose was at our door, come to tell me that Mr Locke had turned up downstairs to see me. Jane could of course be left in the presence of a priest, so I followed Goose to the parlour, where I spent perhaps as long as half an hour in the company – if it could be so termed – of my parents' steward. He'd been in London when the siege had started, which had, at the time, put paid to any business he'd been there to do, and was eager to tell us what he'd experienced. 'Shut up shop,' he said, amazed, more than several times, 'the whole city, shut up shop.' For half an hour or so, Mr Partridge nodded sagely, Goose twiddled her thumbs and Twig chanced some begging, while Mr Locke and I exchanged appropriate pleasantries and any news, such as we had; and then, when he was sufficiently reassured that I'd survived recent events unscathed, I was free to leave him.

My return upstairs coincided with Fr Feckenham's departure. 'And in view of how well we've done today,' he was saying brightly to Jane, 'I'd like to ask the Queen for more time, just a day or two. Given a little longer, I don't doubt we'll find our common ground.'

I could hear Jane's smile in her voice. 'Thank you, father, you're very kind, but, really, as I say, I'd like you to convey for me that tomorrow will be fine.'

There followed a small silence, which I took to be nothing more than his shifting in the doorway to allow me past, but then, gravely, he said, 'My lady, please, I beg you to reconsider.'

She was unmoved: 'You're very kind, father, but, really, tomorrow is my final word.'

Shutting the door on him, I asked her, 'What's tomorrow?' It was easier to ask about tomorrow, just mentioned, than the previous, mysterious night.

She was tidying the table because, had the priest liked it or not, there'd obviously been some consultation of her books. Turning to hang up my cloak, I had my back to her when she said, 'My execution.'

There was no need for that, I was in no mood for jokes and I knocked it back at her: 'Don't say that.'

She paused in her book-shuffling to look up at me but there was nothing in her eyes as she informed me, 'My father was involved in the uprising.'

Her father – the man with the canopy? A man who couldn't even take down a canopy unaided. 'Your father?'

'Involved in the uprising.'

But that made no sense. The bodged canopy-dismantling, and then the shameful skulking from the Tower by which he'd abandoned his daughter: that man was a coward. He'd already been in more than enough trouble for a lifetime and I couldn't believe he'd go looking for any more. I must have misunderstood her. Uprising? I was thinking of Wyatt's men but perhaps she was speaking historically. Perhaps 'uprising'

288

was what she called her attempt to take the throne, although then she wouldn't have been telling me that her father had been involved, because we both already knew that.

'Hence,' was all she said.

Hence? Baffled, I could only repeat it back to her: 'Hence?'

'My execution.' Offered up like that, in conclusion, she sounded almost pleased with it.

But I was stuck, repeating it back to her: 'Your father was involved in the uprising?'

She gave me a small, humourless smile: *Would you believe it?*

Well, no, actually, I wouldn't. I still didn't understand. 'The one in favour of the princess?'

She was busy again, now with the tray. 'The very one.'

She was humouring me. *Stop it. Stop trying to pretend this is nothing.* Because, I was realising, this was something, something had happened, something was happening, even if it wasn't clear to me exactly what, and even if her prissy table-tidying belied it.

She indicated the tray: 'Should we take this down?'

I ignored that. 'Your father wouldn't be involved in any uprising. He wouldn't do that.' Not when a mere six months ago he'd escaped with his life by the skin of his teeth. Not with his daughter, judged guilty of treason, held prisoner in the Tower.

'Well, he did,' she said, and then she was going into our bedroom.

But no, *Oh no you don't,* and, quicker than she was, I got

myself between her and the door. 'But,' I said, 'he'd have to be an idiot to do that.'

She gave me a wry look.

No. Enough. I hated how she was standing there, her emphatic show of tolerance as if I were a toddler on the verge of a tantrum. 'That was for the princess.' My breathing was louder than my words. 'The uprising. That was in favour of the princess.' *You said.*

Wasn't that what she'd said? Yes, she had, I was right about that, I was damn well right and she should admit it. One of us needed to be sensible here; one of us had to get a grip.

She said, 'I need the chamberpot, Elizabeth.'

But no, *no*, she was going to confirm it for me first: I was the one of us who was speaking sense and I needed her to confirm that for me. 'You said Wyatt was for the princess.'

'And he *was*.' She was surprised that I should doubt her.

'Well then.' I stood my ground. I had to have her agree that she was in no danger, no real danger; I couldn't fathom her desire to pretend that she was.

'Well then *what?*'

'Well then, it had nothing to do with you.' That was the nub of it: I'd got there, if with no help from her.

She said, 'My father planned that uprising. My father and a couple of his friends.'

'Yes,' I allowed, 'but not *for you*. He did it for the princess. He just happens to be your father, but he didn't do it *for you*.' Why persist in the denial of it? 'And he'll tell them,' I said.

290

'He'll tell them it had nothing to do with you.' Obviously he would.

'Elizabeth,' she sighed, giving up on the chamberpot, wandering towards the window. 'I don't know what he'll tell them, but whatever he tells them, it's irrelevant.'

But, no, she was wrong there: it was precisely what was at issue.

'One attempt to put me on the throne . . . ' she shrugged, *fair enough*, in the case of a particularly merciful queen, 'but twice . . . ' and again a shrug, but this time huge, a giving up.

'But it's not twice.' I spoke too loudly, had to lower my voice, 'because this one, this . . . uprising' — I hated the word — 'wasn't for you.'

She was exasperated. 'But we don't know that! *She* doesn't know that.' The Queen. 'My father was one of the leaders, and who knows what he was thinking? For him, it might've been for me, and next time it could be. It's too risky for her; I'm too much of a risk, I'm a threat.'

Oh for God's sake, I almost laughed. 'You're not a threat. You're just a girl.'

A girl, though, who would change the world.

'Strictly speaking,' she said, 'I'm a married woman: I could have an heir.'

Oh, well, yes, if you say so. 'The princess,' I insisted, 'the princess is the one she needs to worry about.'

Jane gazed over the green. 'But she can't touch her. Too close to home. And anyway, there's nothing she can prove against her.'

I burst out, 'But there's nothing she can prove against *you*! I mean,' and it was almost funny, 'you were *in here*.'

She looked over her shoulder at me. 'Yes, and why? Why am I in here?' Not a question, not really. And now she turned fully around to face me. 'The Queen very nearly fell. Thousands and thousands of men marched on London. There's no place in England, now, for traitors.'

Which was all very well, but 'She won't do it.' Those various, burly, scheming men, they'd have to face the consequences, of course they would, but 'Not you. You know that. She won't actually do it.' Murder a girl? An innocent girl? A noble-born, serious-minded, Godly girl? Even if the Queen wanted to do it, she wouldn't dare, because she'd never live it down. Why did I feel this was a corner that needed fighting? Why was I shaking so much that I was close to being sick? The Queen wouldn't do it. She was a queen who wouldn't have her cannons fired near civilians, a queen who'd knelt on the grass to take a boy up into her arms, a queen who had said we were all her children. 'Who told you this?' I demanded. *Let's get to the bottom of this.* Who was the source of this disgusting scaremongering?

'Mr Partridge.'

Mr Partridge? Was that what that had been about last night?

'Last night. He told me, and he showed me the warrant.' She was ahead of me: 'And yes, I did check that it was signed.' There she stood, in front of me, arms folded, unyielding.

'But so what?' I said. 'So what if it was signed? It has to be signed but she's bluffing.' Why couldn't she see that? 'She signs a warrant but then she pardons you and then she looks all wonderful and merciful.'

'But she's already done that. She's already pardoned me once. Now, she has to look strong.'

She'd seen the warrant — seen her name on it and, below, the Queen's signature — and then she'd come back into this room and crept into bed beside me and gone to sleep. And when she'd got up in the morning, she hadn't told me. *You hid this from me.* I didn't know her, I realised, I didn't know her at all, and perhaps that was why I said her name, just her name: heard myself say it, just the one syllable.

What she said, in return, was, 'Tomorrow,' just as she'd said it to the priest. The priest: I'd forgotten him.

'That priest's here to get you to recant.'

'Well,' and she was faintly amused at the thought, 'that's what he's *hoping* for.'

Relief washed over me. 'Well then,' I said, 'there you are: that's what this is, all this—' I flapped a hand, to sweep it all away. 'It's all just to scare you into recanting. All you have to do is recant.'

'Elizabeth,' and the look she gave me was kind, 'she's not sending Father Feckenham to save me, or not in any earthly way. She's saving my soul, as she sees it. Doing her Christian duty: sending me to my maker, not to Hell. She's preparing me, or giving me the chance to prepare myself. She's doing it properly, that's all.'

This queen who was anxious to get things right.

'But there's a chance,' I urged, 'you know that. She'll be looking for an excuse, any excuse, anything. If you recant, she has her excuse.'

There was no arguing with that; instead, she looked almost shy. 'But I'm not going to do that, am I.'

'No' – she'd misunderstood – 'no, you just have to *say* it,' as if I were explaining to a child, 'you just *say* you've recanted. Just until you're free and—' Well, abroad, probably, if Guildford had his way. 'Everyone'll know that's all it is.' Everyone except the Queen, the earnest little lady who'd lifted Edward Courtenay off his knees into her arms as if he were still a boy: that lady would believe whatever she wanted to believe, and more than anything she'd want to believe that the Protestant pretender had returned to the fold.

Gently she repeated, 'But I'm not going to do that, am I.'

I laughed because it was so absurd that she'd object; I laughed even as my throat was smarting. 'But you have to, You just . . . do it.' It really was as simple as that.

She seemed about to join me, and got as far as a smile, although it stayed sad. 'But I'd never do that,' and there was a tenderness in it, this appeal to me. She whispered, 'You know that.'

Which was when it occurred to me: 'What happens to Guildford?'

'He goes earlier,' she said, 'before me.'

Goes, and for a moment, in my mind's eye, I saw him leaving through a gatehouse, loping away to what was at least a kind of freedom: there he went, with my blessing.

'Up on the hill, though,' she said, 'not down here on the green like me.'

And my heart got it before I did: my animal-heart, playing dead. Not that it fooled her; her gaze went right inside me to uncover it as it cowered there.

'I'm sorry,' she said, and she was, I could see she was, but if I kept very still then what she'd just said might somehow slide off me, roll away to become nothing and be gone. I should take a breath, I knew; I was aware of a pressing need to take a breath but I couldn't do it with her watching, I couldn't do anything with her eyes in mine, couldn't even breathe. Speak, though, I was able to do, it seemed, because I heard myself: 'Guildford's done nothing wrong,' and that was a fact, pure and simple, incontrovertible, shining there high in the air between us.

She reflected, 'Well, *I've* done nothing wrong.'

I asked her, 'Does he know?' Did he know what they were threatening him with? She knew, now, but did he? There was a chance he didn't, yet.

'Yes.'

'Last night?' Had he, too, been told, last night?

'Yes.'

And how odd and how shaming it was that what hurt at least as much as anything I'd heard was that they'd been together, the two of them, when they'd been told.

She was saying something about having to prepare. But no, I thought, because no one prepares for something that isn't going to happen. 'What are you doing?' She'd gone to the table; the chamberpot forgotten — a ruse, as I'd suspected.

'I'd like to write to my sisters.' So normal, she made it sound, *write to my sisters*.

But no, *No, you don't go writing to your sisters*, and anyway, to say what? She couldn't write to her sisters, meek and mild and studious, because she had to be going to find Mr Partridge and——

Mr Partridge, who'd dragged her from her bed in the middle of the night to show her her own, signed death warrant? Well, perhaps not him, but someone. There'd be others she could go to for help, and anyway, Mr Partridge was no one, a nobody when all was said and done, just an official scurrying around following orders. Jane knew lords, she probably knew every last lord in England, knew them personally, had stayed as a guest in their houses, been rowed around in barges between their houses and actually, come to think of it — and why hadn't I, until now? — she knew the Queen, she was the Queen's second cousin. She should request to see the Queen, and as soon as the Queen saw her——

Gently, she admonished, 'This doesn't help.' My resistance, she meant, my refusal to countenance the threat: it was me who was letting her down, in her view; me, and not the mealy-mouthed bastards who'd have her believe she was about to die. 'I need to prepare.' Her eyes searched mine, concerned for me that I couldn't grasp something so fundamental: 'This is what I've always wanted; all my life, this is what I've wanted.' And there was a suggestion of a smile: 'It's just come a little earlier than I'd expected.'

'No—'

'No, *listen*,' and she took a step towards me, to impress upon me, 'I *want* this,' and there she was in front of me, her bones still with the business of growing to do, not yet at full stretch but folded in on themselves like nascent wings, sappy at the core with a little further to go in their mineral trickle, their testing and teasing of their muscular bindings.

But don't you see? This is a lie, this is a trick, this is how it's done, this is how they get you to walk out there and offer yourself up as if it were your own idea.

'And imagine,' she said, 'just imagine the love, where I'm going.'

But couldn't she see there was love enough for her here? Why couldn't she see that? Anyway, wasn't she forgetting something, someone? 'And Guildford?' Because did she really think he'd be over there in his room enthusing like this to William? He was only roped into this madness because of her.

'Guildford was fine,' she said airily: last night, she meant; fine to be told what they claimed lay in store for him.

How dared she, because that wasn't true and she knew it. *Look me in the eye and say that.* Guildford was for staying alive and fighting it out, and he was only here in the Tower because of her. She liked to pretend otherwise but we needed to face it: he was here because he was her husband. And to make it worse, her husband in name only. Guildford had no wish to die for any cause. To fight for one, yes, or at least argue for it, but not to die. You stay and fight – if, admittedly, from abroad initially: that was Guildford's view. You play them at their own game, if at first from a distance. There was work to be done, was what he believed. Jane should remember what he'd said of the princess's saving her own skin, *no bad thing*, and hadn't he once said to her, *You're no use to anyone if you're dead*. I was going to say it, crass though it was: 'That letter to Dr Harding, you couldn't have written that if you were dead,' and indeed, she'd been so very alive, then, writing that letter. She'd been so utterly herself, she'd been the best of herself, busy doing what she'd spent her whole life preparing herself to do. I'd stake my own life on there having been no emotional appeals in that letter, but instead points, one after the other, dozens, perhaps hundreds of them, and I wouldn't mind betting that each and every one of them had been won.

'But I've written it.' She was puzzled. 'It's done.'

I despaired, 'But there are more people than Dr Harding in the world!'

Again she almost smiled because, 'I can't write them all a letter, can I.'

But she'd get herself martyred instead? No, no, *This is not you*, she was not someone for grand gestures, she was a nit-picker, a pourer of cold water, and *Listen, missy: if you go, the world won't miss you*. Couldn't she see it? A Jane-sized, Jane-shaped hole in the world would achieve nothing. No one would remember her. No one much remembered her even now, a mistake-queen manhandled on to the throne and then just as quickly off it again. The Duke of Northumberland, yes, people would remember him, incomparable ruler of England, but Jane? She was just a girl, and before long, if not already, people would forget precisely which girl: one of the Grey sisters, someone's sister, someone's second cousin.

'This is my test of faith,' she was telling me, 'here, now; today, tonight, tomorrow, and –' that familiar lift of her chin '– I think I can do it.'

But anyway, it didn't matter, none of it mattered because nothing was going to happen and everyone knew it, even Mr Partridge. He knew that nothing would come of it, he knew it would blow over, and I wondered what on earth he'd been playing at, getting her up in the night, getting her and Guildford together. She asked me where I was going and I told her, 'To get someone,' although I didn't yet know who. I just needed to get started, get myself through the doorway and down the stairs and see who I came across.

The ease with which she closed the distance between us was like a dangled rope, a mere flick at the top but a sweeping turn below so that in one movement she'd come for me, taken my hands into her own, drawn me to the window, sat me down and crouched at my feet. She said, 'There are things I need to do before tomorrow. I need to write to my sisters – not much – and I need to pray.'

And I understood: no distraction, which was what I would be if I were running in and out of the room, fetching and consulting people. I understood it even if I wasn't quite ready to concede it.

'And there's something I need to ask of you,' but she relinquished my hands, returning them to my lap, and withdrew to the table to shuffle books, which was, I knew, how she summoned up courage. She didn't look at me when she said, 'Please don't go and see Guildford,' and I hadn't known until then that that was what I was going to do. Because yes, of course that was what I was going to do: go to Guildford, as soon as possible, and I knew I'd manage it with a bribe of some kind or perhaps just good old pleading and, under the circumstances, I'd be granted what I wanted, which was no more than a minute or a couple of minutes in a stairwell or on a wall, or at a door or a window. Anywhere, anywhere would do because I just needed to see him. All I needed was a minute of him.

'Because,' she said, still avoiding my eyes, 'you have to be strong for me, and if you've seen him, you won't be.'

But of course I would; what was she talking about? Her entreaty was a hand at my throat but I could still slip free, I could just say what she wanted me to say and sidle from her clutch and she'd know nothing, be none the wiser, because when was she ever? But now her eyes did come for mine and she said, 'I can't do this without you,' which stopped me dead in my slip-sliding. Had I been able to take a breath, I might've said, *You can't ask this of me*. But of course she could.

She could ask anything of me. She could only ask.

*

Something I did manage to do for her, that night, was lay the coverlet over her when she fell asleep on the floor beside the bed. She hadn't come to bed, she'd intended to stay praying and perhaps she could've prayed in the other room but force of habit, perhaps, kept her at the bedside. As for me, I'd only got into bed because, as the night deepened, I hadn't known where else to be or what else to do. I couldn't think how else to get through all the hours that were stretching ahead and also it would have been unbearably cold to have been any- where else. So I'd got under the coverlet just to keep warm, but, unbelievably, I must have succumbed, because then it was later and I was aware that something had changed. Jane's side of the bed was still unoccupied but elsewhere, some- where in the silence, something had altered. Edging across the mattress to dare a peek through the hangings, I found her hunched on the floor, lifeless. If I left her there like that, she'd freeze – she was probably already half frozen – but she was too heavy for me to lift and, anyway, if I were to try, I'd wake her and she'd go back to praying and surely it was kinder to leave her to sleep. I slid from the bed, drawing the coverlet in my wake, and softly arranged it over her. Then I dressed in my warmest clothes and went through to the main room to open the shutters. There was no light in Guildford's window or leaking around his shutters but that didn't necessarily mean he was asleep, because there was no light in mine either.

I had no need of any light. That night held no terror for me. Jane was right, perhaps, that she had to prepare for the worst, but I didn't. I didn't believe it, and the reason I didn't was that it couldn't be true. The Queen, upriver, would be awake too, I didn't doubt that. *You and me both, Your Majesty.* I would spend the rest of that night held firm against what Jane regarded as inevitable. This was a vigil and there was no one better than me to keep it, the girl who got reprieves. If my time in the Tower had taught me anything, it was how to hold my nerve.

Jane was praying again by five, when I checked; and not long afterwards Goose had the audacity to bring the breakfast tray, its dollop of jam like a severed tongue. She entered the room with none of her usual rumpus, as if she were a normal servant, although a normal servant would have offered up some kind of greeting and she said nothing. Why had she come so early? Outside, the various night-lights had burned away but morning lights had yet to be lit. I wondered aloud, 'Should Jane get dressed?' Because how far were we supposed to play along with this charade?

'No rush, they're running late.' She was expressionless; I couldn't tell what she made of any of it. 'There's fog.'

Glancing back at the window, I saw it coalesced there in the darkness, and realised I wouldn't have seen any light even if there had been one.

When Goose had coaxed us a fire and gone, Jane looked through and spoke as if we hadn't been separated by a night.

'I need to get dressed.'

The praying looked to have been hard work, and I couldn't have despised the Queen more at that moment for putting Jane through this protracted pretence.

Glancing at the table, she asked, 'Has Goose taken the letters?'

Goose?

I turned to the table; the letters to her sisters were gone.

I followed her back into the bedroom and saw she'd already chosen her clothes, not that it had taken much doing because, with the exception of one small garment, she'd be dressing exactly as she had for her trial. Various items of black velvet were splayed on the bed but instead of the jet-jewelled headdress was a coif, a scrap of linen in which to tie up her hair. *Why did you let her dress like this?* Well, this time, Guildford wouldn't be seeing it. *He goes earlier.* His reprieve would come sometime before hers. He might have even already had it, he might already be free.

I helped her to dress and neither of us spoke because there was nothing to say (except, perhaps, *Goose? Really, honestly, Goose?*) and anyway we were too tired. The coif, I left to her: that coif, I felt, was taking it too far and I'd play no part in it. So, she herself was the one to secure her hair off her neck. Then she wanted to be left again to pray.

Back in the main room, someone was knocking at the door: Mr Partridge. He didn't seem to be delivering any reprieve. I'd never imagined he could look so depleted – not our usually jaunty, cock-eyed Mr Partridge – and I panicked that he had bad news of his wife but he was quick past me through the doorway and looking for Jane. He smelled as if he'd slept in his clothes; he too, then, I guessed, had been staying ready for news. I wondered if he knew about Goose and the letters.

I summoned Jane for him and he made a rushed job of the appropriate courtesies before saying why he'd come: Guildford was asking to see her.

And so there it was and there we were, after all that time, the shut-away months of winter and illness, and the siege and yesterday's priest and the long, cold night before this morning's coif with its silky, insinuating tapes and its revelation of a small mole at the nape of her neck. There we were, about to go to see Guildford, to troop out there – somewhere, anywhere – just as we'd always done, so that there would be him and William and Jane and me, just as we'd always been, and together we'd be able to make some sense of what was going on, of how far it was likely to go and what would happen to us and when.

Or if not the two of us, then me: I was going to go down the stairs to see Guildford and there would be nothing to it, just down and through the door and then perhaps a joke about Mass, and the relief was dizzying but Jane and Mr Partridge weren't staring at me because I'd begun to cry but because they wanted an answer. Jane was looking to me for our answer and there was absolutely nothing else in that look of hers but why would there be? She'd said her piece and although she hadn't said much, she couldn't have been clearer. She was wrong, though: *you have to be strong for me, and if you've seen him, you won't be*, but she'd seen how strong I could be and anyway no one needed to be strong because nothing was going to happen. We would be walking away from here and going our separate ways and it was that as much as anything that had started me crying.

But Guildford was going earlier and there was fog. A messenger was coming with the reprieve but what if he lost his way or his horse took fright? What if Guildford had to go as far as Tower Hill before that messenger arrived? There would be hundreds, possibly even thousands of people up there. I'd be back for Jane, and I'd be strong for her – of course I would – and together we'd see this through to her own reprieve, but first she had to let me go to Guildford even if I couldn't think what it was that I wanted to say to him, couldn't remember because it'd been too long and anyway this wasn't the time,

Please, Jane, don't ask this of me, not this: to give up, for her sake, the chance to see Guildford which – whatever happened – would probably be my last. Because had she forgotten how I'd come here in some other girl's dress? I'd come here as a good Catholic girl volunteering to be her companion when really I was a ducker and diver, following my nose, keeping to corners, taking what I could get and believing in nothing and no one. *That's who I am and you know it. I am no good to anyone. You know I am not the girl to do this for you.*

And she did know it, I could see, because there she stood, unflinching but resigned. She'd asked it of me and whatever I should now decide, yes or no, she'd take it; she was ready to take whatever I said, even as she held no hope at all of it being in her favour. She'd known what she was asking of me but had gone ahead anyway and asked. And that, for me, was what did it. If she could ask that of me, then the least I could do was honour it. So, I did: I said no, I made myself say it, which in the end was surprisingly simple. I said that Lady Jane felt unable, in the circumstances—

I didn't quite know what I'd said but I knew that it had been understood and that it was done.

Outside, it occurred to me – too late – that Jane should have stayed in bed. Well, got into it, for a start, and then stayed there, refused to get out. Because what could anyone have done? Any of these men, out here, what could they have done? I should have dressed as Jane because then she could have stayed indoors doing her praying and I would have done this pointless standing around. Because, with the exception of Mr Partridge, how many of these men would have known who I was? Or who I wasn't. None of these men would have known the difference between us two girls.

The daylight in the bailey – on the grass, the stones – was like something coughed up, but at least there was sky, even if the fog made it hard to see: sky, arcing over us and stretching away, full of itself, and somewhere under it, at the turn of an hour or so, were our future selves. Something would happen: someone would come, someone was coming or was even here already but biding time, but I knew I couldn't look because you have to be looking the other way for a reprieve to come. You have to be at its mercy. That's how it works.

Would they really have paraded Guildford all the way up to Tower Hill, just for him to have to come all the way back down again? How absurd that anyone should even have considered an axe for Guildford: a hammer to crack a nut, when all he'd ever needed was taking down a peg or two. *Would* he come back here to the Tower again? Or would they just let him go, then and there up on the hill?

All these men, and we two girls. Every one of the men looked worried. They too, then, were wondering how much longer before they could call it off.

They were taking her with them and I was following, keeping up in case they closed around her and left me behind. Mr Partridge was talking to her and she was answering, attentive and grave. Me, though, I was a mess, breathless and shivery, and perhaps I should've eaten some of Goose's bloody breakfast, should've forced some down. And now there was the priest too, he and Jane greeting each other like old friends: she taking his arm and he gazing into her eyes as if they were lamenting someone else's misfortune.

Where was Guildford? We needed him here, carrying on, kicking up a ridiculous fuss in defence of his wife. What I would've given, then – anything, everything – to see that, just that, as if we were back at the beginning.

Ahead of us was a scaffold, which seemed a bit much, although I supposed the charade had to be convincing, and beyond the scaffold were people, dozens of them, on benches, and were they there because they believed it was going to happen or because they knew it wouldn't?

Jane climbed the steps up on to the platform, taking it too fast, rushing it, *This is what I want*, and I was supposed to be accompanying her but that didn't seem to be happening even though I felt as if I were running full pelt to catch her up.

Had anyone gone to look for the messenger or was I the only one with my wits about me?

She was already up on that platform and being received by a man who I could see – despite his hood – wasn't the fake from the trial, the barge, but nor did he have that impostor's axe. The wheezy little man from the barge would've been a better choice, despite the offputting axe, because this one was too serious, asking forgiveness of Jane, and it was cruel to have him up there like that because then how was he going to look when it was called off?

Jane was addressing the people on the benches but I couldn't hear what she was saying because my blood was hissing in my ears, and then she'd finished and was turning back to me. She had an encouraging smile for me, and her gloves and a book, she was bending down to give me the gloves and the book but I didn't seem able to grasp them so she took the lot – my hands, the gloves, the prayer book – into her own hands and held them together and it wasn't a smile, of course, in her eyes, but kindness.

Then she was up and across the straw-strewn platform and her hands were at the back of her head although it was hard for her to tie a knot because there was already so much there – her bundled hair, the coif's convoluted ribbons – and then, kneeling, with her gown rising around her as if it had been made for the purpose, she reached blindly forward. A man – some man – stepped towards the platform and helpfully, deferentially, took one of her flailing hands – his gloved hand and hers ungloved inside it – to guide it, settle it somewhere before stepping back again, bowing out, apologetic for the intrusion.

Leaning forward, she seemed wary of hurting herself, and why was this still happening? Why hadn't it stopped? It was time now for this to stop before it was too late. Someone had to stop it. Should I say something? Shouldn't I say something? I should say something but suddenly there was a flash and the axeman stepping back and he did have an axe, he had had an axe, he must've had it all along, and what had he done? What had he just done? He wasn't supposed to have done that. *What have you done? You weren't supposed to do that!* I felt I was screaming it but there was nothing besides a burning in my throat and I was down on the ground, there was grass beneath my hands and someone had hold of me and oh Jesus he'd come for me, the axeman had got me and I was next, me next and then he was going to go on and on—

But my name was being said and it was Goose who was saying it, Goose who had hold of me and where had she come from? Goose, red-eyed but not returning my gaze because her frown was for my mouth, which she was wiping with a handkerchief. I was full of '*Did you see, did you see, did you see,*' and she was intoning, 'I know, I know,' but regretful, as if she'd known all along it would happen. But if she'd known, she'd have stopped it, she'd have stepped up there and stopped it: this was Goose, she'd have got up there and put a stop to it.

I was soaked, drenched, I'd taken the full hit of blood in my hair and on my face and in my mouth but when Goose shook me so hard that I grabbed the grass there was none on my hands, and when I rocked back on my heels there was none in my lap. Not blood, then, but sweat and sick. Jane, I remembered, *Jane*. I needed to get to her, she'd gone up there alone; I looked up and she was still there, just as she had been, exactly as she had been but with blood like a beast beside her, rising in the straw and still moving, and there was so much of it, and what on earth had he done to her to cause that much blood? I had to get over there, but Goose was saying no, she was saying my name and she had hold of me. 'I'll do it,' she said, firm, forbidding, 'I'll do it,' and 'See?', releasing me so she could show me what she had, and it was the coverlet from our bedroom.

See?

I said, 'You can't use that.'

'Yes,' she said, 'I can.'

On the far side of the scaffold, people were rising from the benches, shuffling along, going on their way. A moment ago, they'd paid respectful attention to Jane when she'd asked them to pray for her but now they weren't even waiting to see who, if anyone, would clear her up. Goose stood; she had work to do. 'Go,' she said, not unkindly. 'You need to go.'

I couldn't have moved even if I had wanted to, I hadn't the strength even to stay kneeling, but instead folded over, doubled up, forehead to the ground. And there, drawn in on myself, I thought of Guildford. *Guildford; earlier.* If a reprieve had been on its way – *if* – but too late for Jane, could it have reached him? Guildford, *earlier*: would it have gone, first, to him? Was there any possibility that it had reached him in time?

I picked myself up limb by limb, and then it was as if I'd never before in my life taken a step. I didn't know where I was going. The house? Back to the house? The house, yes, because there he was, I could see him there by the door: William. William, raw-eyed, I saw as I drew closer, and in a flash I felt for him and him alone – William, in tears – before the feeling was all for myself because clearly the news was the worst. There was no need for me to hear it but he was already speaking, coming towards me, tremulous and choked but sounding a note of surprised relief. 'He was—' Words failed him. 'Shook everyone's hand . . .'

Calm and dignified, Guildford had been, and suddenly I did want to hear it: Guildford going around shaking everyone's hand. The more I heard of it, the longer I'd be able to keep him there in my mind's eye, doing the rounds up on that hill, graciously saying his goodbyes.

But William stopped, fearful, to check: 'Lady Jane?'

I managed a nod, *Much the same.*

'He said you're to go abroad.'

Abroad, where he'd have gone. Well, maybe one day I would.

'Don't even go back up to your room.'

What?

His gaze was stark in mine: *Listen.* 'You know the Tiger?

just through the—' *gatehouse*. 'Ask for Mr Hamey,' and he was taking one of my feeble, shaky hands, closing it around something small. 'Show him that. Then show it to every-one—' *along the way*.

I opened my hand and there on my palm was a ring with a seal: *Dudley*, it would whisper to Dudley-friends. Safe pas-sage, it would request. But how could I? How could I do it, when even putting one foot in front of the other was too much? Breathing, even. Not crying, though, it seemed.

'Elizabeth,' William said, 'you really should.'

A perfect circle in my hand, as clean as only gold can be. I looked back up at him. 'You?'

He grimaced. 'My wife—' *is Catholic? Refuses to go?* 'You, though,' *you really should*. And then he turned, he was going, leaving me with that ring on my palm, wide open and expec-tant. I put it on my finger.

Jane Grey is believed to have been held in the Tower with two or three ladies or girls, but it's unclear who they were and whether they were constantly in attendance or working to a rota. It has been suggested that Elizabeth Tilney was one of the attendants, and for the purposes of this novel I have chosen to depict her as Jane's sole companion and a constant presence.

Jane did live in the house of the Tower's Gentleman-gaoler, Nathaniel Partridge, and did sometimes dine downstairs with him and his guests. The consensus among historians is that at times she was permitted to meet her husband outside.

I have conflated Father Feckenham's several visits to Jane during her final days into just the one occasion. The letter Jane wrote to Dr Thomas Harding survives only as a printed copy, but the prayer book that she carried to her execution is in the British Library.

ACKNOWLEDGEMENTS

Thanks first and foremost to David and Vincent, for their considerable forbearance while I was very slowly writing this book. Heartfelt thanks, too, to my agent, Antony Topping, and my editor, Clare Smith, for their patience and wisdom, and to Susan de Soissons for her tireless, ever-cheerful efforts on my behalf. Thanks also to Poppy Stimpson, Steve Dumughn, Charlie King, Sian Wilson, Marie Hrynczak, Linda Silverman, Zoe Gullen, Vicki Harris, Richard Beswick and David Shelley, all of whom make working with Little, Brown such a pleasure. And, last but not least, to Carol Painter and Jo Adams, once again, for the frequent lend of lovely Birdcombe Cottage.